...lnight at the Brig...

...thew Sullivan grew up in a family of eight spirited ...ldren in suburban Denver, Colorado. In addition to ...orking for years at the Tattered Cover Book Store in ...enver and at Brookline Booksmith in Boston, he has ...ught writing and literature at colleges in Boston, Idaho ...d Poland, and currently teaches writing, literature and ...m at Big Bend Community College in the high desert ...Washington State. He is married to a librarian and has two children and a scruffy dog named Ernie.

Praise for *Midnight at the Bright Ideas Bookstore*

'With *Midnight at the Bright Ideas Bookstore*, Matthew Sullivan has written – with great panache and suspense – a smart, twisty ...ime novel filled with compelling characters set in a world book-lovers will adore.'

Jess Walter, author of *Beautiful Ruins*

'Matthew Sullivan's debut novel is a cleverly constructed thriller with enough twists to keep readers guessing ... The grim storyline focuses on the dark side of human passion, and the description of the gruesome murder at its centre is not for the faint-hearted – but the feisty heroine and the dark family secrets that are revealed layer by layer make this a compelling read.'

Scotsman

'A page-turner featuring a heroine bookseller who solves a cold case with clues from books – what is not to love?'

Nina George, author of *The Little Paris Bookshop*

Midnight at the Bright Ideas Bookstore

MATTHEW SULLIVAN

WINDMILL BOOKS

3 5 7 9 10 8 6 4 2

Windmill Books
20 Vauxhall Bridge Road
London SW1V 2SA

Windmill Books is part of the Penguin Random House group of companies
whose addresses can be found at global.penguinrandomhouse.com.

Penguin
Random House
UK

First published in the United States by Scribner,
an imprint of Simon & Schuster, Inc. in 2017

First published in Great Britain by William Heinemann in 2017
First published in paperback by Windmill Books in 2018

www.penguin.co.uk

A CIP catalogue record for this book is available from the British Library.

ISBN 9781786090157

Interior design by Kyle Kabel

Printed and bound in Great Britain by Clays Ltd, St Ives Plc

For Libby

All words are masks, and the lovelier they are, the more they are meant to conceal.

—Steven Millhauser, "August Eschenburg"

As always we take up again where we left off. This is where I belong after all.

—Walker Percy, *The Moviegoer*

CHAPTER ONE

Lydia heard the distant flap of paper wings as the first book fell from its shelf. She glanced up from the register, head tilted, and imagined that a sparrow had flown through an open window again and was circling the store's airy upper floors, trying to find its way out.

A few seconds later another book fell. This time it thudded more than flapped, and she was sure it wasn't a bird.

It was just past midnight, the bookstore was closing, and the final customers were checking out. Lydia was alone at the register, scanning a stack of paperback parenting books being bought by a teenage girl with pitted cheeks and peeling lips. The girl paid in cash and Lydia smiled at her but didn't say anything, didn't ask what the girl was doing alone at a bookstore this late on a Friday night, didn't ask when she was due. When the girl got her change, she met Lydia's eyes for a moment, then rushed out without any bookmarks.

Another book fell, definitely somewhere upstairs.

One of Lydia's comrades, a balding guy named Ernest who walked like a Muppet but always looked sad, was standing by the front door, guiding the night's final customers into Lower Downtown.

"Are you hearing that?" Lydia said from across the store, but her voice was too quiet and anyway Ernest was occupied. She watched him unlock the door he'd just locked to let in a clubbing couple who looked drunk.

"They need to pee," Ernest said, shrugging in Lydia's direction.

Outside, a few scruffy BookFrogs lingered on the flagstone sidewalk, zipping up backpacks and duffels, drinking from gallon jugs of water they'd refilled in the bathroom. One had a pulp crime paperback crammed in his back pocket. Another had a pencil on a string tied to his belt loop. They stood together but none of them spoke, and one by one they slumped separately into the city, off to sleep in a run-down basement in Capitol Hill, or on a bench in Union Station, or in the sticky cold of Denver's alleys.

Lydia heard another faint flapping. Definitely a falling book, followed by a few more in rapid succession: *flap-flap-flap*. The store was otherwise quiet.

"Upstairs empty?" she said to Ernest.

"Just Joey," Ernest said, but his eyes were fixed on the corner of zines and pamphlets that flanked the bathrooms where the drunk couple had just disappeared. "Do you think they're screwing in there?"

"He knows we're closed?"

"Joey?" he said. "You never know what Joey knows. He asked after you earlier, by the way. It may have been the longest conversation we've ever had. 'Seen Lydia?' I was touched."

Most days Lydia made a point of tracking Joey down wherever he'd settled into the store—a corner table in the coffee shop, or the former church pew in the Spirituality section, or even under the Story Tree in Kids—to see what he was reading and how he was feeling and whether any odd jobs had come his way.

She had a soft spot for the guy. But tonight she'd gotten caught in the store's after-dinner rush and never tracked him down.

"Lyle is with him, right?" Lydia said. Though decades apart in age, Joey and Lyle were all but inseparable, like two halves of one smart and awkward beast.

"No Lyle. Not tonight. Last I saw, Joey was all alone in History. He had masking tape on his fingers."

"On his fingers?"

"I think he must've cut himself or burned himself. Made bandages with Kleenex and tape." He looked at his watch. "He's not a crackhead, is he? They're always burning fingers."

Lydia heard another fluttering book. The store occupied three cavernous floors, and when it was quiet like this, sound traveled between them as if through an atrium. She imagined Joey all alone lobbing books up there, some kind of bibliomancy or I Ching toss. She'd be the one to stay late and reshelve them.

"Count the drawer for me?"

"Goddamned couple," Ernest said, coming around to the register without unpeeling his eyes from the bathrooms. "They've gotta be screwing in there."

Lydia crossed the store's gritty floors and headed up the wide, tiered staircase that reached through the building like a fattened spine. Ernest had gone through earlier and turned off most of the overhead lights upstairs, so she felt as if she were climbing into an attic.

"Joey?"

The second floor was quiet, shelf upon shelf of books standing still. She continued to the third.

"Joey?"

Joey was the youngest of the BookFrogs, and by far Lydia's favorite. This wouldn't be the first time that she or one of her bookselling comrades had done a final sweep at closing and

3

found Joey knocking books off the shelves, searching for a title that may or may not have actually existed. His glossy hair would be draped over his eyes, and he'd be wearing black jeans and a black knit sweater with the collar just low enough to see the top of his tattooed chest. The wooden floors around his feet would be spread with books about subjects as far-reaching as his thoughts: Sasquatch sightings and the Federal Reserve, Masonic rites and chaos theory. He was a shattered young man, Lydia often thought, haunted but harmless—a dust bunny blowing through the corners of the store.

She liked having him around.

"Joey?"

The third floor was dim and peaceful. Lydia stepped into a familiar warren of tall wooden shelves and followed their angles and branches into different alcoves and sections, each holding a chair or a couch, a table or a bench: Psychology, Self-Help, Religion, Travel, History.

Something squeaked.

"Last call, Joey."

When she stepped into the Western History alcove, she could feel her eyes trying to shut out what she was seeing: Joey, hovering in the air, swinging like a pendulum. A long ratcheted strap was threaded over a ceiling beam and looped around his neck. Lydia's body sprung with terror, but instead of running away she was suddenly running toward him, toward Joey, and hugging his lanky legs and trying to hoist him up. She heard someone's scream curdle through the store and realized it was her own.

Lydia's cheek pressed into Joey's thigh and his jeans were warm with urine. A lump in his pocket smelled of chocolate and she assumed it was a knot of melted Kisses, swiped from the bowl on the coffee shop counter. His hands were clenched

4

into quiet fists and she could see the masking-tape bandages on three or four of his fingertips, but she wouldn't look up again at the popped purple sockets of his eyes, nor the foamy saliva rolling down his chin, nor the blue swelling of his lips.

She could see the cemetery of books that had flapped to the floor as Joey had climbed the shelves, and the others he'd shoved aside to create footholds as he threaded the strap through the ceiling, and still others that had dropped as he'd tried to kick his feet back to stop himself from dying. By now she'd locked her hands together on the far side of his thighs and was trying to lift him up, but her sneakers kept slipping on the wooden floor, and each time she slipped the ratcheted strap cinched tighter around his neck. She must have stopped screaming because a ringing silence suddenly swallowed everything when she saw, a few inches from her face, poking up from Joey's front pocket, a folded photograph of her.

Lydia.

As a child.

CHAPTER TWO

"Lydia?"

Ernest was hustling up the steps.

"Lydia? Where are you?"

Lydia plucked the photo from Joey's jeans. In it she was ten, wearing frizzy braids and a blue cord vest, blowing out candles on a chocolate cake.

"Oh Jesus!" she heard Ernest say as he rounded the shelves into the alcove. "Here, here. Joey, c'mon, c'mon, man, don't—"

In the dim bookstore light, in the stench of Joey's death, in the warren of those shelves, Lydia slid the photo into her back pocket and tried simply to breathe. Ernest—responsible Ernest, who moments ago had been downstairs counting change, guarding the Bright Ideas bathroom from horny club rats, and who half a decade ago, in a previous life, had driven through sandstorms in the Persian Gulf War—Ernest dragged a footstool over and hopped to the top and yelled about an ambulance as his hands went to work. Lydia stepped back and realized that the drunk couple from the bathroom was now standing behind her, holding each other and looking on, and she accidentally stepped on the woman's high-heeled foot and whispered, *Sorry*, and the woman said, *That's okay*, and both of them started crying at once. Someone put a hand on Lydia's shoulder and she shrugged it off.

"Is he moving? Does anyone see him moving?"

The long nylon strap that Joey had earlier unthreaded from a dolly or a cart had a metal ratchet built into it. Ernest released it high above his head and the strap unspooled like a whirring whip and Joey hit the floor.

All went quiet. No one attempted to move him, to defibrillate or resuscitate. Joey was obviously over.

Someone's ride honked on the street out front, and the Union Station sign glowed red against the windows. Lydia felt a sharp stirring in her abdomen, something much more terrifying than sadness or shock, and she stooped to her knees and began scooping up the books that Joey had kicked to the floor, and once she had them all in a pile she began reshelving them because she didn't know what else to do. Books that were pushed too far back she scooted forward, and books that were too far forward she scooted back, and then an older woman with thick glasses who worked part-time at the store took Lydia's elbow and led her toward a couch in the Self-Help section, where she waited for the police, out of sight of Joey's body.

After being interviewed by the reporting officer, sipping a cup of green tea with a coat from the lost-and-found draped upon her lap, Lydia went outside to the sidewalk and watched Joey's bagged body get wheeled on a gurney into the back of an ambulance. She declined a few offers for a ride home and instead caught a slow bus up Colfax Avenue, where she could be alone with Joey's photo.

Her late-night city passed by outside, streetlights and neon glowing over the noodle shops and cantinas, the fast food and the porn, the basilica and the temple, the wig stores and salons. She passed the diner with sixty-five-cent coffee and the dry cleaner's with the ceramic Buddha in the window. Hooded figures drank out of paper bags and a pair of nuns pushed a grocery cart full of blankets. She loved riding the Colfax bus, with its potholes and its people.

Once the bus had emptied out some, she slipped the photo out of her back pocket. Her hands were damp and she felt as if she were breathing through a straw.

Lydia couldn't remember the last time she'd seen a girlhood photo of herself and she was fairly sure she'd never seen this one. The spare snapshots of her childhood had been buried so deep inside her bedroom closet that she wasn't certain they were even there anymore—all of which made Joey's possession of this photo even more impossible. It had been taken during the only real birthday party she'd ever had, two decades ago, in the little bungalow off Colfax where she'd spent her early years, just a mile or two east of here. Inside the photo's yellowing border Lydia was a ten-year-old girl leaning over her birthday cake, deep in a candlelit bliss. She found it hard to believe that her dad had been able to wrangle her curly black hair into those tight braids, and even harder to believe that this joyful little girl was *her*. But unquestionably she was: her big brown eyes, her blue cord vest, her crooked yellow buttons. So much had not yet happened.

Though Lydia occupied most of the frame, there were two other kids in the photo, her only fourth-grade friends. Raj Patel was seated to her right, wearing a light blue jumpsuit with silver buckles and staring with an adoring smile, not at the cake or at the camera but at Lydia, the birthday girl. Carol O'Toole was there too, on her left, but she'd been fidgeting so much that only a blurred corona of her orange hair could be seen. The

9

photo's composition was odd, canted and crisscrossed by twists of crepe paper, and Lydia realized this was because her father must have been trying to get all three of them into the frame as Carol bounced around and scraped her fingers through the frosting. It hadn't worked.

Lydia's stomach churned. Fourth grade, she thought, the same year she and her father had left—*fled*—Denver. And they'd fled all right, a month or two after this photo had been taken, straight from the hospital to the mountains without saying good-bye to a soul.

The bus jostled to a stop in the gut of Capitol Hill. Lydia hopped off and walked the rest of the way home.

In their second-floor apartment, David was still awake. He was perched at the kitchen table, wearing a headlamp and tinkering with a computer motherboard. A soldering iron and a small spool of wire sat on the table near his hands. The counter behind him was crowded with dirty bowls and cutting boards, garlic peels, a jar of olives, a zesting grater, and the lopped stem of an artichoke. The room smelled of soldering flux and baked chicken, and Lydia could hear Cobain screaming in the headphones that cupped his neck. It was the middle of the night but David was acting as if it were the middle of the day, and she could tell that his evening had once again disappeared into whatever project was currently dissected on the table. He tilted his head slightly when she came in, but his sight remained focused on the tiny circuitry below.

"Let me just wrap this . . ."

She planted a kiss on his temple. This was the man she'd fallen for five years back, the guy who'd rather take apart a television than eat nachos in front of it. David wasn't perfect, she knew, and she sometimes was annoyed by the computer cords and old hard drives stacked on a shelf in their bedroom, or the splintery skateboard with its box of wheels and bearings that had been under their bed, unused, these past four years, or the autographed Broncos poster that couldn't be hung near the bathroom because the shower steam could potentially *crinkle Elway's jersey*. But despite such minor irritations, David was truly a pure-hearted guy, an upbeat mama's boy with wavy hair and beautiful eyes who just wanted to split breakfast burritos with Lydia until death. She was glad to have him in her life.

"I didn't get to the dishes," he said, "but there's some food . . ."

As soon as David looked up, he must've sensed something was wrong. He stood and clutched her shoulders.

"Lydia, what happened? Oh shit. Was I supposed to pick you up?"

"It's not that."

"Then what?"

Her gut was swimming. She leaned against the sink to steady herself and told David all about Joey. Except for the part about the photo. She shared almost everything with David—her bizarro sci-fi dreams, her fears about the future, her shifting rotation of phobias and anxieties—but not the ruins of her childhood. Some things were off-limits, even for the guy she loved.

"Oh, babe," he said. "I just assumed you went out for drinks after work. I had no idea. I should've come down there."

David was a fervent believer in comfort food, so without registering how late it was, and without asking whether Lydia was even hungry, he pulled a plate of artichoke chicken out of the fridge and warmed it in the microwave, careful to be precise in cook time and power level (3:05 at Reheat 4). Lydia took the opportunity to slip into the bedroom and hide the birthday photo in the depths of her sock drawer. The microwave beeped just as she was finally washing the smell of chocolate and urine from her hands.

On the Bright Ideas loading dock, Lydia listened to the rhythmic beeps of a truck reversing up the alley. She'd been told last night to take the week off, but here she was pacing with the pigeons behind the bookstore—unable to be away, yet unable to go inside.

The rattling sound of nearby jackhammers didn't help to calm her nerves, but by now she'd grown used to them, just as she'd grown used to the walls of scaffolding and flapping plastic that cloaked this part of town these days. For decades this entire brick district had been a network of underused rail lines and concrete viaducts, honky-tonks and stockyard stomps, and the only residences had been stacked above shit bars with names like Drinks and the Drinking Hole and A Place to Drink. Even the neighborhood's name—Lower Downtown—had always felt fitting because these blocks marked the low point where the city's runoff collected: the soup-kitchen-and-skid-row crowd, the salvage and warehouse trucks, the wastewater sloshing from driveway to sewer grate to the trashy foaming currents of the Platte. It felt then like a city should: reeking of its own past. But change was on the way. The viaducts had been ripped out, cobblestones scoured back to life, and buildings that had sat abandoned for decades were being converted into galleries and apartment lofts. Along with a single brewery and a couple of coffee shops, the bookstore had been one of the first new businesses to move in, and over the course of a few years it had gradually expanded through the lower three floors of a onetime lightbulb factory. (Hence the name Bright Ideas, and the retro bulb that defined its front doors and bookmarks.) The store was growing busier by the month and down the street a ballpark—a ballpark!—was even under construction. Lydia sometimes wondered what she would do when this end of town, with its buried cowboys and hobo stories, began to cast the dull hue of any other.

Not that she would ever quit the store. Six years ago, when Lydia had put on a flannel skirt and a loose-hanging blouse and stepped into Bright Ideas for a job interview, the spotty résumé in her hand held little ripples where her sweat had saturated the paper. The manager that day was a reformed radiologist and country music fiddler with a tidy gray beard, and as he steered Lydia toward a couch in the Philosophy section, her nerves began to settle. When he folded her résumé and placed it on the floor near her feet, saying that interviews around here were a *little less formal than all that*, she let out a gusty sigh and tapped her fingertips together and began to speak of her shoestring travels (Eastern Europe, Southeast Asia), the classes she'd loved in college (World Religions, Renaissance Lit), her many fleeting jobs (orchards and farm stands, hotels and pet shops), and for the first time in a long time she found herself speaking openly with a stranger, and not feeling as if she were splashing through the conversational equivalent of a shark attack. At the end of the interview, in one of the most consequential moments of her life, the manager leaned back and simply said, "Recommend a book to me." The title she picked was telling—*One Hundred Years of Solitude*, as her own years of solitude were coming to a close—but even more telling was the tranquillity she felt afterward as she explored the enormous store, sliding books in and out of their slots, sizing up her new comrades.

She felt typically shy that day, avoiding eye contact and wearing her mild smile, but she could tell from the start that Bright Ideas was just the kind of sanctuary she'd been seeking for much of her life. Her fellow booksellers ran the demographic gamut, from a sixty-eight-year-old ex-nun with a brazen taste for erotica

13

to a seventeen-year-old dropout who, despite the Churchillian monocle tattooed over her left eye, had landed second place on last season's *Jeopardy!* Teen Tournament. They wore their hair dreaded and Afroed, waist length and shaved clean. Some of the older, loftier lefties looked like models from the 1974 Sears catalog, while others wore bolo ties and sassy dresses and hats that could only be described as Parisian. Even on that first day she knew that these booksellers were happier—or at least more tuned in to what happiness really was—than most, which had always seemed reason enough to stay.

Lydia hopped off the loading docks and rounded the corner into the alley behind the store. She was just gathering the guts to go inside, strategizing ways to get through her shift, when the sound of footsteps touched the air behind her.

"You know it's not your fault."

She turned to see Plath walking toward her, dressed in baggy black, fogging the air with a cigarette.

"Do I know that?" Lydia said. "I guess I do."

"He'd be dead no matter what. It's really not your fault."

A woman on the edge of fifty, Plath had worked at Bright Ideas since its opening day, and at other indies and libraries for decades before that. She was a benevolent oddball with unnerving beauty: silver hair cropped close to the skull, wide green eyes, slender arms. She never wore makeup and sported her wrinkles proudly. And she often showed up at work with gifts for Lydia—startling things, like the creepy doll with no hair or the tin of Japanese candies that tasted like meat. Though she didn't know for sure, Lydia assumed that Plath was single because she was too headstrong to get suckered by love, and most men, she imagined, would be made flaccid by her testimonials about Gilded Age vibrators, which she claimed were effective largely because of their threat of electrocution. Lydia sometimes saw

Plath as the woman she might someday become: caring, creative, content—but inaccessible to nearly everyone alive.

"He would've found a way," Plath said, "with or without you. Suicides are persistent like that."

"It just doesn't make sense."

"You were good to Joey," Plath said. "It makes me mad he did this to you."

Lydia felt too empty to speak.

"And the bookstore, too. We were like his second home."

Lydia pulled at a coil of her hair, silent.

"I mean, I loved the guy, I really did, but what the hell, Joey? Now I don't have anyone to talk to about the Bermuda Triangle."

"I'm sure you'll find someone," said Lydia.

"I just don't get the drama," Plath said, lighting a cigarette off of her cigarette. "Hanging himself in the History section? This from a guy who blushed when you said hi? Unless you were Lydia. The lovely Lydia." Plath reached out and held Lydia's shoulder. "I mean it," she continued. "The kid adored you. You were really good to him."

"He was a good guy."

"I know," Plath said. "But the next time he decides to kill himself, he should go backpacking in the winter in his undies. Swallow some cleaning products in a canoe. Just leave you out of it."

Listening to Plath's wandering thoughts, the obvious suddenly occurred to her: Joey had wanted her to find him. He'd wanted Lydia to be the one.

"And he didn't even leave a note?" Plath said.

"No note."

"I'm sorry," Plath said, shaking her head, "but that's like not tipping your waiter."

No note, Lydia thought. Just a birthday photo of me.

"If I was going to kill myself," Plath continued, "I'd leave a note just to get a few last digs in. Insult the guy who took me to prom. Give my parents one last guilt trip. Criticize my ex-husband's penis. Make it count, you know? It's not like you'd have anything to lose." Plath stopped rambling and squeezed Lydia's forearm. "Are you okay?"

"Mmm."

But Lydia wasn't okay. Something had been happening inside her. An old tight knot was beginning to unravel.

"You sure you're okay?"

A hairy wrist tucked into a white latex glove. A white latex glove gripping a claw hammer. A claw hammer spun through with a girl's hair. And blood. Always—

Lydia wiped her eyes on the threadbare sleeve of her sweater, breathed deep for a minute, and waited for the images to fade. She didn't need a therapist to know that Joey's hanging had opened doors long closed.

"So what did David say?" Plath asked.

"What does David always say?"

"The right thing," Plath said. "Makes me *sick* how adorable he is. You should really go home and rest your soul. Spend the week reading with David at your side."

"David's usually more of a *doer* than a *reader*, if that makes sense."

"Spend the week in bed with him then."

"He reads," Lydia said, smiling. "Just not like crazy. It's mostly just the Sports section and crosswords and stuff for work. Last year for his birthday he asked for a programming book called *C Plus Plus*, whatever that means."

"My god, Lydia, that's the saddest thing you've ever said."

"I feel better now."

Plath bit her lips and looked to her hand for a cigarette that was no longer there.

16

"Listen," she said. "I know this is freaky, and I really don't want to add any more chaos to whatever you're going through right now. But . . ."

"But?"

"It was in this morning's paper. The event. The incident. No article or anything, just one of those captions beneath a photo of the scene." Plath grimaced. "You were in it."

"Me? In the photo?"

"In the photo. In the caption. It's too bad you're not the attention-getting sort. This would really make your day."

Plath dived into the black bladder of her purse and retrieved a crumpled newspaper. Lydia glimpsed an image of Clinton giving a thumbs-up from a podium while Gingrich grumbled behind him. Plath flipped the page over. "See? That's you by the door covering your mouth with your hands. Look at your wonderful hair. How do you get it to look so weed-whacked?"

"Oh god," Lydia said, feeling the flush of self-consciousness that arrived at any mention of her appearance: the giant brown eyes that gave her a look of perpetual alarm; the slight curve in her shoulders that gave her a beaten hunch. Though she'd only recently turned thirty, Lydia couldn't help but notice the gray sprigs that had infiltrated her hair and the new lines alongside her mouth that, when she relaxed, gave her the look of a frowning rabbit. She very nearly hyperventilated at the fact that this photo had accompanied a hundred thousand morning coffees. She wondered who had seen it—who had identified her.

"There's the ambulance," Plath said, pointing at the page, "and the gurney and poor Joey in his body bag. Why do they have to use *black* bags for bodies anyway? No wonder everyone's afraid of death. Why not teal? Oh, and did you see what they called Joey in the caption? *Unidentified man.*"

Lydia sighed and glanced up the alley toward the sidewalk,

where a couple of guys were locking a shopping cart to a lamp-post.

"How sad to think of Joey like that," Plath continued. "*Unidentified man.*"

"They all are," Lydia said, and walked toward the wide window with red casing that cut through the store's brick back wall. There they were, already populating the store and not yet noon—an entire world of *unidentified men*: the BookFrogs.

During her first weeks of working at Bright Ideas, Lydia had noticed that not all the customers were actually customers, and a whole category of lost men began to formulate in her mind. They were mostly unemployed, mostly solitary, and they—like Joey—spent as much time in the aisles as the booksellers who worked there. They napped in armchairs and whispered in nooks and played chess with themselves in the coffee shop. Even those who didn't read always had books piled around their feet, as if fortressing themselves against invading hordes of ignora-muses, and when Lydia saw them folded into the corners for hours at a time, looking monastic and vulnerable, she thought of Mr. Jeremy Fisher, Beatrix Potter's dapper frog who was often portrayed reading a newspaper with his lanky legs in the air. They were like plump and beautiful frogs scattered across the branches of the store, nibbling a diet of poems and crackers.

"What are we going to do with you?" Plath said, gently putting her arm around Lydia.

Lydia leaned into her. "I wish I knew."

In other lives many of the BookFrogs may have been professors or novelists, but now their days were spent obsessing over bar codes on toothpaste and J. D. Salinger conspiracies. Early each morning when the store opened, a handful of them always shuffled in to grab the day-old pastries and fill their fast-food cups with milk from the coffee counter. To the inexperienced, many

BookFrogs appeared as derelict or homeless, but to the seasoned eye it was clear that they'd shed themselves of the world, rejecting its costumes and rules in favor of paper and words. For her part, Lydia gravitated toward them with a tenderness that bordered on gullibility, especially those loquacious few who could guide interesting conversations (though, in truth, as was always the case with Lydia, these conversations were heavily one-sided). A few of the BookFrogs were so erudite that their rambling lessons in literature seemed easily as insightful as those that had come from her professors years ago in San Francisco, where she'd cobbled together an English degree. A few others—like the man who made a habit of leaping out of stalls in the bathroom with a plunger above his head—were banned for months at a time, but most were quiet and benevolent, thankful for the chance to read and stare and, most importantly, leave their solitude at the door.

Lydia sometimes wondered if she'd stick around without them.

"Have you seen Lyle yet today?" Plath said, cupping her hands and peering into the window. "He's got to be taking this hard. How was he last night?"

Lydia pulled the newspaper from under Plath's arm and looked more closely at the photo: Joey's body, zippered into darkness, rolling out of the store, his gurney surrounded by gawkers and cops. She could see herself and a few of her comrades, but Lyle wasn't anywhere in sight.

"Lyle wasn't here," she said.

"Lyle's *always* here."

"Not last night he wasn't."

Lyle and Joey, Joey and Lyle: the two BookFrogs were as attached as a couple of matryoshka dolls. Though Lyle was easily in his sixties, he'd taken Joey under his wing years ago, first playing the role of a BookFrog philanthropist, a moneyed patron who supported Joey's bibliophilia, and later as his genuine friend.

It was Lyle who made sure that Joey ate every day, fulfilled his group-home duties, and showed up for his piss tests and parole meetings, but more importantly, Lyle was responsible for steering the kid into that leapfrog of new authors that expanded his inner life. They were an odd pair: Joey was jumpy and battered like a sad, scared puppy; Lyle was tall and prissy like a sloppy British schoolboy. Seeing the pair slouch daily through the store, Lydia often thought of their many iconic predecessors: Ernie and Bert, Laurel and Hardy, Steinbeck's George and Lennie. Watching them opening books before each other's eyes, brushing each other's elbows as they browsed, nodding cerebrally over cups of cooling tea, Lydia had witnessed an affection that she rarely saw in grown men. As far as she could tell, Lyle was the only person—besides perhaps herself—whom Joey opened up to, whom Joey maybe loved. Without Joey, it only now occurred to her, Lyle would be destroyed.

Plath slammed her cigarette into a coffee can and popped a mint.

"Stop it," she said.

"Stop what?" Lydia said.

"Wigging out over Lyle. His absence is *not* your problem."

"Says you."

"Listen, Lydia, I've got to get inside, but promise me you'll stay away from sad men today. Just this once. Just the sad ones. Just stay the hell *away*."

"Promise."

Plath swiped a smoky hand through Lydia's waifish bangs, then joined the dozen or so booksellers who buzzed through the store with pens behind their ears. Lydia watched them rush between ringing phones and computer pods and tried, without success, to shift her mind away from the specter of unidentified men.

CHAPTER THREE

In the Bright Ideas break room after work, Lydia gathered her jacket and satchel, then reached into her cubby and found, tucked alongside her sad little paycheck in its sad little envelope, a scalloped postcard of Pikes Peak. *Howdy from Colorful Colorado!* was printed in a red banner above the massive gray mountain, and below it a caption read, *The Most Visited Mountain in North America!*

The postcard was addressed to her—*Lydia*, no last name, *c/o Bright Ideas Bookstore*—and in fat black ballpoint it read:

> *moberg here.*
> *just if ever you want more.*

That was all, except for the flag stamp and the inky red postmark that, despite its smear, offered a legible origin: it had been mailed from the town of Murphy, Colorado. Mailed to her by Moberg himself. Detective Harry Moberg. Retired. Homicide.

Apparently Moberg had recognized her image in the newspaper last week, which meant that her worst fears were coming true: without her permission, the publication of that photo had opened a portal for travelers from her past. Her arms braced the cubby shelves. She wasn't ready to allow them in.

There was something terrifying about the postcard's arrival, in its verification that Detective Moberg was still alive, still secluded in the same snowy cabin where she'd last visited him twenty years before. And that he was probably still attempting to track down the Hammerman.

—We're going to find him, but we need your help. Understand? So tell me again exactly what you heard. Every sound you can remember, from the moment you crawled beneath that sink until the moment your daddy finally arrived. Lydia, can you do that for me? Think: beneath the sink.

if ever you want more.

She unbuckled her satchel and crammed the postcard inside. She didn't want *more* of that night. She wanted a lot, lot less.

When Lydia stepped into her Capitol Hill apartment after work, the curtains were closed and the only light came from the pair of glowing monitors stacked next to each other on the small desk in the corner of the living room. The coffee table had been pushed aside and David was arching his back on the carpet, wearing pajama bottoms and no shirt. A spiral-bound book of yoga poses was open on the floor. He smiled in her direction.

"Hey," he said. When he dipped back to the carpet a piece of lint stuck to his lips and he sputtered it out.

Lydia was glad to see him, and even gladder to see him occupied.

After a few years of crappy jobs at convenience stores and phone banks, David had taken a job last winter as an IT grunt at a curriculum development company and now spent his days in a windowless office surrounded by programmers and gamers—*indoorsy types*, he called them. At first he'd worried that fifty hours a week at a screen-lit desk would turn him into a bleeding-eyed drone, but before long the idea of getting paid to solve problems clicked perfectly with his tinkering side, and as an act of rebellion against his coworkers' diet of Funyuns and Mountain Dew, he made it a point each day to exercise—hence this evening's yoga.

"Just a minute more."

"Take your time," she said, then set her bag of groceries on the kitchen floor and slipped into their bedroom, a bright cube of windows so overrun by a pair of blue spruce that it felt like a tree house. Their apartment was on the second floor of a converted Foursquare home, and details like this one—not to mention their $300 rent—kept them from leaving the neighborhood and disappearing into some condo complex with shuttles to the slopes and mixers by the pool.

Lydia stood in front of her dresser and opened her sock drawer. When she slipped the postcard into the back, behind her summer socks and the itchy teddy she never wore, her fingers grazed the birthday photo.

Five years back, David had surprised Lydia by hovering next to her at a Broadway bar and reaching over her shoulder for a napkin, a toothpick, and an olive before finally getting the nerve to ask her to shoot a game of pool. His interest in her didn't make sense: David was quite possibly the most beautiful boy in the bar—wiry body, rosy cheeks, lippy smirk—and though Lydia was wearing cutoffs and sandals and a black Bikini Kill T-shirt that left her feeling slightly more comfortable in her skin than usual, she was also cocked sideways by bad gin and tonics, smoking her thirtieth cigarette of the day, leaning on Plath's shoulder, and feeling as if she'd just fallen off a hay truck. At first she acted shy and overly suspicious, as if his hitting on her had been a cruel bar bet, but as she weaved behind him she noticed that his gait was slightly awkward, and that one of his sneakers was dragging a frayed gray lace. Her suspicions faded even further when he leaned into the pool table's green felt and she saw, in a moment that warmed her thighs, that his right hand was a mangled twist of missing fingers. His thumb was there and most of a pointer, but otherwise the hand held a trio of squat little nubs.

A few hours later, during drunken sunrise omelets, she would find out that David had been a *deep-fried mathlete* in high school—his words—when one shitfaced night at a party he accidentally dropped a shot glass into the garbage disposal. He was fishing it out, hand groping the bladed depths, and flipped the light switch above the sink to see better what he was doing. Only it wasn't a light switch.

—My mom told me it made me less of an asshole, he said.

—Then you musta flipped the right switch, Lydia said.

Back in their first months of dating, she'd begun to notice that nearly every woman under forty eyeballed David like he was breakfast in bed. To all these gawkers Lydia felt like his presumed sister, his drinking buddy, the girl who could beat him in a belching contest—until, by chance, their sight fell upon his half-a-hand. She could see it sparkling in their eyes: *Is he holding something? An uncooked chicken breast? A knot of bread dough?* In their worst moments together, Lydia couldn't help but wonder if *it*—his hand—had been their main matchmaker.

But that was early on, and if it was really only David's hand that had kept them together, then by now their relationship would have been long over. As Plath once slurred, "Three missing fingers does not five years make." Lydia agreed: she and David were onto something. She just didn't know what it was, or whether she could handle it.

Negotiating boyfriends had never come naturally to Lydia. As a teenager, when she lived in her father's mountain cabin in Rio Vista, whenever boys asked her to dances or out for a drive she usually quivered and claimed that her father was oppressive to the point of violence. This was a half-truth at best—oppressive, yes; violent, no—but the boys always backed away slowly and settled on those hometown girls who got all their jokes and knew their parents from church. That was okay with Lydia. With the exception of the single hallucinogenic night when she lost her virginity to a metalhead atop a picnic table, this reputation of being *untouchable* protected her through the end of high school. Once she fled Rio Vista and moved to San Francisco—vowing to get as far away from her father as possible—she ramped in the other direction, sleeping recklessly with strangers at first, then slowly easing into a scant selection of boyfriends, none of whom lasted more than a month. Lydia honestly enjoyed this short period of penis-hopping, but with each boy the problem was always the same. After singling her out in the grocery line, the Victorian lit class, the taco shop, they inevitably realized that the armor in which she hid was impermeable, no matter how daring their moves. In different ways, they all wanted to share the space that belonged to her the most, but that was impossible. She was the only one allowed in there.

But from the start David had been different. The first time she'd spent the night at his apartment, she'd awakened alone in his bed and could smell something cooking (burning?) in the other room. She assumed that he was making eggs or french toast, but when she slipped into the T-shirt balled on his floor and came out to the kitchen she found him not cooking at all, but rather using an old iron to wax the pair of skis that were stretched across his countertop. A few minutes later, when she went back into the bedroom to get dressed, she nearly tripped over a dismantled VCR—the huge kind with clunky buttons and fake wood paneling—that had been wired to a surplus military bullhorn, a gift-shop strobe light, and the tube screen of an old black-and-white television. Nearby sat a pile of VHS videotapes (*Rocky Mountain Wildlife*; *Coping Skills for Emergency Responders*). She suspected it all had to do with a rave or some smart-drink electronica video project, but when she asked David what it was, he said he didn't know.

—Just fiddling, he said.

—Does it do anything?

—Not yet. May never. Oh well.

Oh well. She smiled. She never saw the contraption again, but its presence signaled the very *distracted* quality that she realized, in retrospect, allowed their relationship to work. His toothbrush soon appeared in the mason jar on her sink side, his bags of celery and cartons of cottage cheese soon sidled up to her grape jelly and cherry yogurt, and all the while David appeared to have better things to do than obsess over Lydia's hidden inner life.

In the kitchen, Lydia drank a glass of water, put the kettle on for tea, and began to put away the groceries.

Soon David came in, shirtless, barefooted, with that stupid tattoo of a pork chop just below his rib cage that he'd gotten on a high school trip to Mexico. Lydia had already pulled out the cutting board and unbagged an onion and was just piercing its skin when he pecked her from behind.

"You're happy," she said.

"I found a semicolon in the program where a colon should've been."

"Is that good?"

"Really good," he said. "Thousands of lines deep. Boss gave me a clumsy high five. It was awesome."

She studied him for a clue that he was being sarcastic, but he wasn't.

"I just saved our department about a week's worth of headache," he added, fumbling through a basket of fruit. "What about you? Any better at work today?"

It was a question David had asked her every day for the past week, ever since Joey. It still didn't make sense, she thought, what the kid had done. A few days ago while emptying the front counter trash, she'd come across a crumpled wad of yellow crime-scene tape that someone had shoved into the dumpster like an unspooled cassette, and she'd stared at it for a long time, unable to peel herself away, as if its cursive loops might explain why Joey—young, bright, damaged Joey—had climbed the shelves and tightened a strap and stepped into his death. She thought about the books she'd seen him reading in the weeks before he'd died—fractal geometry and microbial art and Petrarchan sonnets—but as far as she could tell they reflected the same tastes, both broad and narrow at once, he'd always indulged. In her search for an answer, she'd even gone up to the third floor earlier today and stood in the center of the Western History section, wondering if his choice to kill himself there, around those titles, signaled some deeper meaning.

Just as she was about to give up and head downstairs to help at the counter, Lydia noticed that the floral chair in the corner where Joey had spent his last living hours had been shoved too far against the wall. When she leaned over to reposition it, lifting and tucking its cushion for good measure, she spotted something tiny and white, about the size of her pinkie nail, sitting in the seam behind the cushion. She reached past a penny and a few oyster crackers to dig it out. A tab of paper. A perfect little rectangle. At first, she wondered if Joey had been dealing panes of LSD that night or cutting chains of paper dolls, but when she placed it on her palm and saw that it had clearly been cut from a book, she thought that he might have left her a suicide note, after all. She held it under the light, anticipating a single word that might tease out Joey's death—*sorry*; *hopeless*; *murder*—but discovered instead that the letters printed on it were fragmented, nearly indecipherable: an almost *e*, an almost *j*, an almost *l*, an almost *m*, some almost others. A biopsy of a page that added up to nothing.

Lydia's hands were holding the onion and the knife, but they weren't moving, and she was staring blankly at the silver toaster in the corner of the counter.

"Work was fine," she said to David. "I guess I'm getting over it."

He nodded, rolling an apple against his palm.

"Listen," he finally said, "maybe this isn't the best time, and I know it's out of nowhere, but can I ask what's up with you and your dad?"

Lydia felt her blood grow warm and her skin prickle cold. David took a bite of apple, then spat the apple's sticker into the sink.

"You're right," she said, suddenly focused on chopping, dicing, swiping. "It's really not the best time."

"His name is Tomas, right?" David said.

Hearing her father's name, Lydia felt like a child lifting the lid of a coffin. All it took was a peek.

"He called this morning," he added. "Just after you left for work."

She could feel her face flush and she quickly made a scene of washing her hands—pumping the soap dispenser, cranking the faucet to scalding.

"He needs to leave me be," she said. "David, did you talk to him?"

"A little."

She looked up from the sink and stared at David for a sign that her father had *told*, that David now knew who she really was: Little Lydia. The bloody-faced girl beneath the sink, the survivor from the evening news. Because no one from her present life knew. No one could know.

"If he calls here again," she said, "please hang up."

"All parents suck when you're a teenager, Lydia," he said, irritating in his calm. "Maybe he's just trying to reconnect."

"This is different," she said, and she could feel a painful bubble expanding inside her throat. "He moved me to the middle of nowhere, then he just checked out. After the age of ten I basically raised myself."

"Okay."

"So hang up if he calls again. Please."

"Okay."

David started to reach for her but turned at the last moment and wiped some crumbs from the counter instead.

CHAPTER FOUR

Lydia's father, a horn-rimmed librarian named Tomas, was a quivering wreck from the moment his infant girl entered the world. Only minutes before Lydia had taken her first breath, he'd been pacing the waiting room at St. Joe's and worrying about his wife, a flush-faced bookworm named Rose, who was down the hall in labor. When an overeager candy striper asked if he was ready to meet his new baby girl, Tomas rushed toward the delivery room so energetically that he'd barely gotten his mouth covered with the surgical mask before barging in. It turned out that the candy striper, still a full hallway behind him, had mistakenly beckoned the wrong new daddy, so Tomas arrived in the cold delivery room during the worst moments of Rose's emergency cesarean. One of the more experienced nurses lunged in front of him and tried to spin him back to the hall, but she'd been too late to prevent him from seeing his newborn daughter get cut from the womb of his dying wife.

At the nurse's insistence Tomas turned away and faced the door, but he refused to leave the delivery room. Behind him the anesthesiologist whispered that someone should take off Rose's wedding ring before the *corpuscular swelling* made it impossible to remove without cutting, and Tomas found himself wondering if he'd meant cutting his wife's finger or cutting his wife's ring. A minute later a different nurse taped the ring into a square of gauze and buttoned it into his jacket pocket while he stood there like a mannequin being readied for display. The ring itself held a dainty silver rose with ruby petals and an engraving along its inner wall. *A rose for my Rose*.

In a dark fog Tomas watched one of the nurses pull a sheet over Rose's body and roll her gurney toward the basement. He wanted to follow the gurney, but the doctor placed his newborn daughter into his arms and told him in a gentle voice that right now his girl needed her daddy. Tomas felt her squirming inside her blanket and began to understand. He held her close and her eyes, oily black, opened up his world.

During those first months, Tomas had nightly deliveries of casseroles and condolences, but one by one, as he returned baking dishes and stuffed bereavement cards into drawers, what little comfort these gifts had brought him began to fade. Because he was ashamed to expose his own ignorance of child rearing, he never asked anyone for help with Lydia, and with the exception of a single parenting book he found on Rose's nightstand, he was determined to figure out all this baby stuff on his own. He scalded Lydia's tongue with overboiled formula. He fed her nibbles of rice cereal long before she could lift her head. In the middle of the night he leaned over her swaddled form and listened to her irregular breathing and had no idea if she was freezing to death or choking on upchucked paste or simply as tuckered as he was.

When the time came for Tomas to go back to work at the local library, he tried placing Lydia with day-care providers all over the neighborhood, but none lasted more than a few days:

this one's playground had a rusty swing set and low fences; this one's shelves held hardly any books; this one's staff looked as if they came straight from the Screw Farm. As far as he was concerned none was up to snuff, so he did what he'd secretly hoped he'd have to do: he brought her with him to work. Where it was safe.

Lucky for Tomas, the tiny branch of the Denver Public Library that was under his watch serviced such an old and forgotten community that its patrons were well schooled in bendable rules. No one would complain about the constant presence of a child because low expectations had trained them not to complain. Volunteers sometimes helped with story hour and shelving, but most of the time Tomas sat behind the circulation desk alone, keeping one eye on his library, one eye on his daughter.

For those first few years, Lydia dawdled behind the desk, rode through the aisles on the bottom shelves of roller carts, and dozed in Daddy's lap as he cataloged. The elderly patrons seemed to stay longer with Lydia around and books were read to her by the dozen. Her learning thrived even more when kindergarten approached and Tomas sent her to Little Flower Elementary, a small Catholic school close enough to the library and their bungalow home that they could walk between them without enduring the expense of a car. Though it was rougher than most private schools, Tomas's fears were assuaged by the *Madeline*-like image of Lydia huddled in a yellow raincoat at the knees of towering nuns, on the safe side of a chain-link fence.

As Lydia grew, Tomas learned to braid her hair and polish her shoes and dress her up in plaid skirts and sweaters. With few exceptions—mainly during the terrible twos, which lasted for one month when she was three—he was pleased with his decision to keep her around the library. She kept herself busy after school by spinning through the records and filmstrips, building bean bag forts, and exploiting the Popsicle sticks and cotton balls of the craft room. Though he'd always believed in the value of solitude—Tomas felt himself like its lonely ambassador—each afternoon when he showed up at Little Flower to pick her up he began to notice that she was always alone, dragging her fingertips along the chain links with rarely a classmate in sight. The other kids swarmed the playground like ants on a pile, and even the nuns smoked in laughing clusters on the steps, but Lydia was always on her own. He began to worry about her solitude, and to wonder if he was somehow to blame.

So it was something of a big deal when they were walking home on a wintry afternoon in first grade and Lydia, kicking pucks of ice along the shoveled sidewalks, pointed at the neon doughnut that rose high into the sky above Colfax Avenue and asked if they could stop there, at Gas 'n Donuts, the bustling gas station/doughnut shop on the corner up ahead.

—For a doughnut?

—for a friend.

—What friend?

—he's waiting for me. with a doughnut.

Tomas looked around as if the street they walked every day had just been unpeeled.

Tucked into Denver's boot like a straight razor, Colfax Avenue was the longest street in America and the most dangerous street in town. It was the place to get a vacuum fixed or eat ethnic foods, to buy secondhand slacks or a bicycle pump, but it also held the city's highest concentration of gun shops, prostitutes, strip clubs, drug dealers, dive bars, and hot-sheet motels. In the single mental snapshot he took while holding Lydia's mittened hand, Tomas counted a dark cocktail lounge, a used auto dealership, a nail salon, a pawnshop, a fabric store, a motorcycle parts outlet, and a nightclub advertising nude Jell-O wrestling.

And a doughnut shop. Slash gas station.

—he's waiting for me.

—With a doughnut. You said.

Tomas was feeling wary and overprotective, to say the least, so it came as a relief when they entered Gas 'n Donuts and were greeted by a smiling woman wearing a knitted scarf and a white apron over a yellow sari. She seemed amused by the sight of this bearded father and his big-eyed daughter, holding hands in winter coats, stomping snow from their feet. At one of the booths along the back wall a chubby boy wearing a red down vest and a matching knit hat was reading some plucky adventure story with a shark circling a sailboat on its cover. He didn't budge when they entered, nor did the few figures hunched over ashtrays and newspapers at the counter. It was late in the day and the display-case trays were mostly empty, their wax-paper sheets holding little footprints of frosting. When Tomas turned to ask Lydia which of the remaining treats looked good she wasn't standing next to him anymore, but rather strolling toward the booth where the boy was reading. Tomas took a seat on a swiveling stool and watched as his daughter tugged off her mittens, cleared her throat, and knocked on the hard cover of the boy's book. The boy lowered the book with half-lidded eyes, far enough to peer over its top, then rested it facedown on the table.

—Nobody's home, he said with exaggerated grumpiness, then started cracking up.

A smile filled Lydia's face as she slid in next to him. A chocolate doughnut waited for her on a plate at his table, just as she'd predicted.

Tomas ordered a cup of coffee from the woman behind the counter. Maybe it was the flowy fabric of her sari, or possibly the drape of her woolen scarf, but as the woman shifted trays and dumped coffee grounds she moved with such fluidity that he immediately pictured her dancing, eyes closed, alone on a colorful floor. He was somewhat ashamed of this exotification, yet as he studied the way her hair was pulled into a bun and speared with something that looked like a painted pencil, his shame was not great enough to halt his fantasy of sliding that thing out with his teeth and letting her thick black hair gush down her back. Beyond the bank of coffeepots, behind a swinging door, the metallic clunk of kitchen work sent Tomas into a mild panic. A man back there coughed.

Of course she was married, he told himself. Just goddamned look at her.

—Your daughter? the woman said, nodding toward the corner booth as she filled Tomas's mug.

Tomas rubbed his beard, embarrassed. He'd been expecting an accent, but other than a certain softness and calm, the woman's voice was as crisply generic as that of anyone else from the mountain West.

—Lydia, he said. Your son?

—Raj, she said.

—Little Flower?

—Little Flower.

The icy windows dripped.

Raj Patel was a sorrowful kid with a shaggy bowl of black hair and an array of polyester jumpsuits with built-in buckles that, from that day forward, would always remind Tomas of zookeeper outfits. Tomas would soon learn that the boy's parents, Maya and Rohan Patel, were second-generation Indian Americans who had been running Gas 'n Donuts for over ten years. When they were teenagers in Southern California their relationship and eventual marriage had been carefully coordinated by both sets of parents—the families had been in the States long enough to avoid using the word *arranged*, though all parties involved knew that was exactly what it was—and ironically, the financial conditions of the marriage were precisely what allowed the young couple to move to Denver, far away from the reach of their families, to buy this deco gas station and replace its repair bays with an unassuming doughnut shop. For all of her immediate warmth, Tomas noticed during their early meetings that Maya's eye contact was typically brisk, offered in passing as she moved between tasks, and when he met her husband, Rohan, he understood why. Whenever Rohan stepped out of the kitchen, his thick hair bursting against a hairnet, his thick gut bursting against a stained white apron, customers shifted up and down the counter and Tomas felt himself shrink. When he learned that Rohan had once chased an early-morning burglar away from the flower shop next door, and another time had grabbed the old Montgomery Ward .22 rifle the previous owner had left in a storage closet—good for popping rats in the alley, but not much else—and thrown himself into the thick of a carjacking at the stoplight up the block, receiving for his valor a zipper of stitches and a reputation as the neighborhood's cranky guardian angel, he felt better about letting Lydia hang around his shop.

From the start, Lydia and Raj found great companionship in their after-school routine of walking together from Little Flower to Gas 'n Donuts, where they would frost and sprinkle their own doughnuts, then sit in the corner booth, playing games or drawing with markers or quietly reading with their sneakers bumping beneath the table. After an hour or so, they'd finish their little bottles of OJ with an enthusiastic *Cheers!*, then complete the triangle of their journey by walking the eight or so blocks to the library to do homework and explore the stacks until their parents were done for the day. Early on, Raj and Lydia had been escorted by a parent on these walks—usually by Maya, who held their hands without realizing the enormous maternal comfort she emanated, especially to the motherless Lydia—but from about third grade on the kids were given permission to walk alone, as long as they promised to stick together and always announce their arrival with an immediate phone call to whichever parent they'd just left behind. Tomas, who had a hard enough time remembering to pack Lydia's lunch box, not to mention her various vaccinations and school events, particularly appreciated the safety and efficiency of this system. He would sometimes look up from the library window and see the two kids walking arm-in-arm and his gratitude would nearly floor him. He was single and reclusive and growing grayer by the hour, yet never in his life had he ever imagined feeling such a fullness of being.

His daughter was happy. His daughter was his life.

And then, deep in the spidery crawl space below Gas 'n Donuts, between mildewed soil and a crusty concrete foundation, a cross-threaded water pipe that had been dripping into the ground for years gradually eroded far enough to begin to trickle, then to drizzle, then to fully flood the rank earthen space. At its worst, the mud pooling below the shop seemed thick enough to swallow them all.

Lydia and Raj learned about the pooling flood one afternoon when the kitchen door swung open and Mr. Patel came cursing through the shop with a vein visible on his neck like a little snake beneath his skin. He had mud all over his jeans and T-shirt from searching through the goddamned crawl space for the goddamned shut-off valve. Mrs. Patel, who'd been overseeing the gas pumps, looked with sorrow at Raj and Lydia, then wiped her hands on a rag. Not long ago, she'd cut her hair short, and now, with an unexpected roughness, she rubbed it with her fingertips. Mr. Patel disappeared into the kitchen, and she sighed and followed behind him.

Lydia glanced across the table at Raj, who looked as if he were trying to disappear between the collars of his mellow-yellow jumpsuit. He suggested that they walk over to the library and get going on their schoolwork.

—maybe we should keep an eye on things here for a bit, she said. since your parents are—

—Killing each other behind the walls?

Lydia smiled. Raj tried to smile too but it didn't work. At one point, Mrs. Patel came running out of the kitchen with a flashlight, locked the register, shut off the gas pumps, flipped around the CLOSED sign, and locked the front door, then ran back into the kitchen with two empty coffee cans. Mr. Patel cursed somewhere below their feet.

Lydia's dad had snapped at Lydia plenty of times, so she was familiar with a base level of household tension, but being around the Patels when they were fighting was a different experience entirely, one that both frightened and mesmerized her. Their fighting felt like *weather*, like clouds had been trapped behind that swinging kitchen door and were presently rolling down from the ceiling. Eventually, though, the storm disappeared beneath the sounds of someone rapping the glass of the doughnut shop door. When Raj ran over to unlock it, a lanky man with a blond mustache, wearing jeans and a jean jacket, strolled in slowly, carrying a hefty red toolbox at his side. He flicked a toothpick and looked around, and even from across the room Lydia could see that his eyes were bright and the color of ash.

—Where's the water? he said in a relaxed voice, as if he were a detective entering a crime scene, asking for the body.

Behind the plumber trailed a girl with a fierce, determined gait, her arms thrown back and chin thrown forward in a way that reminded Lydia of Eloise stomping the halls of the Plaza Hotel. She had irate red hair and a pale freckled face and wore the same red-and-blue plaid uniform dress as Lydia.

39

Carol O'Toole was her name. The plumber's daughter.

—Thought it was gonna be all wet in here, she said, clearly disappointed.

Before Mr. O'Toole disappeared with his toolbox into the storm within the kitchen, he pointed to a stool at the counter and Carol sat down, facing the display case of doughnuts and the bank of coffeepots and stacks of little plates.

As soon as Raj locked up the door and slid across from Lydia again, Lydia kicked him beneath the table: *Carol O'Toole. Carol O'Toole!* They both looked at her linty lollipop of red hair. Carol leaned forward and pulled a fork out of the utensil bin and began cleaning out her fingernails with one of its tines, wholly indifferent to her classmates' presence.

Carol was in the other fourth-grade class at Little Flower and her exploits were legendary. Lydia did not need to remind Raj that during the middle of the science fair last spring, for example, Carol had flushed four apples down the toilet, flooding the bathroom and part of the hallway, then had the guts to claim that her *hypothesis had been validated*. A few months before that, Carol had shown up at the Halloween party wearing a red dress with a fake knife sticking out of her chest, pronouncing to everyone that she was *Annie, only stabbed*. And just a few weeks ago in catechism class, one of the kinder nuns had lauded Carol for how *original* she was in her sinfulness, as if God had yet to announce the commandments that she was breaking every day. Needless to say, Lydia was impressed.

—You're in the other fourth grade at Little Flower, Carol said, pointing at Lydia with the fork.

—yeah.

—So are you, she said, pointing at Raj.

—Yep.

She pointed at the ribbed glass containers of sugar and

nondairy creamer that were tucked next to the napkins where
the Formica table met the wall.

—Grab the creamer, she said.

With the grown-ups back in the kitchen, shining lights into
the crawl space and sighing over the costs of this plumbing
eruption, Raj and Lydia followed Carol out the side door and
into the alley behind the shop. Carol looked around for a
minute, then told Raj to take the jar of powdery creamer and
climb up the access ladder built into the back of the brick motel
across the way. Lydia and Raj had dared each other to climb
that ladder before, but both had always chickened out. Not
today. Today, under Carol's squinting authority, chickening
out was not an option. Raj tightened the buckled belt on his
jumpsuit and took the creamer and climbed.

—Go up about ten feet, Carol said.

He hesitated, hugging the rungs.

—Or get down here and I'll do it. It's probably your nap
time anyway.

Raj climbed. When he neared the top, Carol positioned herself beneath the ladder, then directed him to unscrew the jar's
flippy lid and slowly pour the powder down onto the flame.

—What flame?

—This flame, she said. Then she took a book of matches
out of her pocket and struck one and twisted her wrist until
the whole pack lit with a fiery flash that she held at the end of
her fingertips.

—Go. Go! Go!

With a horrified grimace, Raj began awkwardly sprinkling
the nondairy creamer from on high and it looked to Lydia like a
falling white curtain, threatening to close them off from the rest
of the world, and when it reached the matches a massive flower
of flame began blooming in the air, feeding off the falling powder

41

and igniting the creamer curtain and climbing with a sparkling *whoosh* toward the bottle in Raj's hands. Carol snapped back just as the roll of flames slapped at her face and hair, and Lydia jumped away without looking and landed in the soggy pothole behind her. Within a few seconds the entire flame had dissolved, burning up most of the creamer and filling the air with sticky black specks. Carol tossed the matches to the ground, and Raj panicked and dropped the container from the ladder's height so it shattered into a jagged pile of glass on the asphalt.

The three of them looked at each other. The air was thick with the muddy pungency of burned hair.

—Heckinay, Carol said.

She smiled and Lydia followed her lead, but Raj looked terrified on the ladder, like a sailor clinging to a mast. Almost immediately the doughnut shop's back door opened and Mrs. Patel came out to dump her bucket, wearing a pink spiraling sari and long yellow kitchen gloves. When she saw Raj up on the ladder across the alley and the shattered creamer container below him, she quietly peered back into the doughnut shop to make sure she was alone.

—Pick up the glass, she said in a harsh and hushed voice, before your father comes out and sees you. Then you go to the library. *Now.*

Lydia and Raj picked up the shards and carried them in their palms to the dumpster. Carol pretended to help but really she just knelt next to the mess and made a show of trying not to laugh. Lydia's left sneaker was soaked and gray from the watery pothole, and Raj kept touching his hair and eyebrows to see how badly they'd been singed. As the two of them hustled out of the alley toward the street, Lydia turned back to wave goodbye to their schoolmate Carol, but Carol had already moved on.

CHAPTER FIVE

Lydia was contemplating the birthday party photo when she gazed between the splintered columns of the store's ground floor and saw a woman standing near the entrance, looking around as if lost in a forest. She was short and wide, wore red stretch pants and a *Skate City!* T-shirt, and carried a cane that was bottomed by a tennis ball. The moment she caught sight of Lydia behind the register she huffed loudly and began heading her way.

The woman placed a beaded cigarette case on the counter, lifted her glasses from a lanyard around her neck, and pulled a yellow Post-it note out of her bra. As she squinted into the note, Lydia saw that the part splitting the center of the woman's gray hair was nearly an inch wide. A sad landing strip, shiny under the bookstore lights.

"You're looking for something?" Lydia asked in her kindest voice.

"I think," the woman gasped, "I'm looking. For you."

"Come again?"

"Does that say *Lydia?*" the woman asked.

Lydia looked at the note. *LYDIA*, it said, written in dull pencil.

"It does."

"And you're Lydia?"

Lydia looked at the woman and considered lying.

"Can I recommend something to read?"

"Are you. Or aren't you. Lydia?"

"I am."

The woman paused for a moment and studied her with dissatisfaction. "Look at that ever-lovin' hair," she said. "You got bus tokens?"

"Bus tokens? No, ma'am. I use a pass."

"Good. That's cheaper. Take the Fifteen up Colfax. You might want to write this down. Because I'm not coming back. Take the Fifteen up Colfax. Past Smiley's Laundromat. Get off at the James Dean mural. Walk straight down across Thirteenth. Big brick house near the corner. Bad grass and falling fence. I'm on the ground." She squinted suspiciously before adding, "Joey didn't say you'd be such a pill."

"Joey?"

"Then again," she added, "Joey didn't say much at all, did he? See you after work."

The woman scooped up her cigarettes and planted her cane and went out the door without a browse.

The door in front of Lydia was painted red and covered in scratches. Based on the bank of mailboxes by the entry and the circle of chairs on the porch—arranged around a parlor ashtray that was resting on a stack of phone books—this musty old Queen Anne home had been carved up and converted into a dozen or so small units. Joey had apparently lived in one.

Lydia and David's apartment was six or eight blocks away, and she found it somewhat meaningful that Joey had also ended up living in Capitol Hill. The whole neighborhood was a hodge-podge of different styles and eras and people, all packed close to downtown on cramped streets with fantastic trees. It could be a bit rough and more turbulent than she sometimes liked, especially late on weekend nights, but Lydia loved how walking down a single block she might see a row of subdued Foursquare homes, a sixties-era high-rise, a simple brick deco apartment building, a Queen Anne pseudo-mansion like this one, plus a cross-section of Denver's rich and poor, gay and straight, black and brown and white. It was one of the few places she'd ever lived where she felt as if she were moving while standing still. She wondered if Joey had felt that too.

Before she decided to knock, the door opened and within seconds, without eye contact, the balding woman from the bookstore was escorting her up the staircase.

"Up we go," the woman said.

"Where are we going?"

"Up."

The staircase stretched through the center of the old home. The woman still wore her red stretch pants but her cane was missing and her chapped grip clung to Lydia's elbow as they climbed the stairs. In distant quadrants of the house she could hear doors opening and closing, a toilet flushing, men coughing. She still had no idea why she was here—*Joey?*—but the woman's sense of purpose stifled any desire to ask.

When they reached the landing, the woman stopped and hunched forward, hands on her knees.

"Give me a second," she said, struggling to catch her breath.

"If you wanted to tell me something," Lydia said, aiming to be friendly, "you could have phoned the store. I'm almost always there. Saved yourself the trip, you know?"

"I wanted to see you first. Have a gander. Then if I trusted your looks I was going to let you in. If you seemed high-and-mighty, all of it was going into the trash."

"All of what?"

"The stuff. In his apartment. Someone else has been assigned his place, moving in on Friday, so today's the day it's gotta go. Keep what you want. I'll have the rest thrown out."

"I think you have the wrong Lydia."

"Got it all right here," she said, pulling the yellow Post-it out of her bra. "Lydia. From the bookstore. Joey told me there was *only one Lydia*. Was he wrong?"

"I'm her," Lydia said, feeling her skin go hot and tighten around her eyes. "So this is where he lived?"

"You really don't know why you're here?" As the woman blinked, a growth on her lower lid seemed to scrape her eye. "Then why'd he give me your name? You his auntie or big sister? Because you're too old to be his lover, I hope."

"I think I was just his bookseller."

"Whatever that means," the woman said. "Either way he wanted it all passed to you. An inheritance, you could call it, though honestly there isn't much. The shithead probably burned half of it."

"Burned it?"

"You'll see," the woman said. She climbed the remaining steps and steered Lydia into the dimly lit third-floor hallway. Lydia toed a gray smudge on the carpet and decided it was a onetime raisin.

"Can I ask when Joey arranged this?"

"Long before he died, if that's what you're getting at. But what you really want to know is why. Part of my job is to ask all the boys what I should do with their stuff if they ever get sent back to the pokey. Joey said, *Lydia. From the bookstore.*"

"To the pokey?" Lydia said. "What kind of a place is this?"

"Used to call it a halfway house, but anymore it's 'reintegration something-or-other.' Really, it's a home for wayward boys who are all grown up."

"A home for felons."

"Ex-felons. So you can see the problem. If they get picked up again while they're living here, I'm stuck with all their crap. That's how I know about you." The woman reached for the handle and stopped. "Smell it yet?"

Lydia did: a burned pungent scent, soggy smelling, like a fire pit in the rain.

"What is that?" Lydia said.

"Joey," she said, "in his infinite wisdom, decided to have a bonfire in his kitchen. He contained it inside a trash can, but still. Goddamned fire alarm goes off and he's gone. And I mean *gone*: he never stepped foot inside this apartment again."

"Was that the day?"

"That was the day. Good thing I had a master key and a fire extinguisher or we'd be standing on a pile of charred bricks right now. The handyman is supposed to try to get rid of the stench, but he's waiting on you. To get your stuff. So today would be good. To get your stuff."

"Any idea why Joey would do that?"

"Because even dead he's a pain in my ass," the woman said, brushing past Lydia. She pursed her face and reached into her shirt and jangled a necklace of keys out of nowhere. With a click Joey's door opened.

"Joey overall seemed decent," the woman continued. "He was like a kicked dog, untrusting, so you must've done something for him."

Lydia felt herself blushing.

The woman smiled. "You know, you think they have what it takes to pull it together, and then they go and rob a liquor store or have public sex in a mattress shop or hang themselves in a bookstore. I really thought Joey was different."

Lydia peered into Joey's apartment. The woman let go of her elbow.

"All yours," the woman said, clinging to the railing, heading back down the stairs. "Like it or not, Lydia-from-the-bookstore, the kid chose you."

Inside Joey's apartment Lydia wasn't surprised by the scarcity of furniture—a kitchen island with a single stool, a simple wooden folding chair parked against a simple wooden desk—but she was surprised by how bland his home was. Walls all bare. No photographs on the fridge or desk, no hampers or baskets in the bedroom. And tidy, especially for a guy in his early twenties. She peered into his drawers and cabinets and found them empty except for some folded clothes and basic spices and cleaning supplies. The only thing in his bedroom closet was a black wool suit in a dry-cleaning bag, hanging next to a pressed white shirt and a red tie. She couldn't imagine any occasion for which Joey would need a suit, except perhaps a court date, but it looked brand-new, so she hung it from the front door to drop at a thrift store or pass along to a BookFrog in need.

Next to the door was a small stack of newspapers bound by twine and waiting to be recycled, and on top of the pile was a slim, spiral-bound book with a blue cover and gilded lettering. From the cheap format and the painful title—*The Birds and the Beakers: Forty Years in a Biology Classroom*—she could tell it had been self-published, an educational autobiography, which might explain why Joey had left it in his recycling pile. Her heart sank as she tossed it to the floor below the suit to take with her.

In the bathroom she smelled Joey's pear-shaped soap, felt

the scuffed texture of his bath towel, waiting for something to stand out. Hanging on the wall behind the bathroom door was a framed certificate of completion for some state program called Rebuilding Ourselves, and she was surprised by the tidiness of his signature: *Joseph Edward Molina*. A few knotted garbage bags were piled in the kitchen, and when she unknotted one and peered inside, feeling as if she were dunking her head into a stagnant pond, she found an unfinished box of Life cereal, a dented tomato soup can, a mealwormed bag of buckwheat, a brick of Velveeta, and partial containers of coffee and ketchup and lemon juice and curdled chocolate milk—all thoughtfully prepared for the dumpster, all reinforcing how ready to die Joey had been.

Joey's landlady had left his windows open in an attempt to air out the place, but everything still reeked of a soggy barbecue. Out on the fire escape, Lydia found a small metal trash can holding fragments of ash. Joey's charred papers, she thought, maybe Joey's charred books. She stirred the brittle burnings with a butter knife, but the closest she came to anything legible was the corner of a scorched manila envelope that revealed an emblem of faint letters, discolored but intact: a triangular logo showing a green mountain capped with snow, similar to the one on Colorado license plates and state regalia, along with the faint letters *CODVR*. When she reached into the can to try to pick it up for a closer look it disintegrated into pieces, leaving a gray smudge on her fingertips.

Whatever Joey was burning here, he'd wanted it gone.

From the depths of her satchel, Lydia pulled out the pocket-sized notebook with a sunflower on its cover that David had bought for her birthday last year, after he'd grown tired of finding little scraps of paper on her nightstand, filled with a title, an author, a page number, or a quote. On a blank page, she wrote down the single cluster of letters followed by a big fat question mark: *CODVR?*

As she continued to move through the apartment, it occurred to Lydia that, outside of his favorite authors, she knew practically nothing about Joey. And outside of the certificate he'd left hanging on the bathroom wall, Joey had left nothing behind that might signal his identity. She may as well have been searching through an empty hotel room in any city in any country on the planet.

Joey—a young, invisible, singular kid—had erased himself from the world.

Except for his books, she thought. Which were where?

When Lydia had first stepped into this apartment, she'd been expecting a cavernous personal library, but in fact Joey's entire collection amounted to the single milk crate of a dozen or so titles sitting on top of his desk—that was all. Most of them seemed fitting for Joey (a book on Virgin Mary sightings and another on Sasquatch sightings, one history of Hasidism, three Penguin Classics, a Victorian-era *Child's Story Primer*, a few Vonnegut novels, biographies of J. D. Salinger and Jerzy Kosinski) but a few of them gave her pause, including a dubious collection of pastel poetry, a motivational business bible, and a biography of the Osmond family. She also noticed more than a few favorites that he'd bought based on her recommendation— Henry James's *The Turn of the Screw*, freshly annotated; Alice Munro's *Open Secrets*; Denis Johnson's *Resuscitation of a Hanged Man*; Katherine Dunn's *Geek Love*; Paul Auster's *The New York Trilogy*—and the sight of each made her sigh.

Just as she finished going through them, she saw another book—one she remembered Joey buying—only it wasn't in the crate at all, but rather leaning against the wall that flanked the back of his desk. The neck of his desk lamp was craned toward the wall, and when she clicked its switch the light shone precisely upon the book, as if he'd placed it on display.

A Universal History of the Destruction of Books.

She recalled the day a few months ago when Joey had staggered up to the bookstore counter with this very book in hand, looking exceptionally wispy in his black windbreaker and black dress slacks cut off at the shins. His black hair had been tucked inside a knit hat, but a few strands still clung to his tawny cheeks.

—Can I ask? he said.

Hearing Joey's voice was rare, and when he did speak he sounded hushed, almost stonerly, and often ended his sentences with an inquisitive lilt, as if even he was surprised to hear himself speaking.

—Sure, she said.

Joey pulled a small hardback out from the crook of his arm and placed it between them on the counter: *A Universal History of the Destruction of Books.* A title that had been relegated to the depths of the bargain shelves, where most of Joey's books came from.

—What do you think it's worth, he said, a book like this?

Lydia spun the book in her hand, quite expertly, and looked at the bar-coded label on the back. Though brand-new, the book had been marked down and down and was now selling for a whopping forty-eight cents. Depressing.

—Looks like a really good deal, she said.

Joey flattened his palms on the wooden counter. His hands were long and skinny, scarred across the knuckles but soft.

—I mean what's it *worth*. Not what's it cost.

Lydia stared at him, trying to measure his intent. She took a tiny step back.

—I guess it just bugs me to be paying so little, he added.

Something's wrong in the air, you know, when a book costs less than a bullet. Or a Coke. Values-wise.

Lydia sighed in agreement. Joey touched the book between them, a gentle finger-tap.

—These things saved my life, he said, in nearly a whisper. That's no small thing.

—You're not alone there.

—See, people say that all the time but for me they really did.

Joey pulled off his hat and wrung it between his palms as if it were a washcloth. His eyes appeared so green against his bronze skin and dark eyebrows that they seemed to glow from behind, as if hollowed from jade. He was a beautiful boy.

—I don't know what I would have done without reading, he said. My whole life, really, but especially in prison. You know I was in prison, right?

—I heard that.

Joey looked to his left, then to his right, then gently tugged down the front of his black shirt until she could see the dark outline of a leafless tree tattooed up the center of his sternum.

—Prison, he said. Do you know what they use for weapons in there? *Candy.* Seriously. They make knives out of Jolly Ranchers. And if you heat up a candy bar with caramel and chocolate you can basically burn someone's face off. So I was told.

Lydia nodded carefully but didn't say anything. She wasn't exactly uncomfortable, yet she was aware of how utterly odd this conversation was, in large part because of a silent agreement among the BookFrogs to never talk about their past—a quality that made her the perfect candidate to be their unspoken, unelected, unassuming ambassador. She was all about silencing the past.

—How long were you in? she said.

—Actual prison? From seventeen to nineteen, around two years.

—*Seventeen?*

—Sixteen, if you include all the time while I waited for my sentence. You know what the Pooh-Bah told me on the day of my intake? *Tried as an adult, treated as an adult.* I think he was trying to scare me. It worked.

—Seventeen, she said.

—I know I deserved it, I really did, but it was unbearable all the same. It does things to you, Lydia. Unrecommended things.

—Enter books, she said.

—Yeah. Enter books.

Joey fiddled with the loose threads of his hat, and she thought she should hold on to the moment; she thought he was telling her all of this for a reason.

—Do you want to tell me what you did? she said. It's okay if you don't.

Joey was quiet, but he seemed ready to speak when a chubby businessman with a tie hanging out of his blazer pocket strolled through and bought a daily newspaper and offered Lydia a wink. Joey stepped aside and his eyes, so often buzzing about, went completely still until the man left. She could see his face warming up, growing pink beneath his cheeks. He hadn't put his hat back on and his hair was tied in a knot in the back, and, she noticed for the first time, there were tiny pieces of leaf and paper clinging to its strands.

—It wasn't me, he said. I mean I did it, I'm responsible, but I was just a teenager, so it wasn't really me.

Joey leaned into the counter and began to speak, just above a whisper, and never once met her eye, as if he were talking to a ghost who was just behind her and slightly to the left.

—I try to tell myself it didn't count, he continued. Because I was so young.

—I'm listening.

53

When Joey was fifteen, he was placed in a vocational group home with about a dozen other teenage boys in North Denver. They lived together and did household chores and took classes to learn carpentry and mechanics, spatial relations, basic work skills. They kept themselves occupied by drinking cleaning products and huffing Wite-Out and computer duster and snorting nutmeg or cloves, most of which they would steal on trips to the grocery store and much of which was ineffective at inducing any state but nausea. And a few of them discovered that if they just didn't sleep for days on end—if they lay in bed and poked themselves with needles or pulled their own hair or slapped their cheeks any time they were about to drift off—they could fight their way through the exhaustion and, after two or three days, climb over what Joey called the Wall of Tired and bring themselves beyond the brink and into hallucinations.

One day in May a group of four of them started out and made it twenty-four, thirty-six, forty-eight hours without a wink. They went about their daily tasks, and at night they tried to read sci-fi novels or play video games or do what little they could to work on their certifications—but one by one they began to fall asleep. Except Joey. Joey had made it for almost four days without so much as a nap and soon felt like he was wearing a humongous costume, like a furry mascot stomping around an imaginary playland. He'd gotten so tired that he no longer could feel anything, including being tired, and in the middle of his woodworking class one afternoon he just started laughing uncontrollably and walked out by way of the fire escape and no one stopped him.

The city was alive with things that were not there. Trees had eyes and cars had smiles and the sidewalk was a river of ash. He told himself that he was merely heading home, but of course he had no home, so in fact what he did was wander until dusk, seeking the next levels of his game. When he found a loose retaining wall behind a flower shop and, just below it, a fresh pallet of cinder blocks, he knew he'd found the next level.

He carried the cinder blocks, two at a time, a few streets away to an overpass above the interstate. On the sidewalk he began accumulating the blocks like a kid amassing snowballs. Each move was accompanied by little buzzes and beeps.

—For some reason I decided I hated minivans, Joey said. Minivans became the game.

—Minivans?

—I can't explain it, really. When I was growing up there used to be vans and suddenly there were minivans instead. I don't know. I established a point system based on the color of the van. Remember, I hadn't slept in days.

Joey stood up on the railing, sixteen feet over the interstate, and listened to cars whipping past straight below him, fifty-five, sixty-five miles per hour. And he began dropping cinder blocks on them.

—But only on minivans, he said. As if there was a logic to it.

He would stand up tall enough to see the cars coming from the other direction and then, just as they vanished under the overpass, he would whip around and try to time his drops so the falling blocks would hit the center of the van's metal roof.

—Not the windshield. I didn't want to kill anyone. Apparently.

Over a period of five minutes, Joey hit two vans with his cinder blocks; both thunked straight into the roof. There was something special, he decided, about the way he dangled the heavy blocks high above the highway, then just opened his hand and let gravity take over. The sound of those massive blocks thunking the tops of the vans—the sound was *immense*, like a shotgun blast directly below his feet, only it was accompanied by bright green and blue lights. A side window shattered on the second one. Both vans skidded but regained control and just kept going, and from Joey's vantage on the overpass they appeared to be crawling away from him in defeat. Maybe the drivers were too scared to turn around. Most likely they went straight to the cops. Joey never found out because—

—The third one, he said. The third minivan. I leaned with the cinder block over the railing and opened my hand to release it and watched it disappear straight through the top of the van. A perfect hit. But there were no sound effects this time. No lights. Nothing. It was freaky at first, like I'd imagined the whole thing, hallucinated it, a ghost van, a wormhole van—but then I realized the cinder block had sailed straight through the van's open sunroof. Swish.

Inside the van, a one-year-old girl eating Cheerios from a plastic bag in a car seat had been sitting directly behind the sunroof. Joey's dropped block appeared before her eyes out of thin air and tagged her left knee, then bounced and flattened her diaper bag. The van lost control and skidded into the guardrail and the airbag released and broke her mother's nose. Outside of a fractured kneecap and some cuts and bruises the toddler was fine, at least physically.

—Everyone survived, Joey said, even me. Though I shouldn't have.

Joey was arrested in the middle of the interstate. Because of his sleep deprivation there was some discussion of temporary insanity, but the crime was so reckless and his juvenile record was so spotty that in the end he was charged as an adult. He pleaded down from first-degree felony assault and felony criminal mischief, and was eventually sentenced to forty months in an adult state prison. Because of his demeanor, and because all he did in jail all day was read and avoid even a whiff of conflict, he served just over two years.

—I almost killed a *baby*. How do you undo that one, you know?

Lydia tried to swallow but couldn't. Her eyes felt dry and when she blinked she saw a silhouette of a man looming above her, holding a hammer in the dark. She tasted blood.

—You don't, she finally said.

—And the irony of the whole thing? After all that sleep deprivation, most nights in my cell I couldn't sleep. Serves me right.

—Hence all the reading.

The air between them felt suddenly cold. Lydia wondered what would happen if she were to share the horrors of her past the way Joey just had.

Maybe he sensed the intensity of her discomfort, because he put a dollar on the counter and pressed the wrinkles out of it.

—I would like to purchase this book, he said with faux formality, sliding it before her.

Lydia had never heard Joey speak so freely. She rang up the book and stuck a bookmark inside, and then, maybe out of her own nervousness, she did something she'd never done to a BookFrog before: she reached forward and ruffled Joey's hair. He froze and his eyes went wide, then he grabbed his book and stumbled away. As soon as he rounded the counter, he broke into a little trot, but Lydia couldn't tell if he was happy or horrified.

Her fingers smelled like cat food. She thought absently of her father.

A Universal History of the Destruction of—

Joey.

The smell of old smoke left a prickly itch in Lydia's nose as she leaned over Joey's desk. She wondered why he'd piled all of his other books into a milk crate, while this one he'd left on display. In the tiny tin trash can alongside the desk Lydia expected another cauldron of ash, but instead found a dozen or so wads of tissue, each spotty with small dark drops of blood, as if he'd been suffering from bloody noses or shaving cuts. She recalled the night he died, and the masking tape that had been wrapped around three or four of his fingertips, and she realized that those cuts had happened right here, at this desk. She lifted the can and stirred aside some of the Kleenex, and discovered, at the bottom of the trash can, a few tabs of paper, tiny and white, just like the one she'd found the other day in the alcove where he'd hanged himself. One tab was stuck to a pink knot of bubble gum on the bottom of the can, but the rest were sprinkled around, and when she pinched them into her fingers and looked at them in the light, she saw that these also didn't hold any words, per se, at least not whole words—more like pieces of words and letters, bisected and trimmed until they'd lost their meaning. Lydia brushed them back into the trash and sat silently at the desk.

A Universal History of the Destruction of Books.

She opened the book and flipped through, and soon came across a page that held exactly what she'd been looking for: little holes, little windows, cut randomly into the paper. She began to read.

The incredible, unacceptable fac▮▮▮ ▮▮▮t the Spanish attack reduced pow▮▮▮▮ cultures to ashes. In the Nahuatl language, still spoken today by over a million Aztec descendant▮▮▮▮ word for truth is *neltilztli*, derived from "foundation," and if we look carefully we see that what the conquistadors sought to annihila▮▮ ▮▮▮▮ historical foundations. The Spaniards deliberately eliminated the paintings prepared by the *tlama▮*▮▮▮▮

58

or wise men, on astronomy, history, religion, and literature. In the *calméac*, or higher-education centers, the so-called codices were chanted: "They were taught to speak well, they were taught the canticles." Another poem reflects this idea.

I sing the paintings in the book,
I unfold i
I'm like a florid parrot,
I make the codices speak,
Insid   house of paintings.

Nine or so tiny rectangles and squares had been sliced out of the paper, so that when she held the open book up to the light the page resembled a child's cutout of a skyscraper. Because of the size and dimensions of the cuts, she first assumed that words had been sliced out, that Joey had been cutting and pasting sentences together for some anonymous project, like—good god—a ransom note, or maybe some kind of magnetic-poetry collage. Or a suicide note. But as she looked closer at the holes she saw that there were no missing words at all: the cuts intersected white space and words with no discrimination, so that the words themselves had been largely bisected out of comprehension.

And she noticed something else on the page as well: ink. Rusty red ink, smudged in the periphery of the holes. Only this wasn't ink, she realized as she tilted the book under the light: this was blood. From Joey's fingers.

In something close to panic, Lydia set aside *A Universal History of the Destruction of Books* and grabbed the first title she could from the milk crate. It too was peppered with little windows, as was the next book, and the next book, and the rest—

Little windows, she thought as she clicked off Joey's light and dragged his crate of books with her to the door. Little windows through which Joey was inviting her to climb.

CHAPTER SIX

It had taken Carol's father, Bart O'Toole of O'Toole's Plumbing, several afternoons of wriggling and climbing through that tight little crawl space to replace the corroded valves and update the pipes that had caused the flood beneath Gas 'n Donuts. During those days, Carol came to the shop with her father, and as he worked she managed to slink, one stool at a time, ever closer to Lydia and Raj's booth, and eventually began joining them on their daily walks to the library.

At first, Tomas had celebrated Carol's arrival into his daughter's life, convincing himself that any attention for Lydia was better than none, but it wasn't long before he understood that *this* Carol was *the* Carol—the holy terror he'd heard stories about since Lydia's earliest days at Little Flower—and that his cherished library had now become her new *territory*. One afternoon, he found a photocopy of a girl's squished ass on the floor next to the Xerox machine, followed shortly after by a copy of a five-dollar bill jammed into the cash slot of the Coke machine. Another time, over the course of a single day he caught the kids spinning folk albums backwards on the record player, booby-trapping shelves so the slightest touch would bring a tumble of books crashing down, and cutting coupons out of

1950s-era magazines (*We're gonna get a sweet deal on cake mix!* he heard Carol exclaim). But perhaps most upsetting was that with Carol's arrival, Raj didn't seem to hang around as much. Tomas had found him more than once reading alone on the basement beanbags, looking so solemn and disheveled that it was impossible to miss what was happening: the boy was being replaced.

For weeks Tomas had been trying to err on the side of optimism when it came to Lydia's infamous friend, but this wishful thinking would end one weekday morning in the fall as he was eating toast and reading the newspaper at the kitchen table. Lydia had been uncommonly quiet that morning, ducked behind a box of Raisin Bran, slurping her cereal in a trance.

—You about ready for school?

The messy crash and plunge of Lydia's spoon came to a halt.

—i need your signature.

Tomas folded the newspaper over and looked at Lydia. He resettled his horn-rims with a blink and scratched his beard.

—You need my signature? What does that mean?

Lydia slid up from the table with her head down and jogged over to the hook by the front door where her backpack hung. A moment later she jogged back and handed Tomas a pink piece of paper. Still head down.

—What's this?

—read.

Tomas knew what it was; he just couldn't believe it had come from his daughter. Across the top its heading read *Discipline Sheet*, and further down it explained that *Lydia Gladwell* of *4th Grade, Room 2* had been found guilty of both *Behavioral Problems* and *Disrespect for Authority.* Under the *Comments* section, Sister Antoinette wrote simply, *Inappropriate games during lunch. Last warning.*

Tomas cleared his throat and lifted his chin.

—i got in trouble yesterday for playing a game.

—You and Carol?

—and raj.

—But this was one of Carol's games?

Lydia's neck shrunk into her shoulders.

—Was this one of Carol's—

—yeah.

One of Carol's games. Tomas took a sip of tea and braced himself as Lydia explained that they were playing something called Don't Swallow Your Spit. Apparently the rules were simple: you kept your mouth closed and you pretended you were sucking on an invisible Life Saver and you didn't swallow your spit. She and Raj and Carol had been playing this at the lunch table in the cafeteria, breathing through their noses and making faces at each other as their mouths welled with warm runny saliva, when Sister Antoinette lumbered their way. Raj and Carol managed to jump up to clear their trays before the old nun reached them, but Lydia got stuck at the table, and when Sister Antoinette snapped at her about making such a horrible face while people around her were eating, Lydia couldn't take it anymore. Her mouth burst open. The sound was a wet wallop. Spit slid all over her hands and uniform and the tabletop. Sister Antoinette made Lydia stay behind and wipe all the cafeteria tables with a rag and some vinegar-smelling brown water that, Lydia told her dad at the breakfast table, was far more foul than a giant mouthful of spit.

Tomas lowered his newspaper and leaned into his elbows. Lydia seemed pale as she stirred through her soggy cereal. A puddle of foody milk sloshed out of the bowl.

—Do I need to make you stop playing with Carol?

—raj was there too.

63

—I'll sign it, he said. But no more of Carol's games, understand?

Lydia chewed on a braid of her hair and nodded, but he could tell she didn't really mean it.

There at the table, Tomas could feel his little girl drifting from him, and he began to feel desperate to pull her back. His eyes wandered the kitchen. Their yellow fridge was so covered with Lydia's drawings that he'd lately taken to taping them on the kitchen walls, and now he thought it looked obsessive, even trashy. Somewhere buried beneath all that paper was an old photo of Rose, Lydia's mom, and Tomas found himself missing her so much that his jaw hurt.

—Come with me, he said.

He guided Lydia into his room. From the top shelf of his closet he retrieved a gunmetal box and, for the first time in her life, showed Lydia the letters and cards he and Rose had exchanged for Valentine's Day and their anniversaries. Lydia read each thin penciled note and thick colorful card. Inspired by her focus, Tomas reached deep into his closet and dragged down their honeymoon photo album. And from his old cookie tin of tie clips and wheat pennies, he even unearthed Rose's ruby ring, still taped in its wad of hospital gauze. As he unfolded it and placed the ring in his daughter's palm he imagined her someday-fiancé (a studious boy with wire-rimmed glasses who could kick in some teeth when the occasion called for it) coming to ask for her hand.

—can i have it? Lydia asked.

—Sure, when you get married. At thirty-five.

—deal!

Lydia smiled and was careful as she folded the gauze back around it, and even ran into the bathroom and clipped off a new piece of medical tape to swaddle the gauze and ensure the ring wouldn't fall out. He'd rarely seen her so reverent.

—Things will get better, he said mostly to himself.

But as long as Carol was around, Tomas began to realize, things would not really get any better, and he continued to struggle with the long-term implications of Lydia's new friendship. He didn't understand, in a cosmic sense, of all the kids whom Lydia could latch on to, why it had to be the one who brought a rash to his skin. It just didn't fit—

And then, later that week, he met Dottie O'Toole, Carol's mother, and the world revealed its perfect symmetry.

Of course Tomas had noticed Dottie before she walked into the library that Tuesday afternoon, but before that day he hadn't known she was Carol's mother. She'd only been the starlet from afar, the soft-skinned redhead whose hips swayed when she entered the school gymnasium and whose every tendency seemed designed to disarm those around her. Dottie was in her early thirties, with a swirly bob and sticky lashes and blue shadow that rose from her eyes like wings. The few times Tomas had seen Dottie at school events, she'd been wearing short-sleeved sweaters in colors and patterns he'd only seen on couches—pumpkin orange, aqua green—and always they had a triangle of cleavage cut below the neckline that reminded him of an unzipped tent.

And here she was, close enough for Tomas to smell her piña colada perfume. She reached her hand across the circulation desk and introduced herself.

Tomas hadn't been on a date since Rose's death and he was never good at reading the so-called *signs* anyway, but he was pretty sure that Dottie was clutching his hand for longer than was appropriate. In a moment of pure panic, he offered to give her a tour of the disheveled library. She automatically clasped his forearm with both hands—amazingly—and said in a terrible French accent, *Lead the way, Monsieur Librarian*. He half-expected her to snap her gum.

In the library basement, Tomas was embarrassed to find Carol and Lydia on the carpet, their faces six inches apart, with women's magazines fanned sloppily around them. In their shared collapse they seemed the embodiment of parental neglect, a judgment only made worse by the uncomfortable proximity of a man reading nearby who smelled as if he'd sprayed himself with bathroom air freshener in order to disguise his must. The man's sneakers were tumbled next to his bare feet. When Tomas and Dottie arrived, he squinted grumpily over his Asimov paperback.

—Are they troubling you? Tomas asked him.

—Them? the man said. They're okay.

—You sure?

—They're okay.

—Girls, put the magazines back and we'll meet you upstairs.

To Tomas's great relief, the girls did as they were told.

—Is it really okay for them to hang out here like this? Dottie asked.

—Sure, as long as they're quiet and polite and clean up their messes.

—No, she said, I mean all these sad men reading. It's like a Lonely Hearts Club in here.

When Tomas cocked his head to study her—half-alarmed, half-amused—she was picking at a painted fingernail, apparently finished with the topic. In other circumstances, he might have told her that he'd personally encouraged *these sad men reading* to make the library their diurnal home. And he might have told her that he'd recently been reprimanded by some city bureaucrat who'd discovered the impromptu food bank that he ran out of the library's back door. Libraries were havens for everyone, he might've told her, not just the clean and productive. But his explanation faded under the commotion of Carol and

Lydia clambering up the stairs behind them. Maybe he'd have a chance to explain himself another time.

One damp afternoon a few days after this introduction, while picking up Lydia at the Little Flower gymnasium, Tomas spotted Dottie leaning against a tan brick wall and smoking a cigarette. He opened the door to go inside but she stopped him.

—How's Mr. Librarian today?

They spoke of small things, the Broncos' popularity and the arrival soon of ski season. She offered him a stick of gum and laughed when he folded it in thirds before putting it in his mouth, as if sliding a letter into an envelope.

—Your husband, he said. He's the plumber, right?

She cocked an eyebrow.

—I've seen his truck, he added.

—You've seen it at the library?

—Just around the neighborhood. He works a lot.

—He's never home, Dottie said, but at least he takes Carol on the job with him sometimes. If she had her way, she'd drop out of fourth grade and take over the family business.

Tomas smirked. He couldn't tell if Dottie was staring deep into his eyes or studying the flecked lenses of his horn-rims. Either way, he was nervous.

—At least there's good money in being a plumber, he said.

—Not good enough.

Tomas laughed a little and chomped his gum. Before he went inside to find his little girl, he turned and watched in awe as Dottie pressed the tip of her tongue delicately into her lip.

CHAPTER SEVEN

In her kitchen, Lydia nibbled the crust from her honey toast and waited impatiently for her overworked coffeemaker to finish gurgling. When she looked up, David was there in his towel, red from his shower, smelling of menthol shaving cream. He peered into Joey's milk crate, which sat in the center of their breakfast table, where Lydia had left it the night before.

"More books?" he said, picking up Joey's dusty Victorian story primer and turning it over in his hands.

"Can't ever have too many," she said lightly.

"Seriously. I like your whole book thing. Just having them around makes me feel smarter."

"Now, if we could just get you to read them."

"No need. It's like free IQ points in every room. On every conceivable surface."

"Glad to help."

"Some would call you a hoarder," he said. "But not me. I call you a *collector*."

"That's the spirit," she said.

Lydia looked up the length of David's arm and saw his clean, damp hair and the remnant glow of his shower, and felt the desire to rest her hand on his.

"They're from Joey," she said, nodding at the crate on the table. "The books."

The coffeemaker wheezed and David poured her a cup. She hummed self-consciously, feeling grateful as she sipped. David tilted up the lip of the milk crate and peered at the tumbled titles inside.

"Joey the BookFrog?" he said, and sat in the chair next to her.

"The one and only."

"And his buddy hasn't shown up yet?"

"Lyle? Not yet."

"Fishy?"

"Fishy," she said, then patted the edge of the crate. "Then there's this. Gathered from his apartment. My inheritance, apparently."

"His last good deed," David said, nodding. "It's kind of sweet. He obviously knew you'd appreciate them."

"That's one way to look at it," she said.

"I'm guessing his apartment wasn't paradise?"

"More like the inferno. Listen, I know you need to go, but . . ." She told him about visiting Joey's apartment the night before, and about the books he'd left to her in death and the strange fact that the books had holes cut out of them.

"Holes?" he said.

"Little windows," she said.

"Why would he do that?" he said in that same cerebral tone he used when describing the way he'd cracked a coding problem at work or figured out which sensor in his car was causing his engine to misfire. "I mean, what's the point of giving them to you if they're all cut up?"

"That would be the question."

"Unless there's something to them," he said, and drummed his fingers on Joey's copy of *The Turn of the Screw*. "Because with words cut out it sounds like ransom notes."

"It's not words cut out exactly," she said. "Just little random rectangles. They intersect the letters, so no chance of mining them for, say, a ransom note, or suicide note, or—"

"Or a valentine?"

"It wasn't like that," she said, unsure if this was jealousy or a joke.

"But you're sure the holes are random?" he said. "Maybe there's a pattern somehow, an encryption."

As David spoke, his voice was fading and she could sense him slipping away, quietly scrolling through his mental records of the Enigma device and Fortran punch cards and player-piano rolls and all things encoded.

"Have a look," she said, then handed him the cut-up copy of *A Universal History of the Destruction of Books.*

"Whoa."

"I know."

"Are there others?"

"Cut up?" She rested her hand on the crate. "All of them."

"*All* of them?" he said.

"Some more than others, but yeah, all of them have holes cut out. Rectangles."

David slid the chair back, stepped to the sink, drank a glass of water, and sat back down. Apparently now he was ready.

"This is wild," he said, and then, right to the point: "So why leave it all to you?"

"Exactly. Maybe for some kind of message. I don't know."

David leaned into the crate and shifted around some of the titles.

"Look at this one," she said, and handed him the self-published, spiral-bound book called *The Birds and the Beakers.* Unlike all the others in the crate, this book was *completely* peppered with the cut-out windows, so it seemed as if its pages

71

might simply disintegrate. In its own way this defacement made it beautiful, like a bound pile of paper snowflakes. "This one is definitely the anomaly. Way too many holes to follow any kind of order."

"It looks so sloppy compared to the others," he said, and after spending a few minutes skimming its holes he set it in an empty spot on the table and rested his hand atop it for a moment, as if processing by osmosis. "I have no idea what to make of that one. As for *these* . . ." He stirred through the crate, gently pushing the books around as if they were puppies in a whelping box. Occasionally he'd lift one out and open its pages and trace his fingers over its cut-out holes, and she realized he was seeking a pattern, as if it were a stack of data cards and not a book. "I should call in sick," he said. "This is way better than work."

She knew that if she asked him to, David would gladly bail on work, buckle into the chair next to her, and begin to sort through these piles. In a way, it would be his idea of the perfect date. He'd have a yellow legal pad and a mechanical pencil and a lifetime of puzzles from which to draw his inspiration.

David spent a few minutes sorting through the titles, examining the books from all angles, objectively, as if he were studying an omelet pan or a bike crank. The spine, the cover, the little Bright Ideas label stuck to the back—all of it was worthy of David's investigation.

At one point he looked up from the task and seemed surprised that Lydia was still there. "Are these all from the bookstore?"

"Most are," she said. "All of the new ones I'm pretty sure he bought from me while I was working the register." From the crate Lydia lifted a few books with yellowed pages and scuffed, outdated covers: *The Osmond Family Story*, the Victorian child's primer, a collection of pastel poetry. "These are from thrift stores or yard sales or secondhand shops. Definitely used, anyway. Not from the store. We only sell new books." David picked those up next, turned them in his hands.

"If these are used," he said, "why do they have Bright Ideas labels on them?"

"They don't."

"They do."

"They shouldn't."

"They do," he said, turning them over, one by one. "All of them do."

"Let me see," she said, skeptical.

One title at a time, Lydia flipped over the books and saw that David was right. Not only did the lower corner of each back cover have a Bright Ideas label, but as she looked close enough to read the labels—the title, bar code, ISBN, shelving section, date of arrival, and price—she could see that the information crunched there in tiny type belonged to different books altogether.

Lydia grunted and held her forehead.

"What is it?" David said.

"The labels are all wrong," she said. She lifted the copy of *A Universal History of the Destruction of Books* and tapped the label on the back: *The Bed-Wetter's Almanac*. "This should be stuck on a different book altogether," she said.

"On all of them?"

"On all of them. The new and the old: all have been mislabeled."

Lydia closed her eyes. It was entirely possible, she thought, that *one* of Joey's books could've been tagged with the wrong Bright Ideas label—she and her comrades were, after all, overworked and underpaid—but it was entirely *im*possible that *all* of them had been mislabeled. And swapping labels from book to book made no sense, unless Joey had been up to something really stupid, like exchanging labels in order to pay less at the register, the way teenagers sometimes traded price tags on clothes in department store dressing rooms in order to buy a prom dress for the cost of a thong. But more telling than any such speculations was the fact that *she* was the one who'd sold Joey most of these books, so she knew they hadn't been mislabeled when he'd brought them to her at the counter. Zapping them into the inventory system, she would have noticed that the book on the screen didn't match the book in her hand, which meant that something more than stupidity was happening here.

"You wanted to know what Joey was up to with the cut-up books?" David said. "There's your answer."

"What do you mean?" Lydia said.

David tapped one of the mismatched labels. "That's not an accident. He's pointing you to this book too. Joey is."

"Why would he do that?"

"No idea," David said with a shrug. "But if an answer exists, it's probably in the other book."

"So, what—follow the label?"

"Follow the label. Find the book it belongs to." He looked up at the clock. "Do you want me to stay? I would love to stay. Tell me to stay."

"You need to go."

"Shit," he said, smiling. "I know."

He rushed into the bedroom to finish getting ready, then returned to the table and kissed her. As he gathered his laptop and his jacket and started to leave the apartment, David swirled his bad hand in the direction of the milk crate as if casting a spell on Joey's books. "This is really messed up that he did this to you. I mean it's cool, but—"

"Devious," she said. "I know."

74

"Maybe try not to, you know. Get messed up from it."

"Too late," she said, and though she smiled as if she were just joking, once the door closed behind him and David's absence transformed into silence, the book-lined world of her apartment began to constrict, and Lydia utterly disappeared into Joey's messed-up crate.

CHAPTER EIGHT

Tomas was checking out a pile of picture books to a young mother with a tot climbing up her shoulder when the phone rang at the circulation desk and startled him. He stamped an inky due date on his thumbnail.

—Crap. Sorry.

It was a city administrator on the phone, calling about WinterFest, an annual celebration that had started this morning in the ski town of Breckenridge. At this very moment, Tomas was informed, he was scheduled to be there, parked on Main Street in his branch's rainbow-painted Bookmobile, serving cocoa and handing out library bookmarks on behalf of the Denver Public Library system. The trip had been arranged months ago by the PR people downtown as a sort of goodwill gesture to encourage literacy in the state and to strengthen relationships with small-town libraries, and Tomas had been reminded about it so often that he'd written it in bold red letters on his desk calendar, in his pocket calendar, and even on the construction-paper calendar that Lydia had made him for Christmas and taped to their fridge at home. . . .

Yet he'd still managed to forget. Because that's how this week was going.

—I somehow forgot, he said on the phone.

—You're paid to somehow remember.

Thankfully, the administrator explained, thick with sarcasm, WinterFest would be happening all weekend, and seeing as the town was at least a two-hour drive into the mountains, and seeing as snow was presently tumbling over Denver, and seeing as it was getting darker every minute, he didn't exactly see how Tomas was going to solve this problem except by putting chains on the Bookmobile's tires and driving it there tonight. Yes, tonight. Yes, in the snow. If he was lucky, the librarian in Breckenridge would take the keys and let him go home, and if he was really lucky, someone from the festival would give him a lift back to the city. If not, he'd have to try to find a hotel or catch one of the moonlight buses that shuttled skiers in and out of downtown. On his dime.

—You really want me to drive it there tonight?

—Only if you want to keep your job, he said. Get going.

Tomas looked out the window at the headlights and taillights seeping over the streets and his heart felt hollow. The snow that had begun to fall was getting thicker by the minute, whitening sidewalks and weighing down trees and giving the gray light of dusk an atomic glow. He dreaded the long drive that waited for him out there, but an even deeper dread surrounded the news he'd soon have to break to Lydia: there would be no sleepover tonight.

For the past week, tonight's sleepover had been Lydia and Carol's main topic of conversation, and they'd composed countless colorful lists of everything they wanted to do: make candles out of melted crayons in tuna cans, pop a pot of marshmallow popcorn, tell ghost stories with flashlights after dark—but now they were going to be shattered. Carol couldn't spend the night at Lydia's after all. Not if he had to haul the Bookmobile into a snowy pocket of the Rockies.

Just when Tomas thought he couldn't imagine a worse afternoon, he looked out the frosty library window and saw Bart O'Toole's yellow pickup truck with its cage of racks bouncing into the parking lot, sliding to a halt at just the right spot to block the book drop. Tomas's heart began to pound. He looked around the library and saw empty chairs and empty nooks; almost all of the patrons had gone home, attempting to beat the snowstorm. And then he found himself staring at his watch—4:17, it blinked, 4:17—as if to secure the moment in time, like a doctor noting a patient's expiration.

O'Toole hopped up the library steps, two at a time, looking swift and unshaven and burlier than Tomas remembered. He shoved the door too hard when he came inside, so now it was propped open and cold air swooshed through the library, flapping newspaper pages and kicking the heater into overdrive. Tomas flinched.

—Hey there, pal, O'Toole said.

Tomas jogged around the circulation desk and offered a blundering hello, but before he could think of anything more to say, the girls arrived from the library basement, giggling and excited, wearing blue jeans and striped sweaters and necklaces they'd made from pop-tops. They blasted right past him and latched on to O'Toole's pant legs as he entered the book-lined foyer.

—You'll never guess what, Carol blurted to her dad, as if she'd been waiting hours to share. A boy was bawling at school today. Just *blubbering*!

O'Toole played along, slapping his hands on his knees, stooping down, pretending to be dramatically interested in Carol's classroom gossip.

—it's because he was dying to come to my sleepover, Lydia said.

—Who could blame him? Carol said, rolling her eyes like a diva. I'd cry too.

The girls giggled and Tomas, aware that they were probably talking about Raj, scratched his neck uncomfortably. He'd rarely seen this side of Lydia before—taking such cruel pleasure from excluding her friend—but rather than intervene he stayed focused on O'Toole, attempting to determine the nature of his visit. O'Toole just wiped his boots on the mat, brushed snow off his shoulders, lifted and resettled his blue-jean cap.

—You're really in here all day long? he said to Tomas. I'd be crawling out of my skin.

—I keep busy, Tomas said. Good to meet you by the way.

Their hands pumped and Tomas thought that O'Toole's grip was both strong and mild, exactly like the man. With his other hand, O'Toole held up a pink duffel bag.

—I brought Carol's stuff for the sleepover.

Carol snatched the bag and, with Lydia crouched alongside, unzipped it and began rifling through. Pajamas fell out, and a cassette tape covered with heart stickers, and a bag of rubber bands.

—Buddy, you okay? O'Toole said, leaning forward with a smile and intercepting Tomas's sight. You look like someone shat on your toast.

—Sorry, Tomas said, it's just I had something come up for tonight. Work stuff.

—Work stuff tonight? What're you, a plumber too?

Tomas wiped his palms on his slacks and explained his Bookmobile predicament. He needed to leave soon for Breckenridge and didn't expect to be back before midnight, maybe even later with the snowstorm.

—Bottom line, Tomas said, no sleepover. We'll have to do it another time. I'm really sorry, girls. I know you've been—

The girls sprang from the floor and began to beseech.

—This is not happening!

—you *promised*!

—Hey, O'Toole said, I'll take them over at our place.

—That's okay, Tomas said.

—Really. Dottie and I aren't doing anything. You go do your job in the mountains and Lydia will stay the night with us. We'll make popcorn and cocoa, then tomorrow morning I'll bring them around here. What time's good?

Lydia had never spent the night away from home, and the thought of her first time being under Carol's roof felt too much like turning over the reins to forces he couldn't control.

—I don't think so, Tomas said, looking at his watch, as if his reasons were trapped behind its scratchy face.

—It's up to you, O'Toole said. But just know it's no big deal for Dottie and me. I'm sure Carol's got some extra PJs and a toothbrush she can borrow.

—*Ewww*, the girls chimed.

Tomas tried to come up with a meaningful response, but even to himself he sounded like an uptight weenie, especially with the girls rolling their eyes and O'Toole shushing them for their disrespect. And so with the smell of snow in the air and headlights beginning to pierce the gloom outside, Tomas conceded. Lydia could spend the night at Carol's.

—Come around in the morning and you can help me with story time. Deal?

—deal!

Lydia barely even hugged him before following Carol and Mr. O'Toole out the library doors. Tomas stood at the window and watched the girls running across the snowy parking lot and through the pluming exhaust of O'Toole's yellow truck. As their taillights disappeared into the rising dusk, he thought of

Dottie tucking in his daughter on this cold night, kissing her on the forehead, and with an empty heart he went in search of the Bookmobile's keys—with no idea of the darkness the night would bring.

That evening at dinner, Lydia could not stop staring at Carol's family. While Mrs. O'Toole scooped out plates of macaroni-and-hot-dog casserole, Mr. O'Toole gave the two girls their first sip of beer—straight from his Coors can at the table—and let them eat cold marshmallows with their dinner. Mrs. O'Toole teased him about leaving his plumbing tools all over the house, so he made a big show of dragging his toolbox off the kitchen counter and putting it on the small back porch, and when he came in he sprinkled fresh snow on the girls' heads and laughed like a goof. For all the uneasiness Lydia felt sitting at their table—Mr. O'Toole releasing little beer burps, then winking at Lydia and Carol; Mrs. O'Toole folding and unfolding her napkin—she recognized a certain fullness in their home, in their balance as a family.

Mrs. O'Toole was especially mesmerizing. Throughout the whole dinner, as Carol yammered on about their night's plans, Lydia couldn't keep her eyes off Dottie—the swirling orange shine of her hair, the slight chip in her front tooth, the rings she kept twisting on her fingers—maybe because it was impossible to avoid imagining what she would be like as a mom. All throughout Carol's house, Lydia noticed details that were different from her own, like the glittery pinecone candleholder on the shelf, and the way their orange tablecloth matched the orange flowers in the wallpaper and the orange swirls in the countertops and even the orange yarn of the God's Eye on the wall. A mother's touch.

The night evolved into dirty dishes and television and ice cream, and as bedtime approached, the heavy snow that had been dropping on Denver showed no signs of letting up. Lydia forgot about Mr. and Mrs. O'Toole altogether as she and Carol shoved aside the coffee table and other furniture and set up a fort of blankets and cushions around the couch, smack-dab in the center of the living room. When it got late they rolled out their sleeping bags inside the fort and fluffed up their pillows. With flashlights in hand they listened to Carol's parents murmuring in their bedroom down the hall and falling gradually to sleep. They listened to the snow and wind swelling against the front door and living room windows. Then the girls listened to each other. Inside their warm fort they giggled about the time Lydia had seen Raj's wiener falling out of his soccer shorts, looking like a plucked brown duckling, and they read for a while from Carol's book of scary stories, and soon they decided it was time to tell their own stories—about magic bathtubs and a drain that sucked children through its silver pipes and led them to a world of silver manholes and silver clouds and silver homes—

But their stories were interrupted when the back door swung open and banged hard into the kitchen wall. Back doors always banged like that, except it was after midnight and the door crashed with enough force to strum their ribs a room away. Both girls froze. Lydia wondered if this was some kind of a mean trick Mr. O'Toole was playing, but she could still hear his droning snores at the end of the hallway so she knew it wasn't him. Inside the fort Carol grabbed the flashlights and clicked them off.

—Shhh! she quickly hissed.

Lydia and Carol froze beneath the sagging blankets as someone unknown closed the back door and walked through the kitchen. Into the living room. Mrs. O'Toole had left the hallway light on so that Lydia could find the bathroom if she needed it but the man out there slapped at the switch, turning off the only light. The darkness that followed was immense, but Lydia still had seen, through the slit in the fort:

A white latex glove, tight around a hairy man-hand. In the glove a hammer.

The man out there was gripping a hammer, but Lydia didn't fully register this until later, when the negative space that the hammer had occupied was filled in by her memory: a wood-handled hammer, claw and head painted industrial black. It fit his perfect grip.

The rest of it happened slowly. The Hammerman stepped into the hallway and toward Mr. and Mrs. O'Toole's bedroom. Inside the fort, Carol gripped Lydia's wrist tightly for what seemed like hours, then abruptly let go. By the time Lydia reached out to hug her, nothing was there but a fluttering blanket. From her spot she couldn't see a thing but her ears splashed sights through her mind. She could hear Carol's knees scrabbling over the carpet and into the hallway and she could hear Carol scream-ing *Daddy Daddy Daddy!* The Hammerman spun around and his back collided with the wall, as if he'd momentarily lost his balance. Glass popped and a framed family portrait slid down and shattered on the carpet.

For the briefest moment the house went silent. Until Carol screamed again, and in between she seemed to be struggling for air, pivoting in the hallway, scampering to get away. The Hammerman quickly found his footing and the sounds that followed would follow forever: the man's thick boots trailing Carol and Carol's screams and Carol's screams extinguished.

An egg dropped. Another egg dropped. Another.

Almost immediately the O'Tooles' bedroom door creaked open and Lydia could hear Mr. O'Toole grunting with confusion and then she could hear someone's back crashing full-force into the dresser, the door, the doorjamb. She could hear knickknacks knocked from a shelf and drywall caving in and she could hear man-screams as the eggs began to drop, one at a time, all upon the bedroom carpet.

With the blanket fort limp against her shoulder, Lydia could hear whimpering in the darkness. She thought it was just herself making the noise until she realized that her cries had been joined by other cries down the hall: Mrs. O'Toole, whimpering, then pleading, then shrieking. Lydia heard the box spring squeak as someone lunged over the mattress. She heard the mattress sigh and then she heard eggs dropping all over in there.

In that moment, something rare happened inside Lydia: she stopped herself from knowing. She made a choice not to know, and by doing so she was allowed to unfreeze. Nothing was happening down the hall. Nothing was happening, so why not slip out from under this blanket and make her way over the carpet to the kitchen, through the kitchen to the back door, out the back door and into the snowy night? She found her hands and knees and the blanket sagged over her back and then was gone. As she crawled full speed ahead she looked through the darkness at the orange glow of snow in the back-door window. She swished across the living room, burning her knees on the carpet, and she moved faster now, gaining speed with each slide, and then her forehead thudded straight into the corner of the coffee table and the darkness sparkled with pain. Her face grew wet with blood that dripped into her mouth, but she kept crawling. Her eyes were wet. Her nose and lips and chin were wet. The carpet dropped into the kitchen's cold linoleum and a cereal flake crunched beneath her palm, and then her other palm squished a puddle of melting snow tracked in on the Hammerman's boots. The back door was only a few feet

85

away and the snow out there seemed to uplift through a trance of streetlight but she heard the Hammerman's heavy footsteps coming closer, closer, and before she gave it a thought she was cutting a sharp left and holding a cabinet handle in her fingers and then she was underneath the kitchen sink, squeezing next to buckets and cleaning products and pulling the cabinet door closed and pressing her cheek into the cold silver pipes.

Silence beneath the sink. Nothing was happening out there but he had to have seen her. He had to have heard her. She didn't move, she didn't breathe, and in her silence she thought she heard spilling: a gallon of milk tilted on the hallway carpet, *glug-glug-glug*, mixing with broken eggs like a recipe for her dad's birthday cake.

Minutes passed and the darkness grew wet and heavy on her face. She found a withered sponge beneath her foot so she pressed it against her forehead and it stuck to her skin. She squeezed her knees and rested her elbow on a bucket rim. One of her socks, thick and pink, was missing. On the living room floor. Inside the blanket fort. Just outside this cabinet door. Maybe she would never know.

She heard the approach of boot steps, then a smudge of brightness lit the slit between the cabinet doors: a flashlight, its faint orb erasing the world around it. As he approached the sink his boot steps stopped and his shadow darkened everything. She could hear him breathing and her muscles tightened and the garbage disposal felt like a rock propped atop her shoulder. Inches away she could sense the pressure of his knees against the cabinet door.

Ke-tick. But the door didn't open. It didn't open.

Instead the Hammerman dropped his hammer into the sink and Lydia heard it perfectly next to her ear, steel striking steel. He dropped the flashlight and turned on the water, scalding hot, and she felt the drainage pipe warm against her cheek. Even when it began to burn she didn't pull away. A wave of mildew tickled her nose. The Hammerman rinsed his hands and swiped his fingers through the splash—a drumming-fingertip sound, as if he were pressing spaghetti through the garbage disposal's black baffle. Then he turned on the disposal and its rage of blades chattered Lydia's teeth. This moment—this gurgle of blood and hair and splintered bone whirring inside her mind—this was the only moment in Lydia's life.

This was, some would say, her defining moment.

That night Denver glowed with snow. Plows went out. People slept in.

And late in the morning, Tomas had a defining moment all his own—one that came after Lydia and Carol didn't show up at the library to help him with Saturday-morning story time. As planned.

He read *Where the Wild Things Are* to a few toddlers chewing mittens, and once they bundled up and left he phoned the O'Tooles. No answer. On the radio yesterday Tomas had heard that the state should brace for another *stock show snowstorm*, the annual January cold snap that coincided with the country's largest livestock fair, but he hadn't expected it to blow like this. This was something else. Finally the snowfall was slowing but the wind was icy and relentless, carving drifts in the barren white. No cars were out. No one was in the library but him. The morning was empty and frozen and Tomas was exhausted. Lately he'd been just beside himself and last night's lonely excursion to the mountains had made it all the worse. He'd taken the last ski bus out of Breckenridge and didn't get dropped off downtown until almost midnight, and then with the storm it took him forever to find a cab home. Now he was on his third cup of coffee and still could barely keep his eyes open. Again he stared out the window. The snow out there, a good fourteen inches of shifting drifts, was deeper than he'd realized. Deep enough to call it quits.

With a feeling of gratitude he hung a sign on the door and locked the library and walked over to the O'Tooles' home, ten blocks that felt like twenty as his feet struggled through the billows.

As he walked he could see places where a few brave neighborhood kids had made angels in the drifts or tried to roll a snowman, but none had lasted very long. When Tomas finally reached the O'Tooles' single-story home he found not a soul out front and no footprints anywhere. It made sense enough: it was Saturday morning and Carol was definitely the cartoon-watching type. He whistled through the white driveway and was surprised that Bart O'Toole, with the way he worked, hadn't already been out to shovel a path.

Tomas shuffled up the porch steps and peeked through the little door window. His vision blurred and his breath stopped cold when he saw, on the white wall of the hallway, just below a plastic light switch, a smeared handprint of blood.

The front door was locked, but within seconds Tomas had run around the house and found the back door slightly open, with a dusting of snow blown across the kitchen floor. He crossed the kitchen and lunged through the hallway and found Carol and Bart and Dottie O'Toole dog-piled on the soggy carpet just inside the master bedroom doorway. To say he'd never seen so much blood in all his life would imply that he'd seen blood before, when he hadn't—not blood in the way that this was blood. A gag creaked out of him. The family looked inside out. Pulverized. He pulled on their shoulders and flopped their limbs, searching in a panic for his daughter. He would do anything if—

Lydia wasn't among them, and soon he stood in the kitchen spitting into the sink and tried not to look at the hammer, sticky red, poking up from the disposal like a broken bone. Without thinking he grabbed a damp rag folded on the sink side and wiped his lips and put it back. He wanted to scream for Lydia but remembered that no footprints marked the outside snow, meaning no one had left recently, meaning whoever did this could still be in the house. So he gripped the hammer and stormed through the hall and into the rooms, leaping over the body pile. There was urine in the toilet and a small squat of floating tissue just like Lydia's when she forgot to flush at home. He felt sick and charged through the kitchen and even lunged down the steps to the unfinished basement. Crashing doors. Spinning circles. And finally screaming.

—Lydia!

No one answered.

Back in the kitchen he punched 911 and noticed a few stalks of red hair sprouting from the V of the hammer's claw. The dispatcher on the phone enraged him with her patronizing calm and he was just about to throw the hammer through the window when he saw his own bloody boot prints spread over the floor like steps for some diabolical dance. He noticed the drips here and there, the drizzles, the smears. He paused. The dispatcher said he had ten minutes max before the cops arrived and to sir please make sure you're safe. But with the snow piled in the streets the way it was Tomas thought twenty minutes would be optimistic.

He slammed down the phone even as the dispatcher was still speaking and held his hand over his mouth and looked down the length of the hallway where Dottie's arm flopped out from the pile, stiff and darkening, her hand bent into a claw. He quickly turned back to the kitchen and didn't know why but opened the refrigerator and saw hot-dog casserole and sticky ketchup and crusty buttermilk and god help him, he thought, these were the fragments of Lydia's last meal.

Then from the sink came a sound.

He spun on his heel with the fridge door open and its jars and bottles rattled like church bells. He shushed them with his fingers. The sound of a bird. The faintest of whimpers. Bent in half, nose as close to the floor as he could get without falling over, he followed the whimpers like they were fairy-tale bread crumbs until they stopped beneath the sink and just as he extended his arm to rip open the cabinet door the cabinet door opened on its own. He raised the hammer instinctively, but then Lydia climbed out—her shirtfront soggy from all-night sucking, her face and forehead masked with blood—and she scampered right up his chest and into a desperate hug.

CHAPTER NINE

Lydia scratched the faint scar on her forehead as she walked, head down, toward the Children's section of Bright Ideas. Her beaten leather satchel was slung over her shoulder and Joey's copy of *A Universal History of the Destruction of Books* was tucked under her arm. Today was Lydia's day off, but she arrived at the store twenty minutes before it opened. She loved roaming the stacks when it was early and empty like this, feeling the quiet hopeful promise of all those waiting books—but today she stayed on task: Joey.

When Lydia arrived in Kids, her comrade Wilma, a sharp-tongued and warmhearted eighty-year-old, was standing in the center of the picture book alcove, wearing her usual navy slacks, crocheted turtleneck, and pearlescent glasses. The alcove was still ripped apart from last night's cocktail crowd and Wilma stood at its center, holding a two-foot-tall board book with googly eyes, furry arms, lights, buzzers, bells, and rubber tentacles that bounced toward her shoes like Slinkies.

"Wilma?"

"In what world is this a *book*?" she said, and her mouth was puckered as if she had cat hair on her tongue. "How are you supposed to read *this* to a child?"

"I think it reads itself," Lydia said.

"There goes humanity," Wilma said, then she turned to a shelf of stuffed animals and slapped a sock monkey off his perch, just because.

"Do you know anything about this?" she said, handing Wilma the copy of *A Universal History of the Destruction of Books* but pointing to the label on the back.

Wilma lifted her glasses and squinted at the label, then turned the book over and looked at the cover.

"It's obviously been mislabeled," she said. "Everything okay?" Before becoming a bookseller, Wilma had spent decades working as a grade school librarian, and something in the way she lowered her voice and turned her head made Lydia feel like a wounded child.

"I don't know, to be honest," Lydia said.

Wilma nodded and led Lydia by the forearm into the quadrant of parenting books, then slid out a book with a photograph of a disheveled bed on its cover. In serious font, it read, *The Bed-Wetter's Almanac: Folklore, Wives' Tales, and Cures from Around the Globe.* It was indeed missing its label, but none of its pages had been cut up and it was in perfect condition. In fact, other than its font being slightly larger than usual, nothing seemed to stand out about it at all.

"Is that boyfriend of yours a bed-wetter?" Wilma said, gesturing to the book.

"Only when he's drunk."

Wilma smiled, then grew serious. "This is about Joey, isn't it?"

Lydia nodded, and Wilma gently guided her to the rocking chair near the pop-up books. Joey's favorite seat.

"I didn't like that Joey kid at first," Wilma said, stroking her papery fingers over the nearby shelf of fairy tales, "coming down here and hogging the rocking chair while moms nursed their babies standing up. I thought he was clueless, maybe a bit sinister. I can't tell you how many times I came through here and caught him sitting in that very seat, tilting back and forth, staring at little kids over the top of his book. Creepy, right?"

"I guess," Lydia said. "Joey wasn't really the creepy type, though—"

"But then I realized something," Wilma continued, hushing Lydia with the slightest lifted finger. "You know what you see when you're sitting in that chair? *Everything*. At least everything in the Kids section. And you know when Joey sat there the most? On Saturday mornings. You know what this place is like on Saturday morning?"

"A zoo."

"The busiest time of the week." Wilma pointed to the pair of books in Lydia's lap. "The time he was *least* likely to get any reading done."

"I don't get it."

"He wasn't here to watch the kids, Lydia, and he wasn't here to read. He was here to watch the *families*. For whatever reason, he liked watching the moms and dads and kids interacting. It's a beautiful thing to behold, really. It's enough to keep you young. Most people don't even see it until they themselves are prunes like me."

"That sounds like Joey."

"Once I realized that," Wilma said, "I felt bad for misjudging him. That kid had a giant hole in his heart. And he sat right there to try to fill it."

Lydia gulped, and when she stood from the chair it rocked forward and bumped the back of her knees.

"You haven't seen Lyle, have you?" she asked.

"Now that you mention it," Wilma said, "I haven't. Not since Joey's death."

"Let me know if he shows up, will you?" Lydia said, then lifted the bed-wetting book. "And thanks for this. I'll bring it back in a few days."

"Take your time," Wilma said, walking away. "It's not our most popular title."

Lydia did take her time, standing in the Parenting alcove and studying the two books side by side, trying to figure out why Joey had labeled the one with the other. As far as she could tell, they had nothing in common except that, at some point, they'd both been in Joey's hands. She shuddered and gave up. When she left the Kids section, both books tucked under her arm, Wilma was kneeling on a pillow, reading a picture book to herself, dabbing a Kleenex against her nose.

That kid had a giant hole in his heart, she'd said, and if anyone could measure its depths—could drop a pebble into its well and listen for the *plunk*—it was Wilma.

On the pedestrian mall a few blocks up from Bright Ideas, Lydia sat alone on a sidewalk bench. The morning was cold but sunny, carved with the sharpened shadows of Sixteenth Street.

She set her coffee and the two books on the bench next to her and retrieved a small box of raisins from her jacket pocket. As delicate as a shorebird, she stuck her fingers into the tiny box, moved each raisin to her lips, and chewed. As she nibbled she studied the red box until the sounds of passing traffic disappeared. The woman printed on the raisin box was as she'd always been: young and glowing, wearing a red bonnet and holding her bounty of grapes against a giant yellow sun. Picking, chewing, swallowing, Lydia was a child again. Raisins! How had she forgotten about raisins? The way the smallest seeds stuck in her teeth. The way she felt when her fingers were little and—

A shadow crossed her eyelids. A delivery truck hummed past. A man stood next to the bench.

"Is it really you?" the man said. The sun was bright behind him and Lydia had a hard time seeing his face.

"Excuse me?"

"You are Lydia, right? Of course you are. My god. Hello."

He took a step toward her and Lydia nearly flinched. She thought for a second he had something in his hand, but it turned out it was just his hand.

"Who do you think you are?" she said, but she still had raisins in her mouth, and as usual, she sounded more apologetic than pissed.

"This must seem strange," he said, stepping back. "Showing up like this, no warning."

Lydia's eyes were adjusting to his silhouette in the sunlight and his features soon were clear. His skin was rich and dark, his black hair clean and mussed, and the brown of his eyes was so brown, the white so white, that she felt as if she were looking at a photographic negative. He wore a suede sport jacket, rough blue jeans, embroidered belt. He was slightly chubby but stood sturdy, confident—irritating.

"Lydia? You really don't recognize me? Little Flower?"

Now she did recognize him.

"Oh my god," she said, and her breath gave a little jump when she thought about this man, as a boy, wearing a buckled jumpsuit and gazing at her with adoration. "*Raj?*"

He opened his arms and Lydia, after a quailing pause, stood into a hug.

"Look at us," he said, "both alive."

Lydia took a step back and grabbed the nape of her neck. Her impulse was to sprint down the sidewalk as fast as her awkward feet would carry her—but then somewhere inside she

95

felt a small bright glimmer, and she was greeted with a simple image of the two of them as children, sitting on the carpet in her father's library, leaning back-to-back, encircled by books.

She almost smiled. "I just can't believe you're here, Raj. Because it's been like—"

"Like twenty years."

"Wow. Twenty? Sheesh." She nodded into the cold, then lifted her coffee and moved her books into her lap. "So? Sit with me. Yeah. Sit already."

Both sat on the slatted bench. A pigeon flapped past in the street.

"I saw your picture in the newspaper," Raj said.

"You're not the only one," she said. "You do realize that was like two weeks ago."

"It took me that long to gather the nerve to come down here, to be honest." He nodded in the direction of the bookstore, a few blocks west. "I wasn't expecting to find you on the way."

"I sit out here a lot."

"Lucky for me," he said. His teeth still gleamed, just as they had when they were kids, and his hair was still a shaggy mess, and his skin still glowed. "I wasn't even sure you wanted to see me again. Otherwise, you would have—"

"Otherwise I would have looked you up when I moved back to town? It really wasn't intentional, Raj."

"You don't have to explain, Lydia. It doesn't get more loaded than us."

"No," she said, smiling, "it doesn't."

"We're carrying some serious baggage," he said. "Especially *you*," he added, then gently closed his eyes. "Sorry. That was probably the wrong thing to say."

"Only because it's true," she said, and lightly slugged his arm.

"I guess I'll see you in another twenty years."

Both of them were smiling now, unable not to. Lydia surprised herself by grabbing Raj's hand. She didn't say anything and he didn't either, but after a minute Raj let go and slid over to his half of the bench.

"So, how long have you been back?"

"In Denver? Gosh, like six years?"

"And here all this time I thought you were hiding in the mountains," he said. "Address unknown."

"For a long time I was."

"One day there was a *For Sale* sign on your lawn and that was it for my pal Lydia."

"The plan was to stay in touch," she said, "but then—you know."

"I know."

"I tried."

"I know."

And Lydia was being truthful: when she and her father had fled Denver in the middle of her fourth-grade year for the small town of Rio Vista, Colorado, she'd done her best to write letters to Raj, even if it simply meant letting him know she was alive and safe and missing his friendship. She'd spent more time decorating the letters' margins with flowers and forest creatures than she had on the sullen details of her days. Her father always read and redacted her letters carefully before driving to distant towns—Salida, Gunnison, Leadville—and mailing them without a return address. Since no one could know where they'd ended up settling, Raj never had the option of writing her back.

Eventually, predictably, her letters had stopped.

Lydia looked down at the sidewalk's gray and pink granite pavers, arranged to resemble the scales of a diamondback slithering through downtown. It was quiet between them. She reached across the bench and gave his wrist a little shake.

"It's good to see you again," she said. "I mean it."

"Sorry about the circumstances," he said. "But I'm dying to know what's up with your name. The caption in the paper gave the *Lydia* part. But Lydia *Smith*? What happened to *Gladwell*? You got married? Let me see those hands again. I don't see a ring."

"My dad changed our name back when we moved. We were supposed to be anonymous."

"So you're not married."

"Mmph," she said. "No."

"I'm kind of surprised by that," he said, then crossed his legs and tugged a frayed thread from the cuff of his jeans.

"But involved," she said, though it sounded as if it were a question.

Raj shifted on the bench.

"They never caught him, did they?" he said.

Lydia stared at the argyled mannequins and rainbow kites displayed in the window across the way, and the young woman with a shaved head shouldering her acoustic guitar down the sidewalk.

"Raj," she said, "I'd rather not go there."

"It's old news, anyway."

She thought she should say something more but a sudden lump filled her throat, and up and down her spine she could feel the familiar fronds of discomfort that accompanied most reminders of her childhood. She thought about asking him not to mention her past to anyone, but one look into his eyes—a soft dark brown, like sea glass, and as kind and wary as ever—and she knew her past would always be safe with Raj.

She took a deep breath. "And you, Raj? What are you doing with yourself?"

He shrugged, then pointed loosely in the direction of Union Station. "I live above a bar just over there, where that construction is happening? And I'm a cashier at a copy shop, but I guess I'm trying to be a graphic designer." He opened his wallet and pulled out a card and handed it to her. "I'm calling it my own company," he said, "but really it's just whatever jobs I cull from the copy counter."

Lydia studied the card.

"And what about your dad?" Raj added. "Is he—?"

"Crazy?" she said. "Oh yes."

"They only get nuttier with age, don't they?"

"*He* has, that's for sure."

"Mine too," Raj said. "Both of them. So tell me."

"We aren't speaking," she said. "My dad and I, I guess we're— What's the word? *Over.*"

"Really? Because your dad was so—"

"I'm sorry," she said, "I've just realized." She stood spontaneously and gathered her coffee, then lifted the pair of Joey's books into the air, as if they signified some kind of serious business. "I'm in the middle of something here. Work."

Raj stood too and stuck his hands in his pockets, and for a moment he looked boyish again, brooding and smart and, in the right light, easily as handsome as David.

"Can we do this another time, though?" she added.

"Of course," he said. "I see you drink coffee. We could do that together."

"Yeah," she said. "Let's do that. Soon."

When she was a good fifty feet down the block, she heard him yell, "My number's on the card!"

She spun around and gave him a high thumbs-up, and a pair of passing women in bright ski parkas and bright lipstick looked at her as if she were drunk.

Lydia hadn't planned on heading back to the bookstore any more than she'd planned on escaping from Raj, but now that she was walking in that direction she felt an unexpected mix of clarity and unease. She needed to be done with Joey, she decided, and wash her hands of his death. She'd return *The Bed-Wetter's Almanac* to its empty slot on the Parenting shelves and give serious thought to donating Joey's crate of butchered books to a thrift store. As she headed toward Bright Ideas, she could feel a certain *stride* entering her walk, and she swung her satchel back on her shoulder and slid Joey's books together, cupping them in her palm.

The Bed-Wetter's Almanac. A Universal History of the Destruction of Books.

Lydia spent so much time carrying books up and down the stairs of the store that she was pleased at how nicely this pair fit together. They were simply *snug*, easy to carry, no bumbling or sliding apart, almost like a pair of Lego bricks—

In the middle of the sidewalk Lydia stopped cold. A pony-tailed man jogging with a stroller huffed and veered around her. Lydia mumbled an apology, but her focus was already on the books in her hand.

She looked at the books side by side, spine by spine, back-to-back.

A Universal History of the Destruction of Books. The Bed-Wetter's Almanac.

She pressed the books atop each other. They weren't just the same size, they were the *exact* same size. No lip, no overhang, no difference but the words.

Okay, Joey. Words.

Last words?

Lost words?

Words. Words. Words—

I make the codices speak.

There on the sidewalk she opened *A Universal History* to its first cut-up page—page 128—then she opened *The Bed-Wetter's*

Almanac to its own page 128, which was wholly intact. It was an awkward process—folding back the cut-up book without stressing its spine—but when she slid them together and lined them up perfectly, page 128 on page 128, the little cut-out windows were now filled in by the words and letters of the book behind. A perfect fit.

A key finding its lock. A message from the grave:

you

. Fo

und

mea

gain

ly,

di

. A

, j

CHAPTER TEN

Lydia's skills as a bookseller came mainly, she believed, from her ability to listen. A raging case of bibliophilia certainly helped, as did limited financial needs, but it was her capacity to be politely trapped by others that really sealed her professional fate. From bus stops to parties to the floors of the store, Lydia was the model of a Good Listener—a sounding board for one and all. Strangers and acquaintances and the occasional friend unloaded on her by the hour—add booze and it was every five minutes—and Lydia's main conversational contributions consisted of *Yeah* or *Hmm* or *Great* or *Jeez* or *Ouch* or *Yikes* or *Wow*.

The unloading voice this time belonged to a middle-aged BookFrog named Pedro, a tender man with red suspenders and white sneakers who'd cornered Lydia twenty minutes ago next to the potted ficus in Genre Fiction. Pedro was unable to speak without intense fidgeting, so throughout his entire riff he pruned the tree by hand, dropping one leaf at a time to the wood floor, as if to punctuate his points. He was talking about his favorite sci-fi authors, explaining the worlds they'd created with enough detail for Lydia to formulate spaceship blueprints, and she politely listened—*Yeah*, she said, and *Hmm* and *Great* and *Jeez* and *Ouch* and *Yikes* and *Wow*—appreciating not so much the worlds themselves, but the fact that Pedro had become so lost in their trance that he was unable to stop himself from sharing them. All the while Lydia nodded along, admiring his penchant for details and finding it sweet that he wasn't hitting on her, and probably more than anything, feeling grateful to be focusing on something besides the message she'd discovered yesterday in Joey's books— *You found me again, Lydia*—and the subsequent pair of messages she'd managed to decode before work this morning as well.

Joey's words had scared the bejesus out of her, so Pedro's riff was a calming distraction. Just as she was settling in to hear about another sci-fi system, she peered across the bookstore floor and spotted Lyle dropping down the stairs, sipping from a paper cup of tea.

"Hold that thought!" she said to Pedro. "Lyle!"

By the time Lydia caught up with him, Lyle was already paging through the Sunday *Times* at a tilty table in the coffee shop.

She plunged into the wooden chair across from him. Lyle pressed his glasses to the bridge of his nose.

"Lydia," he said calmly, with an affected Brahmin accent: *Lid-ee-ahh*. "Join me, will you?"

The first time Lydia had seen Lyle, six years back, she'd thought he was an artist of one flavor or another, or at least a New York transplant, because he dressed perfectly for the part: straggling gray hair, half-moon glasses, black peacoat, high-water chinos, plaid shirts buttoned to his neck, and tan-and-white saddle shoes. Easily in his sixties, Lyle was older than most BookFrogs, and Lydia imagined that at some point he may even have led a conventional life. She'd heard through the Bright Ideas grapevine—admittedly, not the most robust source—that he was independently wealthy, and that previous to his existence as a BookFrog, he'd spent a decade at a care facility near Aspen that Plath called "part loony bin, part ski lodge."

Given the amount of time that Lyle and Joey used to spend together, the fact that Lyle wasn't with his friend on the night of his hanging was thoroughly bizarre, a statistical anomaly. Equally odd was the fact that Lyle, who spent as much time at Bright Ideas as any other BookFrog, had left the store around the day of Joey's death and hadn't been back since. For two weeks, Lydia had paid more attention to his absence than to anyone else's presence. Every alcove, every aisle, every couch was missing Lyle's form.

"Lyle, where on earth have you been?" she said, her voice infused with urgency. "What happened to you?"

Lyle looked over the top of his glasses and down the bulb of his nose, somewhere between confused and indignant.

"*What happened?*" he said. "My best friend killed himself upstairs; that's *what happened*. I've been cremating him. Cremating *Joey*. Who did you think was going to take care of the arrangements? The Rotary Club? His suburban parents and his family of weeping siblings? He had no one, Lydia. I was *it*."

"Of course," she said. "I'm sorry."

"You should be."

She was. Of all the thoughts zigging in Lydia's mind lately, the one that hadn't caught her notice was the fate of Joey's remains. Of course there would be the issue of arrangements. Besides which, it hadn't occurred to her that reentering the store was probably just too painful for Lyle.

"He really didn't have anyone?"

"He had me and he had you. Otherwise he was alone in the world," Lyle said, crossing his legs and leaning back in his chair. "If you want to pay respects, by the way, he's at the zoo."

"At the zoo. As in the zoo?"

"Joey liked to walk the zoo on free days. I didn't know where else to put him. I thought about leaving him on a shelf upstairs, with Flannery or Fante or Rimbaud. But I figured there were rules against leaving bodies in here."

"Probably."

"So I put his ashes in a duffel bag and snipped a tiny hole in the bottom and walked the length of the zoo. But I didn't make the hole big enough so there were these tiny *pieces* left over in the bag. I shook them into the grass. But then all the geese thought he was bread crumbs and started charging me. Horrifying, Lydia, the way they gobbled him up. A frenzy. Joey would've abhorred all the attention."

"I can see that."

"I scanned the sky for vultures," Lyle said, dramatically peering at the splintery beams above. "There were children all over the place. Balloon animals and hot cocoa. And here I am dumping Joey. *Joey.* If the den mothers only knew."

"Just tell me why you weren't with Joey that night," she said, and only as the words left her mouth did she realize how sad and desperate she sounded. "You were *always* with him, Lyle, so why not then?"

Lyle stared at her in silence. Without shame, he placed a pill on his tongue and washed it down with a sip of green tea. He dripped the tea bag above the cup and rolled the lump into a napkin and buttoned it into his peacoat to be reused later. He dried his fingertips with a hankie, then folded it back into his shirt pocket.

"Do you ever really watch people in here?" he said. "The way most people browse, it's as if they've stepped into a temple or church. This is not riffling through hangers on the clearance rack or tossing canned corn into the cart. No, this is *browsing*. It even sounds drowsy: *to browse*. Heart rates slow. Time disappears. Serious people turn into dreamers again. They play frozen statues on the floor, chew their fingers, pull the flaps of pop-up books."

"Why are you telling me this, Lyle?"

"Joey loved it here," he said. "*Loved* it. This place gave him something sacred. Gave his mind some quiet. This was his Thanksgiving table. His couch-cushion fort. He could get lost in here like nowhere else on earth. I'm telling you this, Lydia, because in all his life, he'd never really had that feeling before, not consistently anyway. Not to overstate it, but this store was the closest thing to a home that Joey ever had."

"He really had no one?"

"Like I said, he had me and he had you. It's difficult to imagine how a kid like *that* had been so horribly cast into the void, but it happened. Joey was one of those bright, troubled boys who never got beyond being a ward of the state. I'm not sure he even knew the details, but apparently from the time he was a baby he'd lived in a big, run-down house on the north side, somewhere off Federal, and he had six or seven siblings of various ages and backgrounds, and the whole group of them had been adopted by this older couple—Guatemalan, I think, or El Salvadoran—who'd never had kids of their own. Mr. and Mrs. Molina."

Lydia recalled the certificate hanging on Joey's bathroom wall, the only time she'd ever seen his surname: *Joseph Edward Molina.*

"Joey remembered very little about them because he was so young, but he talked about eating a lot of meals outside, and crowding onto a couch with his brothers and sisters and listening to their dad play the trumpet and read Bible stories. And Joey said that he remembered being a happy kid, but that his happiness was very short-lived. When Joey was maybe three or four, his father died suddenly. Joey never got the whole story, just that after his father was gone it became impossible for his mother to keep all those kids around. Financially, I'm guessing.

So *all* of them went back into the system, scattered like chaff, you know, and that was the extent of Joey's experience with family.

"After that, he was bounced from one foster family or group home or juvie center to another. I don't know why no one else ever stepped forward to take him in. Maybe he was a difficult child, or maybe he just wasn't a lily-white newborn, which is apparently the hot commodity in the adoption market, sad to say. For whatever reason, after those first few years he fell straight through the cracks. Imagine if your only threads to family, your only memories of what we call *home*, only lasted as long as your preschool years. It's tragic."

Lydia was wearing a silver pendant of the Monopoly dog that David had given her after they'd decided to wait a few years to get a pooch of their own, and as Lyle spoke she zipped it nervously up and down the chain. Lyle continued.

"By the time I met him, most of the damage was done. This would've been eight or more years ago now, when Joey was maybe twelve years old, and I'd come across him once in a while at this musty old bookshop near the basilica on Colfax. When I would try to say hello, he would ignore me. Not the most socialized teen, but he was born to read. He generally preferred little bookshops to the public library, maybe because he was trying to avoid truancy officers, or maybe because he just liked the vibe. A few times a week anyway our paths would intersect, and every time, just before he left, I noticed that he'd put the book he was reading back on the shelf, pull a black permanent marker from his pocket, and write something small on the back of his hand. After seeing him do this a few times, I asked him what he was writing, and maybe because I was familiar to him by then, he held up his hand and showed me. There, on the skin on the back of his hand, was a series of small black numbers, a dozen or two, most of them fading but a few fresh and dark, and the numbers were divided into four or five even columns with a letter or two up top. I was thinking it had to do with the lottery, or numerology, or some Fibonacci sequence—the type of mathematical illumination that I would later associate with Joey's wonderful peculiarities—but alas, it was far more mundane, and far more sad: he was using the pen to keep track of his page numbers so that the next time he came to the store he would remember where he'd left off. The columns marked the different stores he visited, or possibly the different titles he was reading. Maybe both. I don't recall. What I do recall is that Joey had no money to buy a book, even a used book. One dollar? Two dollars? Four? The boy had *nothing*."

Lyle stared at the exposed brick wall that flanked their table.

"Is that when you—started?"

"Helping him out? Yes, I guess it was. He left the shop that day and I bought the book he'd been reading—*Crime and Punishment*, I believe—and chased him down the sidewalk to give it to him. Joey stood there for the longest time with his hands tucked into his black sweatshirt pockets, looking at me from inside his hood with those crazy green eyes of his, refusing to take it, as if whatever strings I'd attached to it were enough to strangle him. Of course there were no strings, but he obviously had issues with trusting me. So I placed it on the sidewalk by his feet and left. When I saw him again a few days later, reading a different book in the store—*The Metamorphosis*, I think—he didn't exactly thank me, but he did smile, or at least showed me a tooth or two.

"From there, I began to see him around town. I assumed he was going to school somewhere but I had no proof. Once I helped him at the library because he was having some difficulty getting a card because of his age or address or something, maybe just lack of official identification. Sometimes in the spring I'd see him smoking by the lake at City Park, and once in a while I'd buy him a book, or if he wasn't drunk or high I'd stick five bucks in his palm for lunch, or just ask him if he needed anything. We talked a little bit back then, usually about what he was reading, but for the most part we stood silently together, side by side, or roamed the streets with some half-assed destination in mind. An ice-cream cone or a bowl of chili or a pair of winter socks. I thought for a while that Joey had Tourette's syndrome or some kind of involuntary tic because every so often he would release these little whimpering *bursts* that almost sounded like a neighing horse. At first I would ignore it, you know, or I'd ask him casually if he ever went to the community health clinic for a checkup, or if he had any prescriptions I could help him refill, and then one day I realized, with complete embarrassment, that when he made that sound he was *crying*. He had this way of covering it up, of making it seem nasal, or like a stuffy cough, but it was tears."

"I know the sound," Lydia said, thinking about the times she'd heard it while passing Joey slumped in a chair, his face buried in a book.

"Anyway, despite the four-plus decades between us, we began to spend more time together. He seemed to be between different group homes quite a lot, taking this bus or walking that way, in different parts of town. Sometimes I wouldn't see him for a week or two, but when I did see him he'd come right up to me and catch me up on his recent finds. The kid drank too much, and I knew sometimes he was trying to score this or that hit, this or that fix, but he respected me enough to keep all of that separate from me. Then one day he just disappeared. I visited all of his haunts but the kid was just *gone*, and I realized that I had no one whom I could ask. I didn't know where he lived, if he even went to school, whom he was reporting to, if anyone,

110

and it occurred to me that if *I* knew so little about him, if he could disappear from *me*, then imagine how utterly absent he was from the rest of the world. It broke my heart, Lydia. He could've been facedown in the Platte or left for dead in a Five Points alley. I promised myself that if I saw him again I would take better care of him. I'd try to give the kid some self-worth, you know? Anyway, I didn't see him for a long, long time."

"About two years, I'm guessing," Lydia said.

Lyle nodded. "A little over. So he told you about prison."

"He did."

"He was not a violent person," Lyle said, somewhat defensively.

"I know."

"He made a mistake," Lyle said, arching his brow, "and he learned from it."

"I know, Lyle."

Lyle squeezed his hand into a fist. It took him a minute to gather himself.

"Joey found me within a week of getting out of prison. The first thing he did was ask me, in that awkward way of his, to buy him a suit. A suit! I thought, Great! I assumed it was for job interviews and parole meetings, but I never once saw him put it on. I was so glad he wasn't dead in a dumpster somewhere that I gave him a wide berth but made a point of being present. He didn't talk to me about his time behind bars, but he emerged with a whole new cluster of favorite authors. He seemed to have grown up some. He was more hopeful, to be sure. He spoke to me more than he ever had, which made me think that all that solitude in prison, all that silent self-protection, must have scraped away at him. He even began joining me on my daily walks. I thought I would introduce him to Bright Ideas, but it turned out he'd already discovered it on his own. I thought that if I bought him books he'd stay occupied, and he'd be less likely to drink a bottle of cough syrup or drop cinder blocks on the highway. Or—"

"I know, Lyle."

"Or hang himself."

"I know."

Lydia waited for him to continue, but Lyle just sipped from his tea and shifted around his newspaper, as if trying to shake free those two words: *hang himself.*

"What happened that night, Lyle?"

Lyle fished inside his peacoat pocket and dumped its contents on the table. An American flag on a toothpick. A half-smoked cigar. A single nudie playing card. A cough drop stuck to its waxy wrapper. He unpeeled the cough drop and popped it into his mouth, then finally looked at Lydia.

"It's not your fault he died," she said. "I hope you don't think that."

"Joey was horrible to me," Lyle said.

"This is on the day?"

"He was being such a brute. Meaner to me than anyone since the playground. Meaner to me than the jackass in the park who ripped out my earring and split my earlobe for being a *fag.* Joey had never been mean like that. I don't want to remember him like that."

"Tell me."

A cough sparked in Lyle's throat. "For weeks he'd been in the dumps. I kept thinking I'd done something to anger him. I tried to talk to him, but he'd barely give me the time of day. And then came the morning of."

"What happened?"

"It got *bad* the morning of. I got tired of the way he was treating me, so I went to his group home, bracing myself for confrontation, and when he came out and started walking toward downtown I walked right at his side, and when he shoved me away I was undeterred. He was often a quiet, dreamy guy, which was fine, but that day he was kind of groaning and muttering, hissing at passersby and cars, and acting—what? *Indecipherably.* Okay, fine. He was going through something, as we all do sometimes, and I was his friend, so I would stay at his side because that's what you do. But then when we got here, when we got to Bright Ideas— I don't really want to tell you this."

"I found him hanging, Lyle."

"When we got here," he said, "Joey was wearing that baggy black sweatshirt he always had on, and he lifted it up and began pulling books out of his shirt, his waist. Five or six books, at least. I thought— Lydia, I thought Joey was *stealing* books. Only he was taking them *out* of his clothes and leaving them on couches, on shelves, sort of scattering them about the store like he was *returning* them. Like he was *planting* them. I didn't know what he was up to, but I was furious on so many levels. If he was returning them, that meant that at some point he'd stolen them, right? Which meant he was betraying this place that we loved so much. And betraying me, too, because he knew full well that I'd buy the books for him, that all he had to do was ask. And of course there was the risk of him going back to jail over some stupidity. I got very upset, Lydia. Very upset. I made him come out to the alley behind the store and I laid it all out for him: He was a smart guy. He was beautiful. He had his whole life in front of him— You can imagine all I said. At some point I grabbed on to his shoulders and shook him a little, pleading with him. I offered to write him a check, as if I was his father. I told him I'd pay for him to get started in a little apartment if he wanted to try to get out of his group home. I told him I would help him go to counseling or college

113

or move to a different city, but that I just wanted him to be smart and safe and stop doing things that hurt him. I told him I'd give him anything in the world that was within my power, but that he *had* to start opening up to me, otherwise how could I? He just stood there, Lydia, and I was so upset I quite literally started hugging him. I *begged* him, Lydia, to tell me what was happening. It's so humiliating. It's so—"

Lyle fought back tears. He forced himself to sit up straight.

"But the worst thing, Lydia? Do you know what he said to me? He called me an *old queer* and an *old faggot*. He said that all I really wanted was to *suck him off*, that his *cock was the fountain of youth*, that everything I did for him was a way to get some of that *brown candy*. I have to say, Lydia, that snapped me out of it. He humiliated me. Not just because what he said was untrue—it was so totally untrue—but, I'm ashamed to admit, it was something I worried about. Something he *knew* I worried about: I knew people looked at the two of us, this spinsterish old man with a bit of money and this poor street kid with hardly a change of clothes. I was aware that people thought I was manipulating him. But it wasn't like that at all."

"I know it wasn't."

"Anyway, I said some awful things to him in that alley, and maybe he deserved it. I called him *street trash*. I said that it was no wonder he was alone in the world if this was how he treated the people who loved him. He was such a beautiful kid, but the look I saw him wearing that day—he was so *ugly*."

"He wasn't in his right mind, Lyle."

"I know," he said, "but that's exactly why it's so awful, what I did. I'm a grown man. I should have taken the high road, but I didn't. I took the lowest road. I stomped off and left him all alone, exactly as he'd wanted me to."

"And that was the night—"

"The night he took his life. My dear Lydia, *that* is why I have not come back to the store."

Lyle was breathing loudly and staring at an old coffee ring that stained the table. Lydia rested her hand atop his fist.

"Joey wasn't stealing books," she said. "He was cutting them up."

"No. He wouldn't do that."

"He would. He did. Come with me."

It only took a few minutes for Lydia to grab her satchel from the break room and to let the manager know she was taking an early lunch. Then she walked Lyle to a quiet alcove where the education books were shelved. They sat on a couch embroidered with leaves and berries that had been in the store for years and that carried the ghostly imprint of a thousand forgotten readers.

"What did you mean that Joey was cutting up books?" Lyle said in a quiet, cautious voice.

"He was defacing his own books, but borrowing others from the store as well. Taking their labels. Using them as a guide, I guess."

"But why would he? A *guide* for what?"

"For me," she said, and felt the hairs lift on the back of her neck. "He was doing it for me. He was leaving me messages."

"Really, now?" Lyle shifted forward on the couch, rolling this thought around in his head and apparently accepting it. "I'm sufficiently intrigued. Go on."

From her satchel she retrieved a hardcover copy of Denis Johnson's noir novel *Resuscitation of a Hanged Man* and tossed it at Lyle's lap.

"It was in Joey's apartment," she said. "One of the books he passed to me in death."

"Dear god," Lyle said, rotating it in his hands. "The title hits a bit close to home. Intentional?"

"Has to be."

"And that's the message you're talking about—*Resuscitation of a Hanged Man*?"

"Actually, no. Keep looking."

Lyle repositioned his glasses and licked his fingers. He traced his palm sensuously along the spine—the BookFrog equivalent of kicking the tires. He read the opening paragraphs and sighed with admiration, then flipped through the book until he came to the little rectangles, hardly bigger than a housefly, that had been cut from a number of pages.

"What's with the holes?"

"Some kind of cipher," she said.

There on the couch, Lyle studied the novel with renewed vigor, awestruck by the cuts in its pages. She'd thought he'd be more skeptical. "That does sound like Joey, with his New World Order talk and Illuminati leaflets. I hope you never made the mistake of asking him about the Federal Reserve. Or naked mole rats. Positively sinister. Go on."

"I thought it was some kind of puzzle at first," Lydia said, "cutting out the words to arrange into a collage or something."

Lyle laughed through his hand. "Joey doing Dada? Über-freaky." But suddenly he sat up and his smirk turned into a cringe. "The cuts on his fingers—they came from *this*?"

"As far as I can tell," she said. "Look at the label on the back."

Lyle flipped it over and read aloud. "*Alice's Adventures in Wonderland*?" he said. "It's mislabeled. I don't get it."

His face went blank when Lydia extracted from her satchel the annotated copy of *Alice's Adventures in Wonderland* that she'd found this morning on the shelf in Fiction. "The two books are the same size," she said, then stacked them together and held them out for Lyle. Just as she had earlier on her own, Lydia opened the two books to page 34, folded back the cover of the Denis Johnson novel, then lined it up over the Lewis Carroll classic. Again, the little empty windows were now filled with words.

"Read the holes, Lyle. Where new words show through."

Lyle cleared his throat of something phlegmy, then struggled to read aloud:

noon

ewa

. It   ed

out

side   *The*

, ga

tesi

117

was

rel

ease   . D

                                           fr

                        ee

"*No one waited outside the gates . . . I was released . . . free . . .* Is that what it says? Wait—is this real?"

"It's real."

"How do you even know these are messages, though? Couldn't it be, I don't know—something else? Something not Joey?"

Lydia explained how, as far as she could tell, Joey chose the second book because its font was bigger, which made it easier to read through the windows. Then she told him about the pair of books—on book destruction and bed-wetting—she'd deciphered yesterday on the sidewalk.

"He addressed me by name," she said. "*You found me again, Lydia.* And he signed it *J.* And he kept that one separate from his other books, I think, so that I would discover it first, before these others."

"What does that even mean, though—*You found me again?*"

"I found him once when he was hanging," she said, "and again when I figured out his messages. I found his voice, I guess."

"His last words," Lyle said.

Lydia looked at her hands, feeling solemn. "I didn't ask for this."

"I know. But at least we know now what he was doing those last few days. What do the others say?"

"I've only managed to put together two more. This batch"— she gestured to the pair of books Lyle was holding and then tapped her satchel—"and one other. Go ahead. Line up the next pages."

Lyle turned to page 89 of *Resuscitation* and Lydia had to help him fold it open so that only that page stuck out, then place it atop page 89 of *Alice*. Once it was aligned Lyle worked his way through the tiny windows there and on the pages after:

and

, J

us.

tas

Al

one

as

Al   way

son

ly

mo

reg

row

nup

mores

c are

Dan

daw

. Are d

that

Li

few

ould

," Al

way

be

Noon

eo

uts,

I'd

et.

He g

ate

. S

Lydia pulled out the pocket-sized sunflower notebook in which she'd scrawled her morning's labors. "I think he's talking about prison here: *No one waited outside the gates . . . I was released . . . free . . . and just as alone as always . . . only more grown up . . . more scared and awared that life would always be . . . no one outside the gates.*"

"Definitely prison," Lyle said, and then his face fell apart. "But my god, how *depressing*. Finally getting out, and no one being

122

there to meet him. It's awful, Lydia. What a terrible thing. My heart goes out even now, you know?"

"Hopeless," she said. "And then to believe that his whole life would be like that?"

"All he had to do was ask," Lyle said, "and I would've been there."

Lydia dug inside her satchel. "This is the only other one I've figured out so far," she said, then slid an oversized and butchered copy of *A History of the Sect of the Hasidim* she'd found in Joey's apartment over an equally large copy of a fly-fishing book called *Emergers* she'd found shelved in the Sports section. She leaned forward enough for Lyle to see through the windows as she paged through the message:

ids

. W

allows

P

I'd

ers

ch

ew g

Las

s. Y

an k

. M   ynai

lst   ee

Th

. J

us two

be p

ART.

"*I'd swallow spiders, chew glass, yank my nails and teeth . . . just to be part,*" Lyle read. "Well, that's very sweet of him. But where's the rest of it? Just to be *part* of what? The Boy Scouts? The cast of *The X-Files*? The Church of Jesus Christ of Latter-day Saints? I'm sorry. I just can't help but feel insulted here. I gave that boy everything I could."

"Maybe this is about something you couldn't possibly provide," she said. "There's a pattern here, like when he got out of prison. Needing to feel like he's wanted. To feel not stranded—just to be *part*."

"But he was *part*," Lyle said. "He was part of this bookstore. He was part of *us*."

Lyle flipped through the pages and shuddered.

"Why do I feel like Joey is going to come waltzing up behind me at any moment?"

"I know what you mean," she said. "This whole thing is freaking me out."

"Like he's right here, in the space between us, trying to tell us something."

Both looked at the empty cushion between them, then quickly at the floor. Lydia rolled her shoulders and began to flip through the little notebook where she'd kept track of Joey's books, misplaced labels, and transcribed messages. She came upon a page she'd scrawled the other night in Joey's apartment: *CODVR?*

Lyle leaned forward.

"*Codur*? Was that one of Joey's messages?"

She held the notebook toward him. "C-O-D-V-R," she said. "Not a message. It was printed on an envelope."

"Just any old envelope?"

"One that Joey had burned in his apartment," she said.

"Of course Joey would burn his mail," Lyle said. "He probably had a special mail burner, ordered from the back of *Close Encounters* magazine."

"Any idea what it stands for?"

Lyle shook his head and grew serious. "C-O-D . . . it has to be Colorado Division of Something Something. Or Department. Something sponsored by the state. Which could be anything, knowing Joey, with his parole and prison time and his foster families and group homes and social programs." He pointed to a nearby desk. "Phone book?"

Within seconds, Lydia was sitting at the desk, thumbing through the blue pages of the phone book, the section reserved for government entries. Lyle stood behind her, hands behind his back, breathing loudly through his nose. He smelled like moldy lotion. It took her only a minute to find the right entry.

"Colorado Department of Vital Records," she said. "Any idea what they do?"

"Keep records on things that are vital, apparently," Lyle said with a shrug. "Things you can't live without. Like books. Whiskey. Waffles. Film noir."

As Lydia scribbled down the address of the Vital Records office in her little notebook, she could hear Lyle wandering away from the desk and into the depths of the store.

"Ice cream," he said to no one in particular. "Trombones. Peter Falk."

And he continued to murmur his list of vital things—

"Corn nuts. Hot lava. Hitchcock."

—even without Joey at his side.

CHAPTER ELEVEN

The clerk behind the counter at the Colorado Department of Vital Records was in his late forties, a bald burnout with furry eyebrows and a handlebar mustache. A few *Star Trek* action figures sat atop his monitor, and a Koosh ball, and a sticker that said *Not My Circus, Not My Monkeys*. Off to the side of his keyboard sat a microwaved tray of mac 'n' cheese, half-eaten.

"If I give you someone's name," Lydia said, drumming her fingers on the counter, "can you tell me what records he's requested?"

The man looked up from his tray and sniffed. He folded his hands over his belly and bobbed in his swivel chair.

"You're kidding, right?"

"He was a good friend."

"Uh-huh."

"He killed himself. I'm just trying to figure out why."

"Yeah?"

"And he had some correspondence from this office. Only he burned it."

"Okay," he said. "You're not kidding." He leaned toward the button for the numbers board, ready to move on: *Next*.

"Wait," she said. "How about I give you my friend's name, and you give me whatever records you have for him. Just whatever you've got. Can we do that?"

"Just anything?"

"Just anything."

"Listen," he said. "Here's what I can do. If you go up to Broadway, then head just a few blocks south, you'll see the Denver Public Library. It's under renovation, like everything else in this godforsaken city, so you can't miss it. Go inside and ask at the reference desk if they can point you to a copy of the Constitution. The United States Constitution. That might be a good place to start."

Lydia slapped her hands on the counter. "I happen to own a Bill of Rights T-shirt!" she said.

The man twirled his mustache. "You free for drinks later?"

Lydia marched off in a huff, but when she reached the bulletin boards by the door his voice stopped her.

"You have to *be* someone," he said, so she turned and walked back to the counter with her hands at her sides. "Legally speaking. A relative or a spouse or his lawyer—but *someone*. You can't just be you." And then he mumbled, "Adorable though you are."

"What was that last part?" she said, eyes wide, leaning forward, past the point of being patronized.

"Nothing," he blurted, then he pointed at the board hanging from the ceiling behind him. In little plastic numbers and letters, the board listed the documents that the CODVR office could provide, as if they were milkshake flavors at a burger joint. "If you tell me what you want, I can tell you what paperwork you'll need in order to get it. We've got all kinds of certificates and documents, cradle to the grave. Birth, death, adoption, marriage, divorce, dissolution, some immunization and genealogy. A few others too, but they're pretty uncommon."

"My friend killed himself and left me all of his belongings," she said.

"Okay, so maybe a birth and death certificate will be a good start," he said, nodding along, "because you need those for a lot of things. Bring in the paperwork—his will or a copy of his living trust to show you have a right to his records. If you have the notarized original it saves time." He paused, nibbled his mustache. "From the way you're looking at me I'm guessing you don't have anything like that."

"I have a Post-it note with my first name on it, written in pencil," she said. "His landlady pulled it out of her bra."

"Okay," the clerk said, and bit his lips. "Probably not going to cut it." Then he explained that she could always fill out the application request for, say, Joey's birth and death certificates, and she could explain on the application why she needed them, and if she didn't have the right paperwork or legal credentials, then *sometimes, rarely,* one of the clerks would contact her and suggest a different avenue for finding out the information, or even encourage her to apply for a waiver.

"But for a waiver you have to have a good reason," he said, "and it helps to know what you want. And sorry about the whole—you know, earlier."

"You mean the whole asshole thing? Or the whole Kafka thing? Which one?"

"Please," he said, "just one drink."

"I'd prefer not to," she said, then spun around and disappeared into the chilly Denver dusk. The clerk was right about one thing, she thought: it really does help to know what you want.

When Lydia stepped into her empty apartment, the first thing she saw was Joey's black suit hanging like a headless man from a hook on her bedroom door. She startled and nearly dropped her keys, but once she recovered, she found herself staring at the suit with fresh eyes, thinking differently about its presence.

Lyle had mentioned buying this suit for Joey, but as far as he knew, Joey had never even worn the thing. Lydia realized that she was equally in the dark, and that she'd dragged it out of Joey's apartment and brought it here without ever even inspecting it. Feeling queasy and invasive, she turned her head to the side and reached under the dry-cleaning plastic as if it were a hospital gown, then began to grope through the suit's pockets. She was hoping for Bright Ideas labels or little cutout tabs, or maybe even a final note, but found only a single blue foil wrapper that had once held a small sphere of chocolate, probably the same kind she'd smelled melted in his jeans as he'd hanged. Nothing else. Even after throwing it out, she felt sick to her stomach.

After stuffing the suit into her closet, she scrubbed her hands and climbed into a pair of David's Broncos sweats and his ripped *Thrasher* hoodie. Before she'd even finished heating her rice and beans in the microwave, and before she'd even set out the bottle of Tabasco and glass of water on the table in the kitchen, and before she'd even picked out whatever novel would accompany her dinner—eating and reading in solitude being a pleasure she ranked just below sex with David, and just above deliveries of hot Chinese food on cold winter nights—before any such evening rituals took hold, Lydia settled herself at the kitchen table, unbuckled her satchel, and laid out the new pair of books that she'd borrowed earlier from work. If Joey's misplaced labels were correct, these titles would allow her to hear a few more fragments of his disembodied voice.

While Lydia was here dancing with the dead, David was

down in Colorado Springs for a few days, manning a booth at a homeschooling convention. After more than a year working on the lowest rungs of the IT basement, he had recently been asked to represent the company on a trial basis at a few education conferences around the state. *No one gets out of that basement alive*, David sometimes said, so it was a big deal among his programming peers that a coding grunt had been recruited to meet with potential customers. Lydia had been reassuring him for days that he was just the person for the job, but she couldn't help but feel a guilty pleasure tonight in knowing she'd have the apartment to herself.

Lydia pulled her dinner from the microwave and began picking through Joey's milk crate, looking for the cut-up books that she could pair with those she'd brought home from work. Finding the titles on the bookstore shelves earlier had been more difficult than she'd expected. In her sunflower notebook she'd created a list of all the titles printed on the labels on the back of Joey's books, but during her search she learned that many were no longer on the shelves at all; they'd been sold or placed on hold, were missing or on order or lost in some inventory dead zone. Without those complementary titles there could be no messages, but she had enough to stay occupied. At least for the evening.

Lydia picked one of the cut-up books from the crate—a trade paperback of Katherine Dunn's *Geek Love* that she'd personally sold to Joey—and double-checked the label he'd stuck to the back to make sure she was pairing the titles correctly: it belonged to Walker Percy's novel *The Last Gentleman*, one of the books she'd borrowed earlier from the store. When she stacked them atop each other, the two were the exact same size, as expected. In the heart of Joey's copy of *Geek Love*, she found little windows cut into four or so pages—34, 89, 144, 233—and one at a time, she began to slide them over the corresponding pages in *The Last Gentleman* until his words emerged:

My D

add

Y

wast

, he   st

. At

emy

mo

mm   the

Fo

ood!" B   an

ks

and the

"Me?"

talc

ots   and the

L.A.

under

O'Ma

at

then

sand

came

133

my

on

ly,

. He

r.

Lydia flipped through the books to see if she'd missed any holes, and when she was sure she hadn't, she looked at the fragments again—*my daddy was the state . . . my momm the foood banks and the metal cots and the Laundromaats . . . and then came my only Her*—and the last word hooked her sight: *Her*.

She scooched her chair back on the linoleum and the scrape it made felt like fingers strumming her spine. Outside of his early years with the Molina family, Joey had been a ward of the state, she knew that already, and she knew that this was probably a big part of the reason he felt so totally alone in the world. But those last words, *and then came my only Her*, suggested a life after the state.

A life with *Her*. This was new: Joey feeling rescued from that life, feeling saved, by a woman.

Lydia allowed herself to conjure an image of Joey standing behind a twentysomething cutie-pie—flower barrettes and hair cropped short—and bobbing his head to a band at some dim venue, Lion's Lair or 7-South; or both of them rubbing their hands over the bronze claws of the grizzly in front of the Denver Museum of Natural History; or even Joey standing at a courthouse counter in his cryptic black suit, mumbling his wedding vows with chocolate in his pocket. Maybe later, after this relationship had shattered and sent him into a spin, Joey had burned his marriage certificate and his divorce papers—

But then wait, she thought: *Her*.

Now Lydia found herself conjuring an image of the girl Joey had almost killed. Lydia pictured her sitting in her car seat with a mouthful of Cheerios as a cinder block emerged before her eyes and exploded on her knee. Joey's victim was only one year old then, which meant she would be—what? In kindergarten? First grade? Was it possible that Joey had tracked her down after prison, sought her forgiveness, become something like an uncle or a big brother, leading her through the zoo?

But then wait: *Her*.

A sudden, unsettling thought sloshed through Lydia. What if *she*—Lydia—was *Her*? What if Joey had been secretly in love with *her*, and these messages, that photo (just *how* had he acquired that photo?), this whole hanging, was some sort of misbegotten attempt to declare his love? Joey's version of a severed ear.

"Oh, screw you, Joey," she said out loud in the empty apartment. She shook her head and held her hands palm out. "Don't let it be that, Joey, please don't let it be—"

A sudden knock caused Lydia to hop out of her seat. A second knock shifted her sight toward the door. Instinctively she tossed the books into the milk crate and slid it under the kitchen table. She suddenly longed to have David beside her.

Another knock, harder this time.

When she peeked through the peephole, holding a paring knife behind her back, she was startled to see Raj. He leaned against the hallway wall with a swoop of hair over one eye and a box of glazed doughnuts in his arms. With more than a little hesitation she opened the door but kept the chain clasped. She thought she smelled vodka.

"Raj," she said, failing to sound strong. "It's pretty late to just pop in."

Raj looked intensely into her eyes but didn't speak. Since their reunion on the sidewalk the other day, he'd shown up at the bookstore a few times, a frequency that may have bordered on stalky except for the fact that he lived in the neighborhood and was, of course, her oldest friend.

"Come back another time," she said, and started to close the door. "Okay? Earlier."

"I wanted to see you," he said, then added, almost as an after-thought, "and to show you something." He shifted the doughnut box awkwardly in his hands so he could fish something out of his pocket. At the sight of his bumbling, Lydia felt a small glow inside, the spark of an old ember.

"I'm sorry," she said, reaching out to grab his arm. "It's okay. Come in, come in." Raj, she reminded herself, shouldn't need a reason to visit her, even after dark. "I just get a little spooked when David's out of town."

Lydia had no intention of cheating with Raj, yet as he crossed the threshold into her apartment, brushing accidentally against her chest, she found herself wondering whether David would ever cheat on her. She knew she didn't have to worry about his blowing his paycheck at a strip club or a massage parlor—he wasn't the type, as far as she knew—but she sometimes wondered what he would do if he connected with a woman who was more wholesome and cheery than she was, someone who was more his *type*. Maybe because of the education conference he was presently attending, she found herself imagining David sharing wheat-germ muffins with one of those nurturing home-schooler babes, the type who dressed like Laura Ingalls Wilder and chugged milk straight from the udder. She shared more with David than she ever had with anyone—her anxiety around crowds, the nibblings of sadness she often felt in her gut, her penchant for afternoon sex—yet she was fully aware of the one thing she could never reveal: her night with the Hammerman. She just hoped she wasn't pushing him away.

Raj wandered around the small apartment hugging the doughnut box under his arm. His blue jeans were hacked at the shins and he wore tube socks and black leather sandals despite the cold. She couldn't help but notice that he was slightly plump, as he'd always been, yet he was still attractive and had an aura of comfort and solidity. When he paused in front of her books—each one a dusty time capsule of the hours she'd spent within it—Lydia grew self-conscious of her secondhand shelves, doubled up with books, some tripled, and the sight of them left her feeling obsessive and antisocial. But as she studied Raj's profile, watching him hug his doughnuts, she thought he appeared equally obsessive, equally antisocial.

"You do anything but read?" he said.

"Not much."

"Sounds nice."

Raj poked around her apartment, and at one point he stopped in front of David's meager shelf of books—fat programming manuals and a few collegiate musts, like *The Electric Kool-Aid Acid Test* and *Fear and Loathing in Las Vegas*—and picked up a little robot that David had made out of bottle caps. Perhaps Raj was reminded of his childhood, lost now, spent building plastic model cars in his bedroom.

"How are your parents anyway, Raj? They doing okay?"

"I guess they're fine," he said, shrugging. "I worry sometimes about my mom. She never takes a break. She burned her hand recently, really bad this time, but the next day she was right back at work, wearing this mitten of gauze. The woman refuses to take a day off."

"So same as always," Lydia said with a pensive grin.

"Same as always: Dad's a crab and Mom's a smiling wreck. You should stop in and see them sometime. Really. If you can handle it."

"I've driven by," she said, shrugging. "Just never stopped."

Which was true. Countless times, Lydia had passed Gas 'n Donuts while taking the Colfax bus, or riding shotgun with David, or heading on thrift-store excursions with Plath, but her nostalgia for the place had never been strong enough to outweigh her dread of dredging up the past. Despite the paint peeling from its façade, the building itself had remained a deco landmark, with wraparound neon and curved stucco walls and glass bricks lining either side of its entrance. She'd seen Mr. Patel a few times through the street-side windows, slogging around under the smoke-stained American flag that still hung on the wall over the counter. He'd grown a thicker beard and a gut the size of an engine block, and even from a distance she could tell that he still wore those stretched white T-shirts and frayed gray hairnets, and he still carried himself exactly as he had when she was a girl—which is to say he moved through the world like he wanted to kick its ass. As for Mrs. Patel, Lydia had only seen her in passing once: smiling wide and wearing an apron over her sari, politely holding open the door for a customer who was carrying a box of doughnuts and a cardboard tray of coffee—just as she always had when Lydia was a girl.

"I really should stop and say hi," she said. "You're right."

"They'd love to see you. I'm telling you, that place is like a time warp. Nothing's changed."

She watched Raj with a wistful smile. "Don't take this the wrong way," she said, "but you seem the same, too. Unchanged. In a good way."

"Okay," Raj said, nodding with mild amusement, "my turn. Don't take this the wrong way, but I thought you'd be *way* different. You don't seem screwed up at all."

"We're all screwed up, Raj. Modern living."

"But look at this place. It's all so *grounded*. No dirty dishes in the sink. No lipstick on the windows. No pet tarantulas. You really pulled your shit together."

"I work at a bookstore," she said. "That's not exactly corporate law."

"But I expected you to be curled up in an asylum somewhere. I was actually kind of hoping for that."

"So you could save me?"

A grin cracked his lips. "So we'd have more in common."

Raj leaned against the bay window and looked out. From the right angle during the winter, when the leaves were stripped from the trees, the golden dome of the capitol could be seen gleaming in the distance.

"Can I ask you something?" she said, and the words came in a burst, before she had a chance to stop them. "What was it like for you after I left? I wrote you all those letters, but you weren't able to write back, so that's something I've always wondered about. If you even remember, I mean."

"What was it like?" he said, turning his head but not turning around.

"For you."

"Horrible. Not like it was for you, but still really horrible."

"I figured," she said. "That's okay. You don't need to—"

"Let's see," Raj said. "Right after the murders, I guess the worst part for me was knowing what you'd been through but not being able to see you. I begged to go to the hospital, but your dad wouldn't allow any visitors. So my parents and I sat around the shop and watched the news and listened to the rumors, just like everyone else in the city. You wouldn't believe the stories. The Hammerman was scarier than anything. At night he tapped his hammer on our bedroom windows, on the pipes beneath our slumber parties. We pictured him with jet-black hammer tattoos on both arms. After the murders, when Carol's house was on the market, kids in the neighborhood would dare each other to sneak inside and climb under the sink and chant *the Hammerman* ten times. Like *Bloody Mary*? No one made it past five. You couldn't pay me enough. He could've been anyone, you know? Because he never got caught."

"I heard," she said.

"And you came up a lot, too. Always *Little Lydia*, just like on the news. In class we made calendars and recipe books to raise money for you. And the memorial at school—man alive. That was just *intense*."

"How so?"

"People started showing up outside of Little Flower and constructing this makeshift memorial for Carol. All these little gifts, mostly from strangers, just kind of sprouted against the playground fence, and before long the flowers and balloons and ribbons and cards got to be overwhelming. We were encouraged by the nuns to try to forget what had happened, yet all day long, out the classroom windows, we could see strangers piling these reminders against the chain-link. Candles and photos and teddy bears. Posters that people would sign. Then one day it started to snow, that wet, slushy snow that always ruined recess, and Sister Noreen told us to run out to the playground and carry the shrine inside, one stuffed animal at a time, one crayoned note, and soon we couldn't help it, we were all crying, every single one of us, and setting up the shrine on bleachers in the gym. It's such a strong memory, running in and out of the school, all of us in tears together, and the nuns bawling too, and—"

Raj stopped abruptly and blinked for a minute. He seemed as surprised as Lydia about this manic flow of memory.

"I don't know what to say, Raj."

"Heavy-duty, right?" He looped a finger into the back pocket of his jeans. "Anyway, I brought something to show you. I wasn't sure you'd seen it."

From his pocket he pulled out a folded page of a magazine and handed it to her. It was heavily creased and ripped along the margin, and on one side was a faded advertisement for Prell shampoo. On the other, a striking halftone photo from an ancient issue of *Life* magazine, of a little survivor named Lydia, wrapped in a blanket, surrounded by police, being carried down a snowy stoop by her father. The sight of it sent a jolt through her and she let it fall to the coffee table, facedown.

"I'm sorry," he said. "I thought it might be— I don't know."

"It's fine," she said. "It's just hard for me to look at."

"Me too, to be honest," Raj said. "Those first months you were gone were the hardest, probably. That was before I got any of your letters. It didn't help that my parents were already hanging on by a thread. Without you, I realized, I had no life outside of home and the gas station, and my life at home had been a disaster for a long time already."

"I remember," she said.

"Not a great advertisement for arranged marriage, you know, even if it wasn't technically arranged."

"Wasn't there a haircut fight?" Lydia said, somewhat out of nowhere, smiling grimly, glad for the change of subject. "I vaguely remember a haircut fight."

"Oh my god," Raj said, "that was the *worst*."

"Your mom cut off all of her hair and your dad—what? Lost it?"

141

"In a nutshell," Raj said, nodding in a way that seemed half-embarrassed, half-amused. "So do you remember the scene in *Rosemary's Baby* when Mia Farrow cuts off all of her hair? She goes out and gets that pixie cut, right?"

"Vidal Sassoon," she said. "Big moment in the history of hair. Cassavetes played her husband."

"Exactly," Raj said, nodding, impressed. "So Rosemary comes home from the salon, all cute and demure and excited to show him her new short haircut, and do you remember what he says to her? *Don't tell me you paid for that.* I swear to you, Lydia, my dad had that exact reaction when my mom came home with her shiny little— What do you call that haircut? Not a bob, but a Dorothy Hamill thing—"

"A wedge?"

"A *wedge*, yes. My mom was all excited, and my dad basically said, *Don't tell me you paid for that.* Maybe not those exact words, but he was pissed. It wasn't even drastic, right? Every third woman had that 'do. Both of my parents were born in California, but my dad still expected her to be this medieval village woman. For a while I think she even slept on the couch. Anyway, it was really hard on us when you left. My mom always loved you so much."

"I always loved your mom," Lydia said.

"She really couldn't take it," he said. "She'd just gotten so sick of all the violence in the neighborhood, and what happened to you just brought it all closer to home. When I was growing up, you know how she and my dad always kind of babied me—"

"*Kind of* babied you? Raj of the Doughnuts."

"Believe me," he said, smiling. "It only got worse once you were gone. They were so *worried* about me, and my mom talked about not being able to live in America anymore, it was too violent, all that." Raj shifted into his mom's soft voice, no accent, but with long, drawn-out vowels. "*People here are crazy, Raj!* Not to mention all the hassles she dealt with every day on Colfax. Remember, there were always these little scuffles out on the sidewalk, a knife fight at the bus stop one day, or my dad would have to push some drunk out the door or call the police on some asshole trying to steal gas. When she was growing up in Southern California, all of her relatives who'd visited from Gujarat would talk about what it was like back in India, telling her these stories about perfect little villages and the open countryside full of wildflowers and waterfalls—total cartoon, right? A poster in an Indian restaurant. For a while, all she talked about was moving there, but of course my dad refused to even consider it. So then she decided I would go with her, and we'd try to find a business to buy in the village where her aunties and grandparents lived, but my dad put his foot down. I really think that if I would've gone with her, we never would've come back to the States."

"So she went anyway?"

"She did," he said. "I think she just needed a reality check because she came back before long, and her hair had grown out some, and she'd gotten rid of all that women's lib talk. She probably realized that everywhere has its problems, you know? Maybe Colfax wasn't so bad."

"My dad basically had the same reaction," Lydia said, nodding her head, subdued by the direction this visit had gone in. "He did the exact same thing: got out of town the second he could. Rio Vista was his India. Only we never came back."

"I've never really thought about it like that, but it totally makes sense," Raj said. "You can't really blame them, worrying about their kids. Wanting to raise us somewhere safe."

"We were so much happier in Denver," she said, "with the library and the doughnut shop and everything, at least for a while. So much happier—and then we just *weren't*."

Lydia glanced at the magazine page still facedown on the table, and when she looked up she caught Raj staring at her. She picked it up and turned it in her hands. She didn't need to say, *All because of this,* because Raj was looking at the picture now as well, and she could tell exactly what he was thinking: *All because of this.*

CHAPTER TWELVE

The photograph earned front-page spreads across the West and even made *Life* magazine's *The Year in Pictures*, just opposite the image of an American army helicopter tilting away from a crowd of refugees. The freelance photographer, tipped by a pal in the Denver Police Department, popped his shutter just as Tomas lunged down the porch steps of the house next door to the O'Tooles', where he and Lydia had gone to wait for help. The photo captured them plunging through the crowd of paramedics and cops, with Lydia glancing up at the camera, eyes wide with terror, face masked with blood, limbs knotted around her father. A gray blanket dragged behind her, and one of the cops could be seen reaching down to lift it out of the snow.

For days after the photo was taken, Lydia inhabited a hospital room crowded with flowers and balloons and yarn-tied get-well cards. In addition to all the bedside visits from doctors and nurses, she'd been interviewed by a pair of bossy policemen who smoked too much and could never quite figure out how to work their tape recorder. Worst of all, the cops kept leading her dad away from her bedside, and whenever he returned he looked scraped out, as if they were collecting little pieces of his soul in jars somewhere. Before long the policemen were replaced by women who wore turtleneck sweaters and beaded necklaces and looked like teachers. They were kind and brushed her hair and always asked how she felt. She'd look at her dad—fiddling with the bandage on his palm, scratching at his beard—and tell the women that she felt just fine. No nightmares? She'd smile and lie. None that she noticed. No sadness? She missed her friends, was all. No pain? The stitches on her forehead were beginning to itch. Once when her dad was out on a Jell-O run, they asked her if she knew anything about his *special friends*, but when Lydia said *What friends?* they just fluffed her pillow and encouraged her to get some sleep.

Soon Lydia was walking through the hospital lobby, squeezing the hands of nurses as Tomas steered her into the backseat of the used station wagon he'd purchased during one of her naps. He told her to hide under the duffel bags and blankets back there, and doing so felt like the most natural thing she'd done in ages.

—No one's allowed to see us, he said. All part of the deal.

Three hours later the rest of the deal was clear as they dragged their bags into a two-bedroom A-frame cabin in the hills north of Rio Vista. Tomas had apparently arranged to buy the cabin, along with its massive workshop and eight acres of juniper pine, sight unseen. The place had been unoccupied for years and it had cost him practically nothing, but in order to call it home he still had to cash in nearly every cent of Rose's life insurance. Though it would take him another six months to sell their house in Denver, and he spent a lot of that time in a financial panic, never once did he mention returning to the city.

At first, the ten-year-old Lydia thought the move to Rio Vista was an adventure worthy of a storybook. Tomas loaded their grocery cart with TV dinners and candy bags and ordered a set of Holly Hobbie bedroom furniture from the old brick J. C. Penney outlet in Colorado Springs. He assured her that until the following fall—seven months away—she didn't even have to think about school or homework or making friends. Everything about this new life carried the feeling of a dream, especially the tiny town of Rio Vista. The valley smelled of campfires and freezer frost, and Main Street's wooden sidewalks clopped beneath her feet as she ran. Behind town, the Arkansas River roared south, its rocky banks stapled with railroad tracks and mining chutes. The mist rising off the river was so eerie, the mountain peaks so soaring, that she often felt as if she and her father had moved to a paragraph in a fairy tale—

Except that during all of their time together Lydia found it upsetting that they never spoke about That Night, especially because it felt as if it had slithered forward in time and consumed every other night in her life. Sometimes she would hear her father crying in the shower, or she'd catch him pulling the phone into the pantry and whispering in the dark. Once when he fell asleep against a tumble of pillows on the floor, she looked at him over the top of her book—his beard growing gray and scraggly, his wool sweater unraveling, his horn-rims sitting crooked on his nose—and whispered it, just to see:

—the Hammerman, dad. where's the Hammerman?

He groaned in his sleep and she wondered if his nightmares were as bad as her own.

Lydia's fairy tale in Rio Vista fully lost its shine when Tomas, after tapping his remaining savings, decided to take the only job he could find: working as a corrections officer at the state prison on the southern limits of town. When he shared the news over toaster waffles one evening, Lydia was full of complaints. Not only was Tomas *compromising himself*—a phrase she'd heard him say a zillion times—but he would have to be gone all night.

—We all start on graveyard.

—but i'll be alone.

—I thought you were okay.

—i am.

—Then what's the problem?

The problem was, Lydia soon discovered, that being alone all night gave her ample time to think—not only about her seven-month vacation coming to an end, but also about the one thing she wasn't supposed to be thinking about: That Night.

Lydia started fifth grade about the same time that Tomas started his prison job, and during the first week of school, Mrs. Wahl, the busty PE teacher with a platinum lid and satin jogging suits, took special pity on her and set aside time after school to train her in the art of personal hygiene. Ever since moving to the mountains, neither she nor Tomas had shown much interest in taming her tangled hair, and coupled with the forehead scar and the fresh jump in her eyeballs, she'd begun to look wilder than she really was. (In the mirror alone at night, in fact, she sometimes sensed a petrifying resemblance to Carol O'Toole.) But taming her appearance was the least of her worries. Because Lydia was the new kid in town, her classmates tended to either study her every move or want to kick her ass. She didn't quite understand if these scabby mountain kids were supposed to be her friends like Raj, like Carol—god: *Carol!*—but she never had the luxury of sorting such questions out. When they circled her in the weedy lot behind the playground and interrogated her about where she got that forehead scar, she couldn't tell them the truth, of course, and before long she felt like a permanent balloon had been inflated between herself and everyone else on earth.

—welcome to your new life, she'd tell herself.

Each day Lydia managed to survive the ride home on the school bus, and once there she'd open all the curtains and wake up her father. They'd eat pancakes or eggs at the kitchen counter and he'd stare solemnly at the chicken clock clucking on the wall.

Then he'd begin ironing his state-issued shirt and polishing his black ankle boots. She sometimes watched him getting ready and wondered if he was an imposter. Ever since they'd left Denver, he'd been acting less and less like her dad. At first it was small stuff, like when he kissed her good-bye he'd look away too soon, or when she asked him questions he didn't seem to hear her, even if it was important. He'd even begun to look different. Just after taking this prison job he'd replaced his horn-rims with big wire aviator glasses and shaved his beard clean off. With his regulation buzz cut and parted mustache, he looked less like her father and more like (*face it!*) a prison guard.

Although Lydia didn't understand her father's transformation, she knew he would never have acted like this unless things were pretty bad. Which was why she kept it all so quiet, what started happening to her during his nights away.

—You sure you're gonna be all right?

—i'll be fine.

—Chain the door behind me.

His car spat gravel on its way toward the prison and suddenly she was alone in the cabin. Silence surrounding her like an invitation.

The first time Lydia woke up under the cabin's kitchen sink, the sun was rising between the cracks and Tomas was pounding on the front door, calling her name.

—Lydia!

She kicked herself out from under and sprinted down the hall. Before she slid the chain from its clasp on the door she looked around the cabin and it was empty but for her. Of course it was.

When she let Tomas in he patted her frazzled hair and glanced down upon her. He must have noticed something because he tilted her face by the chin, as if examining a shiner.

—i overslept.

—You're late for school.

Then he scooped an ant trap from the kitchen floor and threw it beneath the sink, where it belonged.

As the months spilled forward, Lydia's nights beneath the sink became all but inevitable. Once, twice, three times a week, while Tomas patrolled the snoring corridors of the prison, Lydia would meander through her bedtime ritual with all the enthusiasm of someone changing a toilet paper roll. In bed she'd get lost in a book and chomp through a wad of gum until she could hardly keep her eyes open any longer. Then she'd thumb the gum to her nightstand, click off her bed light, and aim straight for sleep. Sometimes it worked. But sometimes as she slipped out of consciousness, she'd hear creaking in the crawl space or jangling in the fridge. Doors opening. Milk spilling. Her muscles would jolt and she'd snap out of bed, scamper down the hallway, and fold herself safely under the kitchen sink, usually for the rest of the night.

Sometimes when Lydia was hiding in there, she believed that she could hear the Hammerman just on the other side of the cabinet door, his boots squeaking through the snowy blood on the kitchen floor. But mostly what she felt was a pervasive sense of dread and anticipation, as if she were Pippi Longstocking sealed into her dark barrel, just beginning to roll over the lip of the waterfall.

A year of this passed, then two. And then it was a Saturday morning in October and instead of being awakened by her father's keys in the dead bolt, she was awakened by a ringing phone. She kicked her way out from beneath and snapped the phone off the wall.

—I've got to stay on for another twelve.

—dad?

—We could use the money. You'll be okay at home alone?

She looked at the chicken clock clucking: five a.m.

—Or you can go to a friend's house. Wasn't there a girl in your art class?

—i'll be okay here.

Lydia held the phone until its buzz went silent. The dad she'd had in Denver wasn't perfect, but he never would have left her alone so much. Every time she thought of him as he'd been back then—the soft way he entered a room, the tilt of his head when others spoke—she felt incredibly sad, as if the dad in her memory had died that night with all the rest.

The sun was barely a dream in the east and she had the whole day and whole cabin to herself. She walked from room to room in her socks, snooping in the silence, feeling the kinks and aches of her night beneath go away. When she got to her father's room, she sat on the edge of his mattress and opened up the gunmetal lockbox he kept under his dresser. She looked through some envelopes and snapshots, then pulled out a crumpled sheet of brown paper towel, the kind found in school and hospital restrooms. When she unwadded it—expecting a tooth fairy tooth or a lock of her infant hair—she was surprised to see her mother's ruby ring sitting in the crumple like a flower in cemetery soil. He'd finally thrown out the gauze.

As she was packing the ring back in the box she stopped cold and turned her head and wondered if she'd really just heard a man's footsteps in the hallway. No one was there when she peered around the jamb, but her heart was pounding. She checked the front door and it was locked, but even in the daylight the realization that it wouldn't open until dusk tightened the silence around her. A few seconds passed and she was about to feel calm—and then of course she heard it: somewhere in the back of the cabin, an egg splattering on the wooden floor.

The cabinet door clicked as she pulled it closed behind her.

Twelve hours later, above the birdlike sounds that echoed through the sink chamber, Lydia finally heard tires crunching up the driveway. The air around her began to crack and she pushed open the door of her dark box. The lower half of her body was so numb she felt as if she'd been cast in concrete. It was impossible to walk, yet she managed to pull herself up tall enough to peer out the window above the sink.

Outside, at the peak of the driveway, she watched her father, dressed in an unbuttoned work shirt, lifting a heavy cardboard box from the backseat of the station wagon. He walked straight down the slope to his workshop and didn't step foot into their cabin until long after Lydia had eaten dinner alone, taken a shower, climbed into bed, and—finally, thankfully—read herself to sleep.

CHAPTER THIRTEEN

As Lydia awakened and her eyes adjusted to the light, she realized she'd been roused by the sound of snoring. Her first panicky thought was that David didn't snore. She looked at the pillow pile and braided sheets next to her but the bed was strangely empty. When she followed the snores she found Raj on the floor next to her bed, sound asleep in David's sleeping bag.

On the floor, she told herself. Not in the bed. Whew.

She remembered now: Last night they'd talked for so long that Lydia had suggested Raj stay over. He'd taken her up on the offer.

The morning was cold so Lydia decided to lie in bed for a while, but when the phone rang in the kitchen she hopped over Raj without waking him. She was wearing David's sweats and David's hoodie and as she stared at the ringing phone she imagined it was him, David, calling to let her know he was coming home early for sex or bagels.

One room away, Raj still snored. The phone stopped ringing.

As she contemplated coffee she spotted Joey's milk crate underneath the table. She pulled out the pair of books she'd been hoping to decipher last night when Raj's knock had interrupted her. One was a slim volume of poems called *The Devil's*

Tour and she was surprised, as she fanned through it, to find only a handful of tiny windows cut from its pages. This was, as far as she could tell, the shortest of the messages she'd seen thus far. The label on the back belonged to a different book, of course, a brisk novel called *Sula* that she'd borrowed from the store yesterday, and she could feel her vision blur a bit as she lifted it from the table, opened to the corresponding pages, and slid its text under the cut-up poems. When the pages lined up exactly, a few meager words appeared:

my

1.

As

T

me. S

age

, f

In

D

her

. . .

My last message—except Lydia still had a small pile of books in the crate that she had yet to decipher. So while this may have been the last message Joey had carved, she realized, it was not the last one Lydia would decode. Even so, its directive was clear: *Find her . . .*

There she was again: *Her.*

Lydia felt her arms fall loosely to her sides as she realized, with great relief, that the woman in Joey's messages—the *Her* that Lydia was directed to find, whatever that meant—was probably not herself. In the first message, Joey had addressed Lydia directly, had even used her name, so it seemed likely that *Her* was another person altogether. But who?

It was quiet in the apartment, but she could hear the first hints of traffic up on Colfax, as well as birds chirping between branches in the spruce trees that nuzzled her home. When she looked toward the bedroom, she saw Raj wriggling out of David's bag and slipping on his sandals. His hair was a living mess.

Lydia closed the books and dropped them into the milk crate.

"What's all that?" Raj said, coming into the kitchen.

"My inheritance. When someone hangs themselves in the store, they apparently feel the need to leave me a gift."

"Ouch." Raj looked down at the crate. "Can I?"

"I'd rather you didn't," she said.

He shrugged.

"Did I hear the phone?" he said.

"David's coming home today."

"Then I should probably go."

"Probably."

As Raj rolled up the sleeping bag and used the bathroom, Lydia—feeling guilty for denying him access to the crate—opened her sock drawer and pulled out the birthday party photo that Joey had had with him when he hanged himself. Raj was in the photo too, and maybe he'd even know something about it. When he came out of the bathroom, his hair was wet and pressed to the side, and she could smell toothpaste on his breath, and she wondered whether he'd used his finger to clean his teeth or her toothbrush—or, god forbid, David's. He took the photo from her and his eyes widened as he studied it: Lydia blowing out the candles, Raj staring at her, Carol a blur on the boundary of the print.

"Recognize it?" she said.

But Raj didn't say anything, just continued to stare.

"It's us," she said, hoping to break his trance. "Right around then."

"That's what I was thinking," he said, barely audible. "Right around then."

"What is it? The way you're staring at it."

"Just look at me fully crushing on you," he said.

Lydia took the occasion to fiddle in the kitchen—lifting the kettle, rinsing out the sponge—rather than respond.

"Where'd you get this, anyway?" he said.

"From Joey. The guy who hanged himself."

"Really?" Raj said, looking at it again. "What a creep. How'd he get it? Did you have it at the store or something?"

"No such luck," she said. "I'd never seen it before the night he died. Not that I remember, anyway."

The fact was, she still had no idea how Joey had obtained the photo, or why he would have even wanted it. Nothing about the scenario made sense, though she'd wondered about the possibility that a private detective or conspiracy theorist or investigative journalist had somehow enlisted Joey in the quest to uncover Little Lydia's new identity. But that was as far as she'd gotten.

"That's your old kitchen in the photo," Raj said, "so we can assume that your dad took it."

"He must have."

"So then Joey would have gotten it from him."

"From my dad? Okay, but that doesn't explain when their paths would have crossed. Or how."

As Raj continued to study the photo, caught in some loop of memory, Lydia's mind bloomed in new directions. What if her father had persuaded Joey to help him reconnect with his estranged daughter? Or what if he'd enlisted Joey to keep an eye on her?

She felt a chill: *Find her*, Joey's message had said. Find Little Lydia? Maybe she'd been too quick to omit herself—

"You okay?" Raj said, gently tugging a loose thread on her sweatshirt.

"Yeah," she said, collecting herself. "Sorry."

"Was Joey from Rio Vista or something?"

"Joey was from nowhere, as far as I can tell."

"And you're still not talking to your dad? Because you could always just ask him."

"He's been calling," she said. "I just haven't called him back."

Raj waved the photo. "Maybe this is why."

Lydia took it from his hands. Raj pulled up his socks and strapped on his sandals.

"I should probably go," he said.

He walked to the door and opened it but stopped with his hand on the knob. "You know," he said, facing the empty hallway, "the police came to see me after you guys left town. Back in fourth grade."

"Makes sense they would."

"Two detectives. The one in charge and one other guy. This was a month or two after you'd moved, maybe longer. We met in a booth at the doughnut shop after school. It was kind of a big deal. My dad even closed the shop early so there wouldn't be any distractions."

"Why are you telling me this, Raj?"

"I thought the cops were there to ask about Carol, so I was all ready with a bunch of Carol stories and Carol gossip, but they didn't seem interested in her at all. All they cared about was your dad. They wanted to know everything about him. Like, *everything*."

Lydia planted her palm on the textured wall.

"About my dad?"

"The questions they were asking me, Lydia— It was like he wasn't even the guy that I knew. Like they were asking about some other guy altogether."

"Sounds just like him," she said, slowly closing the door, bidding Raj good-bye.

CHAPTER FOURTEEN

Lydia found Plath at the base of the bookshop's wide staircase, leaning against one of the building's scratched wooden columns like a gumshoe on a lamppost. At first Lydia thought her friend was smoking but soon realized she was just gnawing on a Tootsie Pop. Otherwise she didn't appear to be doing anything.

"Very professional," Lydia said, pointing at her lollipop.

Plath smiled and brown drool dripped down her chin. A passing customer covered her mouth with her hand.

"What are you doing, anyway?" Lydia said.

"Lollipop. Ing." Then she dragged her fingers along a stream of spines and sighed. "Remind me never to quit this place."

"Because you can eat lollipops at work?"

"Lydia, you just named the one thing we have in common with strippers. But no, I just love it here. That's all."

"Yeah?"

"Yeah."

Lydia was glad to have found Plath. Plath always made her happy, and today of all days she really needed the boost. After Raj had left her apartment, she decided with uncommon certainty that, for the first time in twenty years, she needed to go see Detective Moberg—to ask about the message on his postcard, *if ever you want more*, but also to ask why he'd been interrogating ten-year-old Raj about her father, and who else he'd cornered in search of information. This felt too huge to hide in her sock drawer.

"Can I borrow your car?" she said. "I need to go to the mountains—"

"Say no more," Plath said, and, lollipop between her teeth, retrieved a jangle of keys from her back pocket and slid one off. Plath had recently shortened her silver hair to just above a crew cut and was wearing big silver hoops that jangled like an optical illusion. "Need a passenger?"

"Not today," she said.

"You sure? How about a shoulder?"

"I'm good."

"How about a drink?"

"About twelve hours too early."

Plath was holding a stack of paper, covertly rolled into a tube. A book cart was parked nearby.

"Is that a returns list?" Lydia said.

"Don't you have mountains to conquer? Go away."

"Let me see."

"Go. Away."

One of the duties shared by Lydia's comrades was to periodically run a returns report through the inventory system and use it to unshelve books that hadn't sold in months and return them to the publisher. The idea was to cut out whatever titles might be bogging down business, but Lydia would play no part in such a cruel practice. In fact, after many failed attempts at rehabilitation, she was no longer allowed to participate in the returns process at all because each time she'd done so she'd been caught intentionally losing pages from her lists or misshelving favored books in order to spare them from the gallows. She just couldn't avoid taking it personally: sending a choice title back to the publisher was like sending a perfectly good pooch to the pound, knowing it would be euthanized.

"This is a business," Plath said, pointing at Lydia with her soggy white stick, "not a library. Sometimes we have to get our hands dirty."

The floor held bits of rock salt and smudged boot prints, but Lydia still knelt next to the cart and bent her head into her spine-reading pose. Her hair crawled into her mouth as she slid out a collection of Grace Paley's stories.

"Put it back," Plath said.

"One copy of Grace Paley will not break the bank."

"The bank? The fucking bank gave up on us years ago. But never mind them, and for that matter, never mind us. Think instead about where your BookFrogs will be if we become a Niketown."

"They're my BookFrogs now?"

"They've always been."

Lydia groaned and continued to browse through the cart.

"What are you looking for anyway?" Plath said.

Lydia hesitated for a moment, then pulled from her back pocket the small sunflower notebook where she'd written lists of Joey's labels.

"These."

Over the past few days, she'd managed to cross six or seven off the list and enter their corresponding messages but was still having difficulty finding the remaining titles. Lydia explained to Plath that most of the books on the list were still in the inventory, yet they hadn't been on the shelves when she'd looked.

"And they may be missing labels," she added. "There's that."

Plath glared. "What're you up to, you little snake?"

For a moment Lydia considered telling Plath about the cut-up books that Joey had bequeathed her, but she was hoping to make it to Moberg's cabin in the mountains by the afternoon so she wouldn't have to drive back to Denver in the dark. She bit her thumbnail until it tore right off, then she stuck it into the corner pocket of her jeans. Plath was staring at her when she looked up. "I don't even want to know."

"Can I ask you something?" Lydia said. "Joey never said anything about being married, did he? I'm trying to figure out if there was a girl, you know, in his life. In his past."

"Besides you, you mean?"

"I'm serious."

"Listen up, heartbreaker. Joey was absolutely not married," Plath said. "He was pretty adorable, sure, in a cuckoo's-nest kind of way, but he didn't wear a wedding ring, and you could tell by the lone-wolf look on his face that he wasn't entangled."

"Well," Lydia said, "someone sure broke his heart."

Plath gestured at the notebook in Lydia's hands. "Check backstage for your list of books," she said. "If they've come through without labels, they're probably sitting on a shelf back there, waiting to be processed. And enjoy your trip today. You know what they say: *the answer is in the mountains.*"

"Not to this question," Lydia said, waving her notebook as she walked toward the swinging doors that led to the bookstore's warehouse.

Unofficially called the store's backstage, the area beyond the doors was a different world altogether, a shambolic cavern of wooden tables and cardboard boxes and ubiquitous piles of books. Lydia had learned early on at Bright Ideas that stepping back here ensured an amplification of both intelligence and surliness. Many of her backstage comrades were bibliophiles who'd been so disappointed by people that they now sought as little human interaction as possible. Other comrades disappeared backstage gradually, one shift at a time, when their faces hurt from smiling too much and they could no longer take responsibility for what they might do to the next person who asked for directions to the bathroom. They were like flight attendants who'd bumped their hips on the seat back one too many times; like English teachers who'd graded one too many essays. Lydia thought someday she might find her own home back here.

She drifted until she spotted Ernest taping boxes closed at a table. She'd only seen him in passing since the night of the hanging, just over two weeks ago, when he'd stood on the stool and unspooled Joey's noose. He was wearing overalls and a gold nose ring and the kind of puffy plastic earphones that her dad's library patrons used to plug into record players. The moment he spotted her he tugged the headphones off and looked around to make sure they were alone, then dove right into a hug that was both unexpected and gruff.

When he stepped back he seemed flustered, embarrassed.

"Have you had a wink of sleep?" he said, unabashedly desperate. "I mean since Joey. 'Cause I can't fucking sleep."

"It's been spotty for me, too," she said. "I've been trying to stay occupied."

"I can't even go out there," he said, gesturing to the store. "Fucking Joey. Thanks, dude. What did I ever do to him?"

Lydia gave his shoulder a squeeze.

"What can I help you with, Lydia?"

"I'm looking for books that are missing their labels," she said. She'd been expecting some skepticism, or a barrage of questions, but Ernest just nodded.

"They've been piling up," he said, talking as he walked her

around a large wooden table and pulled a stack of books off a shelf that flanked it. "I've been flaking on printing new labels. They've been showing up back here all week, one at a time, like debris from a plane crash."

"More than normal?"

"I don't know what *normal* means anymore," he said.

"Can I see?"

Ernest stepped aside as Lydia studied their spines. In the pile she found four that were from her list—four that she needed to fill in Joey's cut-up pages.

"I'm going to take these," she said, lifting them sideways so he could see their spines, a Scooby sandwich of titles, "but I'll bring them back tomorrow." As she tucked the books into her satchel, she turned to Ernest. "Joey didn't mean you any harm."

"I know," he said, "but that doesn't make it go away." Then he disappeared into his earphones and rested his head atop the table, facedown, as if to stake his claim on this space backstage—as if to prove that he wasn't going anywhere.

Although Lydia was now over sixty miles southwest of Denver, climbing toward the snowy peaks of the Continental Divide in the rattling Volvo she'd borrowed this morning from Plath, she didn't sense the usual nourishment brought on by a drive to the mountains. Maybe because all of her focus was on the postcard of Pikes Peak tucked into the defroster vent, right in her line of sight: *just if ever you want more*, it said.

For the past hour, Lydia had been puttering in the right lane with the truckers and the poor, feeling nostalgic about all the times in her teens and twenties that she'd climbed onto a bus alone with a backpack full of books, bananas, and a change of clothes, eager for the tremble of the road. Back then these journeys had always been about the one-way exit, the awareness that her environment needed to change, that there was substance and freedom in abandonment. But this journey felt like it was leading her straight into those very things she'd always headed away from, and much of the pleasure of the road was gone, replaced by overflowing ashtrays and anxiety. She felt uncertain about what she'd do when she arrived at Moberg's cabin, but one thing she knew for sure: of all that had been troubling her lately, the detail that made the least sense was learning that Moberg had visited the doughnut shop to quiz Raj about her father. What did her dad have to do with the Hammerman investigation, especially months after they'd gone into hiding in Rio Vista? It didn't make sense.

As she drove alongside the Platte, watching its currents curl and splash over rocks and logs, Lydia realized that she hadn't seen Moberg in person in over twenty years. Back then, her father had made arrangements with him for full cooperation in the ongoing Hammerman investigation, as long as Little Lydia didn't have to make any more trips into Denver. He didn't want her to be traumatized any more than she'd already been. Luckily, Moberg owned a weekend cabin in Murphy, a small town midway between Denver and Rio Vista that could act as their meeting point. She and her father had only gone to Moberg's getaway once, when despite her insistence that she hadn't seen the Hammerman's face, she'd been called to his cabin to look at yet another album of police department mug shots—lopsided men with facial hair and missing teeth, none of whom she recognized. Moberg had seemed forlorn that day when he sent her on her way.

Her hands were tight on the wheel as she veered through town and up the snowy back roads. She'd just spent twenty minutes at the Murphy Police Department using her postcard and her persistence to convince the cop on duty to give her directions to Moberg's cabin. When she finally made it up his overgrown road, she recognized the place with the dim glimmer of something only ever seen in a dream, and she knew she never would have found it on her own.

The wagon wheel. The wooden chicken. The rusty wheelbarrow in the snow.

The small cabin, creosote and pine, was built against a steep mountainside. Its windows were blocked by foam panels, and a thin ribbon of smoke rose from the stovepipe.

From the moment Moberg yanked open the door and squinted into the winter sun, wearing black jeans and no shirt, Lydia knew she'd ended up on this splintered porch for a good reason: she was facing the mountain-man equivalent of a Book-Frog. She remembered Moberg as massive, well over six feet tall, with corduroy suits, wavy brown hair, and sideburns that spread along his jawline. Now he was *entirely* bald. No eyebrows, no eyelashes, not a hair that she could see on his chest or belly. An image of Brando playing Kurtz trickled through her mind. His eyes bulged like boiled eggs.

"I would've called," she said, "but your number is unlisted."

"No shit. What do you want?"

She held up the postcard and said, "More, I guess."

Moberg squinted through a rip in the screen.

"I saw your picture in the paper," he said. "I shouldn't have sent that."

"But you did. Can I come in?" she asked, attempting a smile.

"I don't have anything for you."

"Don't you at least have coffee?"

"Coffee," he said. He thought for a moment. "I do have that."

Moberg didn't invite her in, but he did turn around and walk purposefully down the hallway. Lydia took this as an invitation and pulled open the screen door. The floor was industrial linoleum so filthy with grime that for a moment she thought it was gray carpet. The wood-paneled hall bowed with water damage. She could hear him clicking on a gas stove and opening cupboards. Out of politeness she heeled off her snowy sneakers and left them by the door.

"Wait in there," he said from behind a wall.

In there, past the kitchen, was a single room with a small wooden table and two wooden chairs. A woodstove hunkered near the table. An empty aquarium sat on the floor. Books—mass-market mysteries—were stacked eye-high against all four walls.

Moberg appeared, holding a weathered spiral notebook.

"Be a few minutes on the coffee," he said.

He smirked at something above her head.

"You here for you?" he said.

"I guess so."

"It's yes or no. Is this for some newspaper article or true-crime book? *My Night with the Hammerman.* Or you here for you?"

"Just for me."

"Not to solve it, I hope."

"To solve it?"

"Are you playing detective or just sorting out your head?"

"I don't know that there's a difference."

"Shit," he laughed, then laughed harder. "Shit!"

When the coffee was ready Moberg presented it on an orange plastic cafeteria tray. He offered her sugar cubes.

"You want answers," he said, "but if I had answers the case would be closed instead of twenty years cold. Can I just tell you that during my whole career I saw maybe five murders get solved this long after? Time passes. People forget. Evidence is tainted. Once a murder loses its context it's nearly impossible to find anything new. Sometimes science will catch up but don't count on it here. DNA this and DNA that. Everyone wants it. Worse than faith healers. Snake handlers. I hope you're not counting on anything like that."

"I'm not sure what I'm counting on," she said.

"Maybe just peace of mind. You won't get it but that doesn't mean it's not worth seeking. I'll give you all I got. Then you go."

And he did. As easy as that, Lydia was listening to Moberg recall his memories of working what he called the O'Toole Family Murders. His tone was cold but his words were clear. Not a story, but a case. Not an experience, but a file. The act of watching him scan through his notebook, then comment on his notes out loud was unlike anything Lydia had ever been through. She appreciated his rationality because it allowed her to view the evening, for the first time ever, with something close to detachment, and she periodically had to remind herself that she'd been there, in the house, on the night when all of these details gained relevance.

Like the talcum powder: traces of it on the O'Tooles' back doorknob, the light switches, the kitchen counter. Likely from latex gloves, packaged with talc to keep them from sticking together. No viable prints, so he apparently wore the gloves the whole time, even as he rinsed his hands after. Probably didn't take them off until he was well outside the house.

The murder weapon: A standard twenty-ounce claw hammer, manufactured at a plant in Gary, Indiana, and owned by one of the victims, Bart O'Toole. He'd scratched his initials on its oval base, just as he had on most of his tools: *beo*. The hammer had likely been removed from the metal toolbox on the covered back porch, or possibly from the victim's plumbing truck, or even his unlocked garage, at some point before the murders.

The pot: two grams of low-grade marijuana found in Dottie O'Toole's dresser drawer, along with a film canister of seeds and a Proto Pipe.

The boom box, or whatever you want to call it: sitting atop the fridge, no longer working. Nothing immediately peculiar about it, but under closer inspection it was discovered to be wet inside: drips tipped out of it when it was tilted to the side. Possibly it had been brought inside after being left in the snow.

The footprints: Left by a pair of Sears & Roebuck work boots, steel toe, heavy traction, size 10½. Common size. Footprints throughout the house showed no irregularities in the soles. Investigators found that no fewer than 116 pairs of that boot, in that size, had been sold at locations around the city in the six months before the attack, and an exhaustive series of interviews found that not a single clerk had noticed anything anomalous about any of said transactions.

The coat: Bart O'Toole's hooded utility jacket, which turned up in a roadside ditch on the north side of the city two months after the killings. The jogger who discovered it found O'Toole's name on a receipt inside a pocket and called the police. Trace bloodstains on the sheepskin lining suggested the Hammerman put it on before leaving the house to cover up the blood staining his own clothing. All of the blood could be traced to the three deceased.

The flashlight: an Eveready economy model, ribbed aluminum, well used, found on the kitchen floor. No initials, but like the hammer, the flashlight could have been taken from the toolbox or plumbing truck or garage. According to the survivor ("That would be you"), the Hammerman turned off the only light before beginning his attack, leaving the house entirely dark. Inconclusive whether he used his flashlight to illuminate the killings.

The hole in the drywall in the hallway: Not so odd, except the presence of gypsum dust along the top of the baseboards below and granules on the carpet showed that the hole had likely been made within a week or so of the attack and the dust had been mostly, if not effectively, vacuumed up. Someone had hung a framed family photo over the hole, but the picture of course shattered and fell that night, leaving shards of glass in the hall.

The survivor, specifically the survivor's blood: Drips of it found in a smudged path on part of the living room carpet and across the kitchen floor. Blood came from the forehead laceration suffered when she was crawling to hide and bashed into the corner of the coffee table. Much of the blood trail had been smeared around by the time the police arrived, but that night, when the drips were fresh, the killer had somehow missed seeing them. Even with the aforementioned flashlight—

"Wait," Lydia said. "What are you saying exactly?"

Moberg looked up from his notebook.

"Just that you cut your head pretty bad and bled a path from the living room to the kitchen sink. But somehow the Hammerman didn't notice it."

"Because otherwise he would have found me?"

"Presumably. The rest of the place was a slaughterhouse. Bloody footprints up and down. Pools and spatters like I'd never seen. But none of the victims had been killed in the kitchen, so it's just a bit far-fetched that he didn't notice a trail of fresh blood leading directly under the sink where you were hidden. That's all."

Lydia felt her belly lurch as she attempted to process Moberg's implication.

"Shall I continue?" Moberg said, then did so before she could respond.

Lydia listened to Moberg's clinical voice, able to stomach all of it, until he began to share the autopsy notes about Carol: *one solid blow to the frontal, two solid blows to the maxilla, one glancing blow to the left orbicular, two blows to the left temple—*

She heard eggs drop and said, "Stop. That's enough."

Carol O'Toole. *Carol.* Of all the images that peppered her head, Lydia had the hardest time with the single glimpse of Carol she'd caught when her father had led her out of the kitchen shortly after scooping her up.

—Don't look, her father had said, squeezing her to his chest. God, don't look.

But before they rounded the corner to cross the living room she'd peeked over his shoulder and there was Carol in an open doorway down the hall, hanging half out of her parents' pile, her red hair and pale skin encrusted with blood, her skull opened so wide it didn't register as her skull until many seconds later, when Lydia was in the O'Tooles' mudroom, so cold she could hardly move, so scared she could not erase—

"That's enough. Please."

Moberg closed the notebook with all the nonchalance of closing a menu. He sipped his coffee and frowned.

"What you're really after isn't in my notes," he said.

"What am I really after?"

"The biggest cat in the doghouse was you. We could never figure you out."

"Me what?"

"Why you," Moberg said. "Why *not* you, more like. Why he didn't kill you."

"Because I was hiding."

Moberg stared at her until she began to feel hot, as if under a glaring spotlight.

"You ever play hide-and-seek with kids?" he said. "You play

hide-and-seek with kids, you know where they're hiding but pretend you don't."

"You think he knew I was there."

"Let's just imagine for a minute that the Hammerman *didn't* hear you climbing out from the blanket fort and crawling toward the kitchen, and *didn't* hear you crash into the coffee table or open the sink cabinet and shove aside some cleaning products and squeeze yourself inside. You *still* managed to drip a trail of blood that led straight to your hiding place. Sounds to me like a dog not barking in the night."

"Meaning?"

"Just that there is one fact in this case and one fact only: you were spared. I'm sure of it, little girl."

"I was *hiding*," she said.

"Someday when you're not depressed you should read some eyewitness accounts of massacres," he said, unflinching. "More times than not when someone survives it's not out of their own cunning. The gunman firing into the facedown crowd doesn't make six headshots and accidentally pass over the single survivor. He *chooses* the survivor and the game is to purposefully miss. There are few accidents with power like that."

"What are you saying?"

"You can pretend you had some angel on your shoulder, but the fact is he walked into that kitchen covered in blood, holding a dripping goddamned hammer, and let you keep your life. Even left his flashlight burning on the kitchen floor, probably so you'd have a bit of light in your hiding place. You came here for truth? Well, that's as close to truth as you're gonna get."

Lydia felt her hands grabbing at the back of her neck, as if something was crawling there, but something wasn't. She felt her memories being rewired.

"Like it or not, Lydia, he helped you hide."

Just thinking about being swallowed beneath the sink, she was immediately greeted by a musty smell, and in the dark of her mind she could feel the hulking disposal, the pipes coated with fuzz, the pair of webby shutoff valves. And she could hear the O'Toole family dying—their breaths going guttural, then silent; their flesh growing heavy; and their bones settling with a crack.

Ke-tick.

"You know I tried," he said, and Lydia wasn't sure what he was talking about. He avoided her eye and his voice hovered near a whisper, as if some unspeakable secret had gotten the better of him. "They wouldn't let me go after him. But I tried."

"Go after who?"

"This is the powers that be," he said, "all the way up to the capitol's golden dome. They thought it would be a PR nightmare for the department if I was wrong. And everyone thought I was wrong. I'm not saying I was right. But the man had more to hide than anyone."

"Who?"

"Your daddy."

"I should go," Lydia said, but when she stood up a rush of fireflies pocked her sight and made her sit back down.

"You mean you've never considered this? What could that shy old librarian possibly have to hide? Turns out plenty, but I was discouraged from pursuing any of my discoveries. Threatened, more like. You don't want to hear this, you'd best go. I don't get to talk much."

"I would know if it was him."

"Or you'd convince yourself it wasn't," he said. "Remember the simple truth that you're alive. Think about it: what madman would have no qualms about slaughtering a mommy and a daddy and a ten-year-old girl, but then grow a set of commandments when it came to killing the little friend sleeping over?"

"It wasn't my dad," Lydia said, picking a gray stain on the floor to stare at. "He'd never do something like that. Besides, the guy—the Hammerman? When Carol went scrambling down the hall he practically jumped through the ceiling. I heard the whole thing. That family portrait shattered and slid down the wall because he crashed into it when Carol *surprised* him. Because he wasn't expecting her. Maybe he didn't know there would be any kids there. My dad, on the other hand, knew Carol and I would be there. So it wasn't fucking him, okay?"

Moberg lifted a ballpoint from the table and leaned into his notebook and scrawled for a minute. Then he set down his pen and spoke.

"That's something," he said, "but listen, murder is a sloppy business. Full of grunts and stumbles and bashing around. If he crashed into the wall it was probably due to adrenaline quivers or being on the cusp of killing your little friend. The worst kind of rush, you know? Or maybe he was expecting she'd hide and he wouldn't have to kill her at all. Like she wasn't part of his plans. Maybe he had to change those plans when suddenly she was screaming right at him."

Lydia listened to herself breathing.

"You're wrong."

"Heard that before," he said. "Tell me something once again. Did you see the Hammerman's face? That night, did you?"

"The lights were off," she said, "and when he came into the kitchen, all I saw was his flashlight between the cabinet doors. But I would know if it was my dad."

"But you didn't see the guy," he said, "so it could've been anyone. Did you know your daddy had no alibi? That's reasonable enough given that he was a single father with no social life outside of his groupies at the library, but still, no alibi is a good place to start."

"Of course he had no alibi," she said. "He had to drive the Bookmobile through a snowstorm for that festival in the mountains, otherwise he would have lost his job. That had to take all night."

Moberg peeled open his notebook and scanned the pages with his finger.

"He dropped off the Bookmobile in Breckenridge, then took the last ski bus into downtown, caught a cab, and made it home around midnight, even with the snow. That gave him plenty of time to walk over there. It coincides with the timeline. But the next morning, when he discovered the O'Tooles' bodies, that's when the real inconsistencies began. He stumbled upon the crime scene, up there with the most repulsive in the city's history, and what did he do? Shoved the bodies around. Piled them aside, claiming to have been searching for you. Convenient then that he had the victims' blood all over his clothes, his face, his hands. You know we picked pieces of *brain* off his shirt collar? Brain as in brain. We found bloodstains inside his *pockets*. But moving the bodies wasn't enough, so he stormed through the house, touching everything in sight. His fingerprints were everywhere and bloody. Which brings us to the murder weapon. When we got there that hammer had been smeared so much by his sweaty hands that all the latent blood basically turned into paste and ruined any chance we had of lifting a viable print—other than his, of course. On the phone with the 911 dispatcher, he made sure to announce loud and clear that he was holding the very hammer that sure as hell wiped that family out. Called from the kitchen like ordering a pizza. Doesn't look too good, does it?"

"I'm sure there's a reason," she said.

"It doesn't look good," Moberg said firmly, leaning forward in a pose that was as threatening as it was assertive. "Listen,

175

I'm not doubting your sincerity here. And you may not want to hear this, but when you map out the serology of that crime scene, you know what you get? You get the distinct blood of the three O'Tooles. Then you get your blood on part of the carpet and the kitchen floor and beneath the sink. Then you get one other person's blood—"

"My dad's," she said. "Because he cut himself."

"When he was looking for you. I know. I've heard it. At some point after the killing, the Hammerman had dragged Carol's body partway down the hall to just inside the bedroom doorway, right where her parents died, probably so she couldn't be seen from the front window or door. Maybe he thought it would give him some time. And in the morning your dad showed up, didn't see you anywhere, so he began searching for you, even going so far as to shove aside the bodies in case you were piled beneath them. In his panic, somewhere in there he cut his hand, most likely on broken glass."

"But he told you all of this," she said.

"He sure did."

"So what's the problem?"

"The problem is that your dad's blood wasn't on the *bodies*. It was only on *one body*. Dottie's. No one else's."

"That doesn't make sense," she said.

"No shit it doesn't."

A plume of spite swelled in Lydia's chest. Whatever she'd been expecting by visiting here, it was not this.

"Are you saying—" she said, but had to restart. "When you say my dad's blood was on Dottie's body, were there other signs? I mean, do you mean that—?"

"Nothing like that. I mean his blood was on her neck and face and shoulder and wrist and hand. And nightie. If it was just that, or just his tracks, or just your hiding, or just the hammer—

176

If those were the only oddities, I may have written all of this off as coincidence. But there's more. I don't need to tell you that, after the murders, your daddy fled the city as soon as he could. He wanted to protect you. I get that. But the thing that always got me was his silence before he left. At the O'Tooles' he stumbled right into the heart of the crime scene, knew all three victims, yet he had little to say about anyone involved. Tell me that doesn't stink. The only way we were going to get any information out of him was to press charges, but that idea was crushed from above. Little Lydia had been through enough. Just ask *Life* magazine."

"I *had* been through enough."

"I know you had. Which is why in all those years, in all those press conferences, not once did the department ever raise public suspicion about your father. It might be that your misery gave him his freedom. You could be mayor of Denver with a history like that, I shit you not. But you see my point about your daddy."

More than anything Lydia saw how desperately her dad had tried to insulate her, to keep her safe, to erase a night that couldn't be erased—at least before settling in Rio Vista, where he became a different man.

"Maybe you were just frustrated," she said. "No suspects were turning up so you settled for the cliché: blame the parents."

"That's exactly what my colleagues in the department said. And for a while I believed them, because maybe all this circumstantial crap was really just in my head. For a time I let it go. I tried to focus on fishing and trains and a merciful God. But then a few months after the murders we got a phone call from the O'Tooles' neighbor. You remember her? Agatha Castleton, a lonely old woman who'd lived across the street her whole life. I'd tried interviewing her twice before, but like the rest of the city she just seemed crippled by dread. Like the Hammerman was just waiting to get her next. I left her my card in case anything came up."

"And it did?"

"The day before the murders, around lunchtime, Agatha was eating a sandwich by her window and guess who she saw whistling up the sidewalk and knocking on the O'Tooles' front door? A man who looked and dressed just like your daddy. Which isn't all that strange, given that you and Carol were such buddies, but the two of you were in school all day. So what was he doing there? Think about it. The murders happened late on Friday night, and your daddy had been at the crime scene Thursday at noontime. When I asked him, by the way, he told me he was just dropping off Carol's mittens, which she'd left at the library. Said he stuck them in the mailbox on the porch and left."

"Carol was always losing things," Lydia said, almost smiling.

"Remember the Hammerman turned off the lights during the attack," Moberg said. "The flashlight may have helped him find his way around in the dark, but the attack was so methodical that he was probably also familiar with the layout of the house, maybe because he'd been there before. A small detail, but it's important. Now take a look at this."

From the back of his notebook Moberg pulled out a single black-and-white page torn from an old real estate catalog. It had been folded into quarters and its seams were beginning to tear. On each side was printed a dozen advertisements for properties, each with a small description and a photograph of the place for sale.

"What do you see there?" Moberg asked.

Lydia studied the ads and found herself mildly distracted by how inexpensive the homes were and by how much her state had changed. Then she noticed that all the places were in the mountains—some weekend cabins, some year-round homes, some dying farms and ranches.

"Turn it over."

When Lydia did she had to hold the page in the direction of the light to be sure of what she was seeing, but there it was in the lower left corner of the page. A small smudged photograph of her father's house in Rio Vista, with a brief description: *2 BR A-frame, mtn. views, 8 acres, lrg. shop, school bus route. $19,950.*

"That's your home in the mountains."

"Where'd you get this?"

"That's not the original that you're holding. The original page is somewhere in an evidence box in Denver, sharing a shelf with a bloodstained hammer. The original was found crammed in the bathroom trash can, water-damaged to the point of being almost unreadable."

For a moment Lydia felt as if she was sitting in a rocking chair, about to teeter over.

"You found this in the O'Tooles' bathroom?" she said.

"We found it the morning after the murders. Based on the other items in the trash, it had probably been there for a day or two. I'm guessing since your dad's Thursday visit. You know, when he dropped off those all-important mittens."

"You're sure?"

"Positive."

"Fuck."

Moberg chuckled. "Yes," he said. "Fuck."

Lydia looked again at the image of the cabin where she'd spent most of her teenage years, the unhappiest years of her life. And she tried to determine whether the uneasy feeling she had at the moment was due to Moberg's insinuations or to the memories evoked by this crumpled vision—or both.

"It makes no sense," she said. "We moved into the cabin

because of the murders. So why would the O'Tooles have a picture of it?"

"This is the question," Moberg said. "Your father was up to something bigger than mittens over there, no doubt. Of course he claimed there were no interactions between them except those having to do with you and Carol. And there was no one alive to say otherwise. My first thought was that he and Dottie O'Toole had something going on. Lord knows she sowed her oats, but one look at your dad— I mean, did the guy ever wash his hair, let alone tie his shoes? It's pretty obvious he wasn't exactly her type, a fact made loud and clear through Dottie's Tupperware circles. Did you know at the time she was screwing one of the Broncos? Third string, but still. Of course anything is possible, but I've always placed high doubts on Dottie going near a man like your dad. As did everyone else I interviewed."

"Go on," she said, reluctant.

"What seems more likely to me," Moberg said, planting his elbows on the tabletop, "is that Bart O'Toole and your dad were up to something. That O'Toole needed a legitimate face for something he was putting together under the table. The problem with Bart is that almost everything he did was off the books, so it was hard to know whether he was working for lowlifes or he was a lowlife himself or just another asshole who wanted the good life without having to pay taxes. There were plenty of plumbing calls in the dead of night, but that doesn't mean he was up to no good, you know? Maybe he needed your dad to sign a loan or to launder some paperwork, to milk the city or squeeze a contract out of the state. Maybe the cabin in Rio Vista was supposed to be collateral, or some kind of tax scam related to his plumbing venture. But no matter how deeply I dug I could never figure out the connection between them. I puzzled over the possibilities for months, going through public records and

IRS files and library budgets, but nothing panned out. But to find a picture of your future house balled up in the bathroom trash can? That's always been the answer without a question."

"Did you ever bring him in?" she said.

"As a suspect? Never. I talked to him plenty in the weeks after the murders, but barely ever beyond that. The last time I saw your father was after you moved to Rio Vista, when you came here to the cabin to check out photos of suspects. I was hoping the different environment might encourage him to open up, but I couldn't even get him to make eye contact with me. You'd know better than I do, but it seemed to me that he started losing it up there in the mountains. Maybe it was the altitude."

"They always blame the altitude."

"That or guilt," he said. "Eventually my superiors in all their wisdom forced me to come up with hard evidence or else steer clear of him, mainly because they didn't want to bring any more attention to the fact that the dreaded Hammerman was still at large."

"But you obviously didn't give up on the case."

"I'll tell you, I've lost sleep just wondering if we missed something. Some detail none of us in the department ever turned up." He shook his head as if to rattle away the possibility. "It wouldn't surprise me if we screwed it up somehow. Missed something. Because anyone who stepped foot in that house? Let's just say I saw grown men lose it there, embracing each other as if they themselves had lost a child. One guy gave up his career in homicide and transferred over to property crimes. Just couldn't deal with the magnitude of evil. That place was a bloodbath. It was hard to be there."

"I know."

"I know you know."

Moberg stared hard at Lydia, and this brash acknowledgment left her grunting with discomfort.

"You can't imagine the number of leads that came across my desk," he said, more contemplative than she'd expected. "Ask me why I'm single. People sent me their grocery-store gossip and church scandals, all of them convinced that the Hammerman was their creepy neighbor or their bastard husband or their asshole boss. Even now it's an open sore in the city—the Hammerman still at large after all these years. Can't blame people for wanting to be part of the great return to order, I guess. I just wish . . ."

Moberg's voice trailed off and he fiddled with his pen.

"Anyway," he added, "that's all I got."

Lydia stared into her empty coffee cup.

"If I give you a guy's name," she said, swallowing hard, "could you tell me if you ever had any dealings with him? Not necessarily with this case, but later. Maybe even years later."

"What guy?"

"Joey, maybe Joseph. Last name Molina. Lanky kid in his early twenties with long black hair. He spent some time in prison for dropping cinder blocks onto moving cars. Petty crimes before that."

"I'm guessing this is the suicide who got you into the newspaper," he said, a statement, not a question. "Even the sickos blur. But no, I don't recall any Joe Molina."

"You're sure?"

Moberg seemed irritated by the possibility that he'd forget a name.

"No Joseph Molina in any of my cases," he said. "I could look into him for you if you'd like." He turned to a blank page in his notebook and spun it until it was in front of Lydia, then he rolled a pen her way. "Spell out the kid's full name and your phone number. If I find anything out, I'll call."

After Lydia scrawled down the information, she stood and gestured toward the hallway.

"I should go."

"Yes, you should."

She sat on the floor and fumbled to get her shoes on. As she stepped out to the snowy porch, Moberg became a bald silhouette on the far side of the screen.

"Listen," she said. "I appreciate your—"

"Don't," he said. "I just ruined your fucking year."

CHAPTER FIFTEEN

After leaving Moberg to fester in his lonely cabin, Lydia drove full speed, fuming and confused, in the direction of her father's home in Rio Vista. She snapped off the radio and cranked the heater, oblivious to the blur of trees and rocky slopes around her. She felt terribly uneasy about what Moberg had told her, but also committed, after more than a decade, to finally facing her father. Because if Moberg was right—*my god*, she kept saying, *my god*—the time to see her father had finally come.

Lydia stopped at a roadside gas station and plunged the pump nozzle into Plath's Volvo. From her back pocket she retrieved Moberg's folded postcard and turned it over in her hands. She listened to cars crunching over knobby ice and the wind flapping the gas station signs and finally began to recognize what she was doing to herself. She wasn't going anywhere but home. Back to Denver and David and Bright Ideas.

Out here in the world, watching the rolling digits of an outdated pump, she felt like a cult member who'd broken away from the compound. This was the land of potato chips and oil leaks and bathroom keys screwed to blocks of wood. *Reality*—that's what this was—and back there, in Moberg's cabin, was a bubble of delusion.

Her dad was not the Hammerman. He may have been a misfit and a loser and an easy target—he may have even developed a shell of ice when she needed his warmth the most—but that didn't make him a murderer. He wasn't the Hammerman, she told herself as Plath's car jostled back toward Denver—he simply was not.

David was still at work when Lydia arrived home, so she was momentarily startled to hear a man's voice speaking in their kitchen.

Detective Moberg. On the answering machine.

She'd driven away from Moberg's cabin not four hours ago, returned Plath's car to the bookstore, grabbed a quick bean burrito, and here she was already back in his contaminated world. She waited for him to hang up, then pressed Play on the machine.

"... Is this Lydia I'm talking to? Well, okay, Lydia. I made a call for you on this guy Joseph Molina. Sounds like you already knew about his criminal record, mostly small stuff, teenage boy stuff, in and out of various juvenile institutions and programs for punks. But I did find something out that might be of interest to you. You already know he was charged with felony assault and criminal mischief for that whole highway stunt, but did you know he served his time at the state correctional facility in . . . you guessed it: Rio Vista, Colorado. Know anyone else who spent a lot of time at the prison there? I think you do. Something stinks here, I'm sorry to say. Be careful, even if he is your daddy."

Lydia sank against her living room wall. It made perfect sense now, how Joey had come upon her birthday photo: Joey was a felon, her dad was his guard, both at the prison in Rio Vista. She felt naive for missing the link yet was acutely aware that knowing about this connection was not the same thing as understanding it.

Draped across the back of the chair at her kitchen table was her beaten leather satchel, holding the latest assortment of books she'd gathered from the store. She pulled them out and placed each title on the table in the kitchen, one at a time in a small grid, as if setting up mah-jongg tiles or a game of solitaire. Then she dragged over Joey's milk crate of butchered books and started pairing and decoding, wondering all the while whether her father was hidden in here too, peering out from Joey's paper windows, somehow spying on her life.

"There's nothing here for me," Lyle said, barely looking up at Lydia from his slump in the chapel's single pew. The chapel wasn't really a chapel but a secluded alcove in the back of the bookstore's second floor that contained the Religion and Spirituality section. Little baskets of sheet music and pocket-sized devotional books were spread around the floor, and an old wooden church pew with Celtic carvings split the alcove's axis. "These shelves might as well be empty," he added, dragging his sight over the books, as lifeless as a tub of ice. "None of it brings him back, you know?"

"I know, Lyle."

With his greasy hair thinning by the month and his schoolboy pants thinning at the knees, Lydia couldn't help but notice how sad Lyle looked in that pew, and how utterly alone. As she slid in next to him, he began lifting the pile of books in his lap, one at a time, as if they were cue cards: *The Jew in the Lotus*, *Hindu Proverbs*, *Care of the Soul*, *Signs & Symbols in Christian Art*, *The Madonna of 115th Street*, *God: A Biography*. "All this Supreme Being stuff is so *intimidating*," he said.

"Maybe this will help," she said, unstrapping her satchel and retrieving the pile of books she'd spent the morning decoding. She handed over Joey's cut-up biography of J. D. Salinger, plus a novel called *Who Will Run the Frog Hospital?* that matched the label on its back cover. If anyone could help her find some clarity about Joey's messages, she reasoned, it was Lyle. Besides, it might do him some good to involve him in—in whatever she was involving herself in.

Lyle took a deep breath and sat up straight. He lined up the pages with admirable expertise.

Tw

. I

ces

, he

sto

Le M

y hear

t. The

firs

Tim

eis

pen

t, my

lie

felo

"Ok

ing   for

it   when f

In a   al

fo

und its

. He, too,

kit

way a

again

and

with

it

, too m

yl

. If

fe

. . .

Lyle read Joey's message aloud with a lot of stuttering back-tracks. "*Twice she stole my heart . . . the first time I spent my life looking for it . . . when I finally found it she took it away again . . . and with it took my life . . .*" He placed his palm dramatically on his chest. "I feel better already. It's like a goddamned *elixir.*"

Lydia didn't know if Lyle was talking about feeling cured by this distraction or hearing Joey's voice again between the pages, but she was glad to see him perking up.

"At first I thought Joey may have been married," she said, thinking of the Vital Records office with its menu of marriage and divorce documents. "Especially with the new suit in his closet and so much focus on this woman in the messages. Like that one about being saved by his *only Her*."

"Joey the romantic," Lyle said, then lifted his head toward the ceiling as if the idea were a balloon he'd just released into the air. "Brokenhearted Joey, killing himself over a girl. *Twice she stole my heart*. I buy it, but I don't *quite* buy it." He read the message again, flipping back and forth through the pages to make sure he hadn't missed anything. "That's not to say it isn't genuine. It's just not the Joey I knew."

"But then I came across this," she said, and pulled from her satchel a cut-up copy of *Wise Blood* followed by a recent reissue of *The Crying of Lot 49*.

Seeing the novels side by side, Lyle raised his brow.

"A deadly combination. Now we're getting somewhere."

It took some effort but Lydia opened the books to the cutouts and handed them over, and Lyle slid the novels together and began to read aloud:

Dr

op

Me

from the

Ask

y. Dr

op

," Me

on   th

, eh?"

igh

away

, so

1.

On

gas

I'l

and

inside

a.m.

. In

, I

Van

"That does not really say that," he said. "*Drop me from the sky . . . drop me on the highway . . . so long as I land . . . inside a minivan?* Sounds like something Neil Young would hum in a bathroom stall. Joey and his minivans, my god. If he was still alive I'd encourage him to open a dealership." Then Lyle held up his hand and closed his eyes, gently humming, as if he were watching Joey's methodology fall into place, window by window, on the inside of his lids. "It's very self-destructive," he said after a minute. "But a minivan? Maybe Joey just wanted a family."

"I think so," Lydia said, unable to stop a small bounce of celebration. "It's like he was obsessed. Remember the one about him eating spiders or glass or whatever *just to be part*? Maybe to be part of a family."

"Or to start a family," Lyle said, "since there's a woman involved?"

"Sure." Lydia flipped open her little notebook to a scribbled page and handed it to Lyle. "This pair I deciphered last night. Two novels. *The Black Book* and *The Secret History*."

Lyle cleared his throat, then read her writing aloud. "*Drowning in blood I may never breathe again*. Well, that's a bit dramatic." He wiggled his fingertips and grimaced. "*Drowning in blood?* Spooky too."

"*Drowning in blood*," she said. "Again he seems to be pointing me toward family. Bloodlines."

"Pointing you?" Lyle said.

"Pointing us."

Lyle seemed pleased by the inclusion. As he flipped through Lydia's notebook, seeking the other messages she'd transcribed, Lydia's thoughts looped back to what Wilma had observed about Joey, the way he'd spend his Saturday mornings sitting in the rocking chair, staring at the families in the Kids section. Lydia imagined Joey silently projecting himself into their lives. He must have believed that the best he could do was to observe them from the outside, to press his fingers on the far side of their glass. It occurred to Lydia that he may have hanged himself because he'd spent his whole life trying in vain to find a place that, for him, was never allowed to exist.

"What's that one there?" Lyle said, gesturing to the rolled-up copy of *The Birds and the Beakers* poking out of Lydia's satchel.

"This would be the gem," she said, "our Rosetta stone, if only it had a label." She flipped through it for him, displaying pages peppered with so many holes that they resembled a shotgun target. "It was in his apartment, too. It's so cut up I'm surprised it hasn't dissolved in my hands."

"So there's no label on the back."

"Which means no book to pair it with," she said, handing it over for him to examine. "So now it's indecipherable, a lock without a key."

"Maybe try pairing it with *Finnegans Wake* or *The Ursonate*."

"It was on top of a pile of newspapers by his front door," she said. "I thought they were for recycling, but I'm thinking now I should have grabbed them. Maybe the newspapers held the answer, you know?"

"They wouldn't have helped," Lyle said. "This is what Joey used to practice with. Look at the first pages. They're a real mess, rips and slices all over the place, not to mention little spots of blood where he'd cut his fingertips. Clearly impossible to decipher. But by the time he got to the end of the book, he was cutting out some pretty little windows. This was his practice round."

Lydia looked at Lyle with admiration. "I'm glad I found you," she said.

"Me, too," he said. "All of this is pure Joey. It's like he was attempting to *become* his books. His deepest self. His final act. Joey's books were Joey's solace, so doing this, inserting himself so *personally* into them, may have been the only way he could profess his burdens to the world. To *you*, Lydia. I mean the kid killed himself, and this was his way of—I don't want to say *justifying* it, but maybe attempting to communicate the process that led him to such a hopeless state. Like windows into his soul. Pure Joey. Pure Joey."

As Lyle hummed, Lydia found herself thinking about the dark tattoo of a tree on Joey's chest, and about trees becoming wood and wood becoming paper and paper becoming pages—

"The question is," Lyle added, leaning forward in the pew and peering over his spectacles, "what are we supposed to make of it all?"

"That he had a broken heart?" she said.

"Broken beyond healing," Lyle said. "And family?" He got up from the pew. He slid out a book on angels and another on chakras. Then he pressed his palm against a row of spines.

"Family law," Lydia said, nearly spontaneously.

Without turning around, Lyle's head lifted.

"*Family law*," he agreed.

Lyle clearly knew what Lydia was referring to: the period, within the past year or so, when Joey had become obsessed with books on family law. Joey's obsessions would sometimes border on rude, such as when he'd waltz up to her while she was scanning books at the counter, or making a recommendation to a customer, and accost her with whatever subject he was presently interested in.

—Guatemalan textiles.

—Vaudeville fiddlers.

—Dominican plantations.

—Knitting with dog hair.

And Lydia would stop what she was doing and tell him where to go ("Second floor, Anthropology") or, if she was free, join him in the hunt.

—Family law.

"What about this?" Lyle said, then he returned to the pew and crossed his legs and met Lydia's eyes, as if he were greeting her at a church service. The limp gray yarn of his hair dangled against his glasses and a thumbprint blurred his left lens.

"Joey's only family gave him back to the state when he was just a toddler, right? So was Joey researching family law in order to learn about his rights as a kid whose adoption went belly-up?"

"Because he was looking for the Molina family?" she said.

"The Molina family," Lyle said.

Lydia recalled the story Lyle had told her about Joey's earliest—and only—family: he'd been taken in as a baby by Mr. and Mrs. Molina, one of a cluster of children they'd adopted, and then, with Mr. Molina's unexpected death—brain tumor? Aneurism? Gunshot?—Mrs. Molina found herself unable to afford the children they'd adopted, so Joey and his siblings had been turned over to the state: discards of the foster system, victims of broken adoption.

"If Joey was trying to reconnect with Mrs. Molina," Lydia said, "or maybe even with his siblings, he'd want to know what his rights were. If any."

"He was so young when he was given back to the state," Lyle said, "he probably wouldn't remember any of their names or where they lived. He'd need help if he was going to find them."

"He'd need his adoption records," she said. "Probably his foster records too, and maybe even Mr. Molina's death certificate."

The realization hit Lydia hard enough to make her sink into the cool curve of the pew: she thought about the Vital Records office, with its labyrinth of documents—and its obnoxious flirting clerk—and realized that at least now she knew what to ask for.

As she gathered her books to leave, Lyle returned to browsing the Religion and Spirituality shelves with widening eyes.

"Maybe there's something here for me after all," he said.

CHAPTER SIXTEEN

Raj showed up at Bright Ideas late in the afternoon, just as Lydia was heading out to the Vital Records office. He was wearing jeans and a puffy down coat, rusty orange, and a black knit hat.

"Walk with me?" she said.

"Anywhere."

"Shut up," she said, and fake-punched his gut.

They walked up the Sixteenth Street pedestrian mall and hopped the shuttle bus through downtown. They stood close to each other in the crowded bus, comfortably quiet, their jackets brushing, their hands holding overhead rails, staring out the big windows at the souvenir shops and fast food, the theaters and clothing stores, the schoolkids and the kooks. Dusk was coming, and the tall, three-legged globe lights that lined the mall began to blink awake like pulp UFOs.

She couldn't help but wonder whether Mrs. Molina had known that Joey was searching for her, fishing in the wells of his past, and whether she'd want to know that the boy she'd adopted years ago had hanged himself.

What mother would, and what mother wouldn't?

Her thoughts wandered to her father. The librarian, not the prison guard.

By the time she and Raj hopped off the shuttle near the capitol, the sun was close to setting and the winter sky was bruised and black. Soon they could see the columned white scoop of the City and County Building, and the blankety mounds of the homeless gathering on its benches and walls. She filled Raj in on the basics of Joey's messages as they walked. When Raj heard about the broken adoption, he scratched at his head.

"Broken?" he said. "Meaning the people who adopted him gave him back to the state? Can you really do that?"

"So I hear."

"What, did they keep the receipt or something? No wonder the kid was a wreck."

No wonder, she thought.

In the Vital Records office, the mustached clerk who'd asked her out for a drink on her last visit recognized Lydia the moment she walked in. He'd added a rubber octopus and a pink Power Ranger to the collection of small toys lining the top of his monitor, but otherwise he appeared the same, down to the coagulated tray of mac 'n' cheese sitting next to his keyboard like a prop. He sized up Raj, who sat, legs crossed, thumbing through a cooking magazine.

"I know what I want this time," Lydia said as she approached him.

"I know what I want, too," the clerk said.

"Joseph Molina. His birth records and anything you have on his foster care. Once I have those details, I'm hoping to get his foster father's death certificate, if possible—is that possible?"

"Okay, let's back up," he said, rattling his head. "You did say foster care, but I think you mean his adoption certificate?"

"Both, I guess."

The clerk rubbed his mustache.

"Foster care records are kept with Human Services. Unless the foster family formally adopted him, in which case we should have a record of that. *Should*. Should."

"He kept his foster parents' last name," she said. "Molina."

"So it's worth a shot," he said, and rested his fingers on the counter in front of her. "But I have to tell you, the adoption stuff gets complicated. Both requests require applications and documentation, and I can tell you now, they are highly unlikely to waive any of the paperwork. Not when adoption records are involved. Sensitive stuff, you know."

"I'd still like to try."

The clerk leaned down next to his desk and began to pull out the catalog of forms she'd need to fill out to get the request started.

"Just one date," he said as he handed the pile over. "Let me take you to my high school reunion. All you have to do is *that*, whatever you're doing right now. Just show up and stand next to me and do *that*."

"What, feel uncomfortable?" she said. "I'm flattered, but no. Unless my boyfriend can come, too."

The clerk smiled. "Just promise me you won't hold it against me if none of this works out," he said. "We have to be really careful with the mutual consent laws."

"The what-whats?"

"Oh boy," he said. "Let me see if our adoption liaison is free. Irene. She can explain all of it and lull you to sleep in the meantime."

And explain she did. Lydia sat in her office down a tiled hallway, next to a crusty old drinking fountain, and listened as Irene—a big, compassionate woman in a loose flower blouse and polyester pants—explained in exhausting detail the state's adoption laws, the required documentation, the court filings that are part of the final steps. When it was Lydia's turn to speak, she told Irene all about Joey's suicide, and Joey's bequeathal, and her desire to trace his foster family, and—making her case here—that she wanted access to his records largely so that she could let Mrs. Molina know that her child had killed himself. Irene nodded along and seemed moved by Lydia's story, even somewhat alarmed.

"You don't have much of a chance," she said, "legally speaking. But I can help you fill out the application and see if there's anything we can do on this end to get you closer. If your application is approved, we'll pass you up the chain."

"There's a chain?" Lydia said. "You mean this isn't the end?"

"You'll have to file an affidavit with the court and a judge will determine whether Joseph's records can be unsealed. And it has to be by mutual consent."

Mutual consent, she explained, of both the birth parent and the adopted child—or, in this case, the deceased child's representative.

"If a child who was given up for adoption wants to find his birth parents," she said, "they file a records request with me. If the birth parent *also* files with me, we can open the records and share their contact information. Otherwise the request sits under lock and key, often without ever seeing the light of day again. Most of the time, this is a one-way ticket into a locked drawer. Both parent and child have to want this, for obvious reasons. Otherwise, you can imagine the disruption."

Lydia stared blankly at Irene, scratching her upper lip.

"Broken adoptions make it all more complicated," Irene added, "but if that's what is happening here then it will be in his records."

"Which I can't see."

"Which no one can see."

"And that's why you're here?" Lydia said.

"That's why I'm here," Irene said, then she explained that her job was to make sure the legal bases were covered and to facilitate the process with both parties.

"And if one of the parties was in prison?" Lydia said.

"There are ways," Irene said. "With an agreeable warden and good behavior, there are ways."

She couldn't be sure, but the way that Irene just scraped at her mascara with her pinkie nail, not to mention her lack of surprise at the question, left Lydia sensing a tell.

There are ways.

She immediately imagined her father, at the bottom of the prison pay scale, miserable in his misbuttoned corrections uniform, passing documents through the bars to a young felon named Joey. The two of them occupied such remarkably different sectors of her mind that she felt herself wince. They made no sense together, yet there they were—*if* they were.

"But you can't tell me if Joey Molina ever sat in this chair?" Lydia said, watching for Irene's twitch.

"I can't tell you that," Irene said, straight-faced.

If this was a game that she played, Lydia respected how delicately she played it.

For the first time Lydia noticed the industrial-sized box of Kleenex on the corner of Irene's desk, and it occurred to her that this was a room full of tears, both happy and sad. Irene handed Lydia a clipboard and an eight-page application, and as Lydia attempted to fill it out, she felt pained by the blanks she was leaving behind. Over and over she found herself checking the box that said *Other*, then explaining in tiny tight scribbles why she, of all people, should be allowed to access Joey's adoption records despite her lack of documentation. She felt self-conscious about writing down her job history and all the places she'd hidden before returning to Denver six years ago, and felt even more self-conscious when she came to a spot in the application that asked for the names and addresses of references who had known her for more than five years. Irene tapped away at her keyboard with long painted nails. Lydia tapped her pen on the application. Finally, she leaned over and looked down the hall, where she could see Raj with his legs stretched out, audibly yawning, reading in his waiting room chair. She wrote down Raj's name and number as her primary reference, and put David second.

"Please don't get your hopes up," Irene said as she skimmed the application a few minutes later. "I will tell you that it helps your case, pardon me, that Joseph is passed away. Opens up a few possibilities. Otherwise I'd probably discourage you from even applying."

Lydia went to speak but faltered when she noticed on the corner of the desk, surrounded by Irene's collection of tiny ceramic chickens, a glass goblet brimming with chocolates. Little spheres wrapped in shiny blue foil.

"Help yourself," Irene said, nodding toward the treats.

Lydia quietly declined. She didn't mention that she hadn't had a bite of chocolate since smelling the melted knot of it in Joey's jeans as he hanged, nor that those blue foil wrappers looked weirdly familiar.

"People sit in that chair for all kinds of reasons," Irene said. "But in all cases what they're really hoping for is a ticket to time travel. Usually it's a worthwhile trip in the end, but sometimes the journey is far harsher than they could ever imagine. Sitting there, where you are, is an enormous step in a lot of people's lives. The chocolate helps, is all."

Irene slid the application back to Lydia.

"Use your current name," she added in a low voice, "but also your *former* name."

Lydia felt her face growing hot.

"I'm sorry," Irene continued. "Both names need to be on there for this to be considered. I'm just trying to help."

"How did you—?"

Irene placed her ringless hand atop Lydia's fist, like a starfish swathing a mollusk.

"You have that kind of a face, even after twenty years. I'm very sorry about what happened to you. I'll do everything I can to help, Lydia."

Lydia snatched up the pen and scrawled *Lydia Gladwell* under "Former Legal Names," then passed the application back across the desk.

"Like I said," Irene said, "don't get your hopes up, but I'll do what I can. Lord knows you deserve it. You were a very brave little girl."

As Lydia stepped out in the hallway, feeling raw and anxious, Raj came down the hall to meet her.

"What happened? Lydia, you look kind of . . . not well. Like somebody died."

"I think," she said, "that Joey was here. In that office. Right around when he died."

"Whoa. Did she tell you that?"

"Chocolate did."

Raj looked at her with concern, then held her forearm. As he guided her past the counter, the clerk sat up straight and stared at Lydia as if she were a statue, something he might prop in his garden.

"Oh, and guess what?" she said to Raj. "You are now officially my *Primary Reference!*"

"Oh baby," Raj said loudly, throwing his arm around her shoulder. "You're goddamned right I am!"

The clerk grumbled to himself as they left.

Three hours later, Lydia and Raj were stepping into Lydia's apartment, warmed by the beers and bowls of noodles they'd consumed in a Colfax hole on the walk home. David was working late, wrapping up a conference in Fort Collins, so he wasn't expected for a few more hours—or was it tomorrow? Lydia couldn't remember. She could, however, remember that he and Raj had yet to meet.

Raj was sidled up to the coffee table, grinding his knees into the carpet, and losing his sixth game of Uno when the phone rang. As soon as Lydia heard it, she sensed that it had been ringing all day, echoing through her empty apartment. She walked to the kitchen and answered.

"That you? Christ, you're tough to track down."

"Who is this?" she said, cupping her mouth with her palm. "Is this—Dad?"

"It's real good to hear you, little girl."

Little girl. Lydia slammed down the phone.

"Was it David?" Raj asked, looking up. When she didn't answer he went back to shuffling the cards.

Lydia ran to the bathroom and splashed cold water across her face.

little girl little girl little girl

First thing tomorrow, she promised her dripping reflection, she would call the phone company and change her number, and if her father found her again after that she'd consider moving into a new apartment altogether. She planted her hands on the sink's edge and felt her fear transform into anger, and without drying off her face or thinking through the consequences, she stormed out of the bathroom and dialed her teenage phone number. Raj looked up from the table but didn't say a word.

"Thank you, sweetheart. I know that's a hard call to make."

That's how her father answered the phone, a sweet greeting that derailed her intentions—*please stop calling me!*—and left her, after an eternity of silence, spinning in the tracks of small talk. She and David still had a corded phone and she stretched it into the bathroom, closed the door, and sat on the toilet. She thought she'd immediately question her father about the birthday photo and Moberg's suspicions, but he didn't give her the chance.

"I hear there's a new library," he said quickly, as if he were going through a list of topics he'd scribbled on his palm. "And a new ballpark under way, and a real home team that's not the Denver Bears."

"Tell me why you're calling," she said.

Her father's response took time. She could hear Raj shuffling and reshuffling his child's game somewhere far away.

"I have a hundred reasons for calling," her father said, "but if I had to pick one it comes down to being proud of you."

"Proud?"

"I mainly wanted to tell you that."

"You don't even know me."

"I know enough."

"I'm a bookseller, Dad."

"Well, you're not a prison guard is more how I see it."

Lydia felt her eyes close. Felt the roof lift. She slid to the bathroom floor.

Not a prison guard.

During Lydia's childhood, being a librarian had been as intrinsic to his identity as being a father, so his choice to leave the library behind and become a prison guard was, as she'd framed it in a thousand teenage fights, a *selling of his soul*. His transformation had been alarming: it began with the drastic shift in his appearance—the mustache and sunglasses and uniform—and amplified over time until there was little difference between the man he was at work and the man he was at home. Beginning in middle school, whenever Lydia swept the cabin floors, he'd taken to sitting at the kitchen table, sipping his coffee and scrutinizing every swish of the broom as if they were on a cell block. On the rare occasions when she got in trouble at school—always for minor offenses, like missing the school bus or forgetting to do her algebra homework—he would remove her bedroom door from its hinges as a punishment and once even tried to take away all of her *extraneous reading material*. Around that same time, with the exception of the occasional back-pat hug that felt more like a playground clapping game than a paternal embrace, he simply stopped showing any affection for her at all. But maybe even worse than anything was the oppressive silence that had finally swallowed their home. After they left Denver, he just hardly ever spoke anymore about anything.

Even as an adolescent, Lydia knew that those were trying times for her father, and she knew she didn't have the answers to the vexing questions that life had thrown at him. Far from it! But then *not* having answers had always been the point: the point of her childhood, the product of her hours in the library, the sum of his philosophy when she was a little girl. You leave yourself open to answers, he'd always taught her. You keep turning pages, you finish chapters, you find the next book. You *seek* and you *seek* and you *seek*, and no matter how tough things become, you never settle. But in becoming a prison guard Tomas had settled as dust settles, as lost hair settles. He'd settled like the bones of the dead.

And so while Lydia had always half-expected this phone call,

208

in all of her fantasies she'd never expected this: Tomas's terse acknowledgment that his choices had defiled their trajectory as a family. She had a hard time knowing what to say.

"Can you tell me one thing?" he said, breaking the silence. "We used to talk, so why not anymore? What is it I did that's bugging you so much?"

She could feel years of accusations leaning forward on her tongue, waiting to be unleashed, but at the moment only one felt truly urgent.

"Detective Moberg thinks you were involved with the murders."

Her dad was silent for a minute before saying, "You saw him?"

"I went to his cabin."

"You believe him?"

"I don't know."

"Doesn't surprise me he'd think that. He's always had it in for me. Apparently still does."

She waited for him to continue, but he didn't, and his refusal seemed so stubborn and suspicious that she found herself slipping into a different line of questioning. "How well did you know Joey?"

"Who's that?" he said.

"Joey Molina. He was one of your prisoners."

Her father paused on his end long enough for doubt to swell through her.

"Joey was your *prisoner*," she said, "in *Rio Vista*."

"Wait—are you talking about Joey the Bookworm?"

"Joey Molina."

"That sounds right," he said. "Just a kid? Skinny, black hair, caused some kind of a car accident? Sure, I know Joey. Question is, why do *you* know him?"

"From the bookstore."

"Huh. I guess that makes sense. The kid is just a phenomenal reader."

"He's dead."

Silence.

"He hanged himself," she added.

"Joey?" he said, barely able to get the words out. "He's dead?"

"He died with a photo of me sticking out of his pocket."

"A photo of you?" Tomas said.

"From my tenth birthday."

"A photo of you. No, he didn't. Tell me he didn't—"

"He did," she said.

Silence.

"A birthday photo," he said, "and you're blowing out the candles?"

"Why'd you give him a photo of me, Dad?"

"Oh, Jesus. Lydia? Did he do something to you? Did he *find* you?"

"Why, Dad?"

"I don't understand what's going on here," he finally said. "Let me think. Let me think."

Lydia could hear Raj out beyond her bathroom door, shuffling cards.

"So you didn't hire Joey to keep tabs on me?" she said.

"I worry about you like you can't even imagine," her father said, "but I wouldn't do that, not in a million years. Is everything there okay? Tell me he didn't hurt you, Lydia. Please, just—"

"I'm fine."

Her dad sounded so concerned, so honest, it was hard for Lydia not to believe him.

"Sweetheart? I really don't see why Joey would have tracked you down. I talked about you a lot, so maybe he wanted to meet you."

"So you did give him a photo of me?"

"I showed him some pictures at my desk in the prison, but I don't know. Maybe he took one. I guess I knew it was missing, I must have, but I didn't ever really pursue what that meant."

For the moment she decided to let it rest. Maybe her dad really was just a sad old man reaching out to his daughter, and maybe Joey had done whatever he'd done all alone, without any help. Maybe.

"I need to see you," her father said. "Can you and I get together?"

"Things feel too mixed up right now," she said.

"You're not alone there. But I need to see you, Lydia. Please."

"Honestly?" she said. "The other day, after seeing Moberg, I started driving toward Rio Vista but turned around. I guess I wasn't ready for that."

"Okay."

"I'm still not."

Lydia sighed into the phone. She was contemplating hanging up when her dad spun the conversation into a new direction.

"Does David know about this whole thing with Joey?"

"David?"

"He should be taking precautions. Who knows what Joey was up to. Or who else was involved. Let me talk to him, will you? I'll feel better about it if I don't have to worry about you."

Lydia froze. "You aren't talking to David."

"He's a nice man, your David. Sounds from here like he's treating you okay."

She looked around her bathroom, at David's razor on the sill, his black shampoo bottle in the shower caddy, a few of his hairs on the porcelain sink, and suddenly felt disturbed by how deeply entwined their lives had become.

"Tell me you're not talking to David," she said.

"I understand you're worried. But don't be. He's a nice man, like I said."

She'd known her father had been trying to get in touch with her but also assumed that David had been curt with him in their exchanges over the phone. But apparently not.

"You cannot speak to him," she said.

"He knows, Lydia. You hear me? David already *knows*. That should change things, I would think."

"You told him?"

"Of course not," he said. "We talked about it, but then we talked about a lot."

"You talked? When?"

Her father waited.

"Answer me," she said, more shrill than she'd intended. "How much does David know?"

"Everything, Lydia. He knew everything long before he and I ever talked. He's a stand-up guy. Maybe give him credit—"

"Don't call here again."

Click.

In the living room Lydia scooped up Raj's cigarettes and lifted the window and climbed out to the small section of shingled rooftop that sloped over the porch. It was bitter cold tonight, yet she hardly noticed that she was wearing only a beaten gray T-shirt, jeans, and holey woolen socks. Under the lights below a man was walking a potbellied pig and the pig sprayed piss all over a fallen trash can.

For the next hour Lydia smoked on her roof alone, hardly able to feel the frozen air around her. At one point Raj leaned out to check on her, but she shook her head and he disappeared back inside. Through the barren trees she could see the cartoonish reach of the Cash Register Building over downtown, and she could hear cars tearing past on Colfax, their studded tires waiting for winter's final thaw.

She thought back on her years with David and reassured herself that, with the exception of the memory of those hours beneath the sink when she was a ten-year-old girl, she'd given herself entirely over to him, and still that hadn't been enough. He had to take the one thing she'd wanted—the one thing she'd *needed*—to keep for herself. And then to discuss it in secret with her father only added to the betrayal.

Before long, a gray sedan bounced through the potholed street below and backed into a parking space. David climbed out.

Lydia's heart jumped and she crawled through the window. Raj was still inside, reading the newspaper with his feet on the coffee table.

"Was that David?" he said, scratching his cheek. "On the phone."

"He just pulled up, Raj. Sorry about all this, but you should go."

Raj grabbed his coat and hat and hugged her before slipping out. She imagined him brushing past David on the stairs.

The apartment door had barely closed before David had it open again. He set his bags on the couch and tried to kiss Lydia on the cheek, but she dodged his lips.

"Okay," he said, his breath hiding beneath clean mint gum. "Did I do something?"

She grunted. Part of her wondered if she just didn't care enough to fight, as if David had just given her the reason she needed to abandon this version of her life.

"So," David said, leaning to catch her eye, "are you going to tell me what's happening here?"

She pulled on a sweater and a pair of sneakers, scooped up her jean jacket, and walked past him to the door. He began to reach for her, saying words she could scarcely hear, but she shook him off and pulled away.

"Lydia? *Please* talk to me."

As she stepped out of their apartment, her voice ripped through the building: "Don't *ever* talk to my father again!"

CHAPTER SEVENTEEN

L ydia stepped inside the Supper Club, a steamy, velvety bar a few blocks from Bright Ideas where her late-shift comrades almost always ended up. Her hands and feet were so cold she could barely feel them, but the jukebox was cozy with crooners and sliding into a buttoned red booth made her feel warmer already. All she really wanted tonight were some comrades with whom to drink—there were always comrades with whom to drink—and in due time she was four hot toddies deep, listening to them chat about bounced checks and student loans and eviction notices, the cheapest vacations they'd ever taken, the worst rural Greyhound stations, their previous lives in Buddhist monasteries and Catholic convents and the American military, the best way to sprinkle Top Ramen's magic golden flavor powder into a boiling pot of noodles without it clumping into paste. She heard someone say, "Never shop at a place with a parking lot," and she couldn't have agreed more.

The night had been going well enough for her to have almost forgotten why she was plunging her face into hot whiskey when suddenly one of her bespectacled, ponytailed comrades dragged the drunken bliss right out of her.

"Hey, bad news," he said. "We had to make Hi Guy leave the store tonight."

"Hi Guy?" she said. "You kicked him out?"

"It sucked. I thought you'd want to know."

"Hi Guy?" she said again, and slapped her forehead.

"I know."

Hi Guy was among the sweetest of the BookFrogs. A lanky man in his fifties, he parked himself most days in an old orange chair in Bright Ideas' magazine section and muttered a gleeful *Hi* to anyone who came within five feet of his stretched-out legs. Over and over, *Hi, Hi, Hi*, with rarely another word. For whatever reason—Plath theorized it was pheromones—no one else ever sat in that chair, even when Hi Guy wasn't around. He had beautiful teeth and shiny skin and flotsam in his hair. His eyes were milky and Plath once told Lydia that he read books upside down—that he was born with upside-down eyes. Plath wasn't kidding. Lydia wasn't so sure.

"You really made him leave," she said. "Hi Guy?"

"He wrapped one of our newspapers around a fifth of gin and sat there drinking it," he said, "which was, you know, whatever, but then an hour later he pissed his pants and started falling all over the place. He crashed into a fancy lady drinking her fancy coffee. She got burned. Not burned-burned, but made uncomfortable, which for a power tool like her was as bad as getting burned."

"Where'd he go?" she said.

"I steered him toward the train station but I doubt he made it. It's cold out there tonight," he added, downcast.

Then Lydia was standing up, listing to the left.

"I'm just gonna check real quick," she said, as if she were just running to the bathroom, and the next thing she knew she was slamming her drink and wandering alone over the icy

216

sidewalks of Lower Downtown. Someone said, "Lydia fucking rocks," as she teetered out of the bar.

Her long rubbery legs seemed to drag a few feet behind her, and by the time they caught up she was scanning the rows of benches inside Union Station. She lifted blankets and newspapers off snoring faces—*sorry, whoops, sorry*—but none belonged to Hi Guy. Soon she was circling the streets and alleys around the station. Finally she found him, huddled against a low cement wall that bracketed the plaza of an office building.

"Hi Guy?"

"Hi."

He groaned and rolled under a ripped gray blanket.

"You okay?"

"Hi—" he started to say, but his voice was interrupted by vomit. Lydia knelt next to him and wiped his cheek with her sleeve. She asked again if he was okay and he sighed *hi* and gently closed his eyes. She put her hand on his shoulder and looked out at the traffic lights bobbing on their wires, and then she heard herself talking about David's collusion with her intrusive father and this lost city of her childhood, and how she'd spent more time hiding beneath sinks than anyone she knew, maybe anyone in history, and she vowed to read *To the Lighthouse* again and to give *Gravity's Rainbow* another chance—

"Don't cry," he said.

She stopped talking and only then realized her cheeks were wet with tears and freezing cold. Somehow Hi Guy made her feel safe, so she nodded and told him all about Joey, about finding him hanging and finding his books and his messages and his suit—

"I'll take that suit."

She looked at him. "You want Joey's suit?"

"His adoption suit."

217

"*Adoption* suit?" she said, craning over him. "What does that mean?"

"That's what he called it. He wore it to meet his mama."

Lydia felt her enthusiasm fizz and with it a flash of sobriety. Hi Guy, with his days upon days of meditative sitting, would certainly have seen more happening between the bookstore's cracks than anyone else. It wasn't surprising that he knew Joey had been tracking down his foster mother.

"You're talking about his foster mom? Mrs. Molina?"

"Not foster suit." His eyes fought to stay open. He stretched his legs until they rustled a twiggy sleeping bush. "*Adoption* suit."

"His *biological* mom?"

Hi Guy nodded.

"Did they meet?"

Hi Guy shook his head no.

"Broke the boy's heart. Standing on Broadway in that badass suit. Like prom king. But. She. Did. Not. Show."

Hi Guy closed his eyes until he'd stored enough energy to speak. "Kid had *nothing*," he mumbled, then his eyes stayed closed and he fell into a coughing fit and didn't say anything else. Soon he started snoring. His shopping cart was parked against the plaza wall, and inside it she found two right-handed mittens and a few wool blankets and a sleeping bag. She sunk Hi Guy's hands into the mittens, triple-wrapped his body, and gently rolled him near a steaming sidewalk grate where he'd be warm.

Though Lydia was drunk and cold enough to contemplate spooning up to him, instead she wandered in the direction of home. Before long she found herself lost in a forgotten neighborhood north of downtown. The streetlights were mostly shot out and the storefronts trapped behind cages and chains. Awnings flapped in rags above her, looking like windblown pages. She rambled through the dark. When she saw a man standing in the middle of the sidewalk a block or so ahead, looking massive and menacing, she cut into a nearby alley. The man had been standing still and seemed to be staring right at her, though in truth she couldn't tell if she was looking at his back or his front or if he was even a man at all.

She snugged her satchel closer. She listened for his footsteps but heard nothing. At the end of the alley she turned right, and this street seemed even darker, more desolate, than the last. She walked faster. She heard somewhere a percussive train. She smelled the horsey grind of the Purina factory. A block or two ahead she could see the red glow of a giant neon Benjamin Moore paint sign and she knew there was an old jazz joint nearby, so she sprinted toward the sign, feeling chased, hearing footsteps echo off the low brick and stucco buildings around her. She didn't stop until she found the bar and made it inside and even then she rushed past all the people drinking and eating late-night burritos and, with no shortage of gumption, called David collect from a pay phone by the bathrooms.

"I'm coming," he said as soon as he answered, but it was difficult to hear him over the jazz, so she shouted the name of the bar into the receiver as if casting a desperate spell: *El Chapultepec!*

"Got it!" he shouted. "What's wrong, anyway? Lydia—what *is* it?"

"You *knew*."

"I knew?"

She rested her forehead on the side of the pay phone, against layers of graffiti stickers.

"You *knew*, David. About *me*."

"Just sit tight. I'm on my way."

She ordered a beer and stood by the door, sipping and

splitting her sight between the sidewalk outside and an old lady on a small stage playing a stand-up bass and wailing into the smoke.

When David's sedan pulled up in front, Lydia slid into the passenger seat, still holding her bottle of beer. She took a slug and parked it between her thighs.

"You okay?" he said.

"I don't want to do this," she said, shaking her head.

"Do what, Lydia?" He flapped at the air between them. "*This?*"

She turned away. Outside, passing trees were skeletal with winter.

"You sounded scared on the phone," he said. "Did something happen?"

"I'm fine. Just cold."

He turned the heating vents toward her and steered through downtown.

"Listen," he said after a while, "I have a few things I need to tell you."

"Does it have to be tonight, David?"

"You don't have to say anything, but it has to be tonight," he said. "For starters, I just want to be clear that I'm not mad at you—"

"*You're* not mad at *me?*"

"For hiding your childhood from me, Lydia."

"Is that so?"

"*You* might be mad," he said, "but I'm not. Just listen. I'm sure you have your reasons for keeping it to yourself."

"I do."

"But honestly I'm a little hurt that you don't feel like you can share this stuff with me. It makes me feel like the asshole boyfriend, like you can't trust me, or like I'm doing something to keep you in your place. I'm not that guy, Lydia."

"I know you're not," she said, staring out at the streets, lamp-lit and cold and empty of life.

"Besides which," he said, "your dad didn't tell me anything that I didn't already know."

"You really already knew?" she managed to say, unable to take her eyes off the taillights glowing like embers in the darkness ahead.

"About Little Lydia? I really did."

"That's shitty, David. It's humiliating."

"I grew up here too. The Hammerman was part of my childhood. More than Blinky the Clown or John Elway. I was terrified of him. We all were."

"When did you figure it out?"

"Two years ago, maybe? I saw one of those 'On This Day in Denver' segments on the news. As soon as they showed that famous picture, the one from *Life* magazine, I could tell the girl was you. You look totally different now, of course, but I've seen that same expression on your face. I think you were at the bookstore, so I called you right away but you weren't free. I guess I decided not to call back."

She waited for him to go on, but he left it alone.

"Is that why you've been so nice to me?" she asked.

"I hope not."

Lydia wasn't sure if this made David a better or worse person, or what this now meant for them as a couple.

"Was it on one of your work trips?" she asked, more meekly than she'd intended. "When you met my father?"

"I didn't plan it. He'd been calling a lot, so when I found myself driving near Rio Vista an impulse carried me to a phone book. It seemed the right thing to do. I asked him to meet me at an ice-cream shop on Main Street. I bought him a coffee. He didn't have any money. Scratch that. He had four cents."

"Four cents."

"He emptied his pockets to show me. He didn't know there was an ice-cream shop in town. I got the impression he hadn't been out in public anywhere except maybe the grocery store. I mean in years. He hasn't worked in a while, apparently."

"What did you talk about?"

"Not much. He seems like a really lonely, isolated guy. He really needs someone."

"You shouldn't have snuck around me like that."

"I know," he said, "but he's your only family. I wanted to meet him."

Lydia touched the cold window glass. David glanced sidelong at her as he drove.

"He said he was going to keep calling," he continued. "He really wants to see you. What if we were to go visit him together? Take a weekend—"

"You know," she said, "I'm just not ready for this."

"I just think—"

"I'm *really* not ready for this, David."

"Fine."

They stopped at a red light and waited for it to change. The manholes steamed below.

"Are you going to tell me about the guy who's been calling?" David said. "After you ran out tonight he left a bunch of messages on the machine, wanting to know if you were okay."

She kept staring straight ahead.

"His name is Raj," she said. "I'm not screwing him."

"Raj," he said. "Okay."

"We've held hands. As friends. He slept in your sleeping bag one night. On the floor."

"Of our bedroom?"

"We're friends, David. As kids we spent every day together."

"Before?"

"Before."

David rolled his shoulders and breathed through his nose.

"Joey had a picture of the two of us," she said, as if it were a natural fact. "Of Raj and me, when we were ten."

David didn't respond.

"When he died, he did," she added. "In his pocket."

Now it sunk in. David dropped his gaze from the windshield and his hands went limp on the wheel.

"Watch the road," she said, "watch the road."

"Am I hearing this right?" he said, squinting into the dark. "This guy Joey dies with a photo of you and your pal Raj, then Raj comes barging into our lives, interrupting everything, and you don't think that's *suspicious*? You actually *trust* this guy?"

"Of course I trust him," she said, though in truth she'd never given such skepticism any thought. "Besides. It wasn't just the two of us in the photo. It was Carol O'Toole, too. The girl who—"

"I know who Carol O'Toole is. Everyone knows who Carol O'Toole is." He looked at Lydia sideways. "How did he get a photo of you?"

"How did Joey? He was in prison in Rio Vista. One of my dad's inmates, apparently."

"So your dad—?"

"Knew him. Yeah."

"But *why*?"

"I don't know," she said.

"Seriously? I mean, why would this con have a photo of you as a kid? That's warped. If I was you, I'd—"

"Stop. Stop." She felt a rising panic and thought she might be sick. "Pull over, David. Please. Now. *Now.*"

David whipped onto a side street and parked in front of a small brick house with a flickering porch light.

"What is it? You okay?"

Lydia was having a hard time catching her breath. She unbuckled her seat belt and gripped the door handle.

"Hey," David said. "Hey. What is it?"

She rolled down the window. Took a few deep breaths. David tried to wrap her in a protective hug, and after a time she tried to hug him back, but her muscles refused to loosen. She realized she hadn't been this scared in ages, not even when Joey—

"Hey," he said. "You're fine. We'll be fine."

But she knew she wasn't fine, knew they wouldn't be fine.

He tried to hand her a water bottle, but she lifted the beer from between her thighs and drank from it instead. As she did, she noticed that his windshield was growing little laces of ice, the night outside working its way in.

"I'm sorry," she said, wiping her face and closing her eyes as he drove her safely home.

CHAPTER EIGHTEEN

The first time Tomas ever spoke to Joey was in the middle of the night, when he was patrolling the prison's echoing corridors. Because Joey had been charged as an adult but was still a juvenile when he came in—not quite seventeen when his sentence began—he was kept on an unpopulated block of level three that was separate from the other prisoners. He wasn't totally isolated, but his nearest neighbor was eight or ten cells away. During meals and exercise he was segregated from the adult population as much as possible.

When Tomas shined his passing light into Joey's cell on that first night, he saw the young man sitting on his pillow in the corner of his cot, huddled in a gray wool blanket. His black hair was draped along his forehead, not quite covering the bumpy acne beneath.

—Are you the Librarian? Joey asked, so quietly that Tomas almost didn't hear him.

Because Tomas had made the mistake a decade or so earlier of telling one of the other COs that he'd once worked as a librarian, his colleagues and many of the prisoners started calling him that—*the Librarian*. There was indeed a library in the prison, smaller than some of the storage rooms, but it was run by the warden's nephew and Tomas's role in its operation was minimal. He'd been given his own desk in a back corner where he sat alone for a few hours each week, in the quiet of the night, cataloging any books that had been donated to the prison.

—I used to be.

—Can I ask you about a book?

—You can try.

Joey had recently read *Slaughterhouse-Five*, he explained, and he wanted to know if Tomas knew anything about becoming *unstuck in time*, as the character of Billy Pilgrim had. He sometimes wondered if that was exactly what was happening to him.

—Not scientifically speaking, Joey added. Emotionally speaking.

—Okay. I could see that. Feeling unstuck like that. In time.

So they started talking. Despite his own laconic tendencies, Tomas was surprised to find that he had quite a lot to say to this young inmate, especially on the matter of time and its impact on a person's soul as it bent and stretched between one's existence and one's memories, and Joey seemed keen to listen. He didn't seem to Tomas like the kind of kid who dropped cinder blocks onto moving cars.

Each shift when Tomas walked his rounds, he would find Joey sitting up in his cot, unable to sleep, waiting for his visit. As far as Tomas could tell, he'd become Joey's only meaningful human contact, and in a way, Joey had become his. Maybe because he'd been living alone for a decade by then, Tomas talked and talked, sharing stories about Lydia and Raj, about the library and the doughnut shop, and when he was standing against those bars in the dark, telling Joey all about his life before—his *real life*, he always called it, back in Denver—it felt at times like Joey was the one helping him.

Of course Tomas never mentioned the O'Tooles or the Hammerman.

The day that Joey turned eighteen was an eventful one. For starters, that morning, as Tomas was ending his shift at sunrise, Joey was gathering his folders and his notebooks and heading out to the courthouse in Salida for some hearing or other that had to do with his legal coming-of-age. When Joey returned to the prison that afternoon, his solitary cell on level three had been emptied out and he'd been moved in with a skinhead from Lubbock who, within fifteen minutes, had beat the living shit out of him—broken ribs and nose, bruised cheekbones, split lips and brow—purportedly for reading any book but the Bible. Rather than trying to figure out a safe spot to move him, at Tomas's urging, the correctional counselor and warden agreed to allow Joey to move back into the isolated cell he'd recently moved out of, just as soon as he was released from the infirmary.

When Tomas shared the news with the bandaged Joey, he suggested that the kid do some decorating of his cell since he was hopefully going to be there for the remainder of his sentence.

—Make it more homey, Tomas said. Plus the Pooh-Bah might be less likely to move you around if you make it your own.

—Make it my own?

—Usually people hang up photos or something.

—I have no photos, Joey said.

—They don't have to be of family or friends, you know.

—I have no photos of anything. I don't really get it, to be honest. I never have.

This was one of the toughest moments Tomas had ever had while working in the prison: having to explain to this brilliant kid why people took and kept photographs of their lives.

—I think it comes down to capturing happiness, Tomas said, before it gets away. Other things as well, but usually happiness.

—Does it always get away?

—Has for me.

Joey nodded along, but the walls of his cell remained bare.

Not long before Joey was to be released, two years into his sentence, Tomas was assigned to work the graveyard shift on Christmas Eve, but he didn't mind. He'd worked enough holidays to know that those shifts were different, and that even the prison on those days could feel more like a community than an institution. They'd play Christmas carols over the PA system and give the inmates more time for phone calls and chapel and holiday shows on television. Joey didn't participate in any of these attempts at festivity. But Tomas wanted to provide him with some semblance of cheer, so when he did his rounds that night he arranged to let Joey out of his cell and he led him, in shackles, down to his desk in the back of the prison library. He threaded his ankle chain through the chair and loosened his cuffs a little and gave him a popcorn-and-honey ball the size of a small globe that he'd made for him at home. As Joey peeled back the wax paper and bit into the sticky popcorn, Tomas pointed to the stacks of cardboard boxes that lined the wall opposite his desk.

—Those are books, he said. You can choose a few. Any ones you want. A gift.

—You don't need them for the library?

The books had all been donated, Tomas explained, castoffs from thrift stores and estate sales, and 95 percent of them never made it to the prison library's spare shelves.

—No more room. And, to be honest, not much interest.

Joey ate through his popcorn ball and looked around. On a corkboard behind the desk, near sheets of departmental phone numbers and a printout of the library's classification system, Tomas had pinned a dozen or so photographs that he'd culled from his gunmetal box at home.

—That's Lydia? Joey said, pointing to an old photo of a tod-dling girl in a pile of leaves.

—That's her. From that spot there we could hear cars on Colfax every few seconds: *Whoosh. Whoosh. Whoosh.* You get used to it.

After two years of Tomas projecting his memories through the bars as if they were old home movies, Joey had had all the context he needed to understand the people and places stuck in time on the glossy photos before him. Tomas gestured to pictures of Lydia in various Halloween costumes (Nancy Drew, Cleopatra, Mrs. Piggle-Wiggle), of Lydia sitting on the steps of the library, and one of Lydia with her friend Raj and a redheaded girl—barely in the photo—leaning over a chocolate cake at her tenth birthday party. Looking happy.

—That's the boy from the doughnut shop? Joey said.

—That's him. Lydia's best friend.

As the carols faded from the crackling speakers, Tomas focused on the task at hand.

—Let's get you some of these books before I get in trouble.

He stooped to his knees and began sifting through the boxes.

—Thought you might like these, he said, handing back a small pile of sci-fi paperbacks. Bradbury, Heinlein, Clarke.

Joey licked his fingers to avoid getting the sticky popcorn on the books, and looking at him Tomas felt the kind of affection he might have felt for a fallen son.

That night, after Tomas locked Joey and his new books back inside his cell, the kid seemed more fragile than usual, more shaky, and Tomas found it difficult to walk away and leave him alone on such a lonely Christmas Eve.

CHAPTER NINETEEN

Lydia stood beneath the stinging shower, attempting without success to wash away the ungodly hangover pulsing through her eyeballs. When she stepped out of the bathroom—dizzy and hungry, wondering how she was going to make it through a nine-hour shift at work—she found a sympathetic message on her machine from Irene, the counselor from the Vital Records office.

She braced herself as she learned that her application for Joey's adoption records had been rejected.

"*Sorry,*" Irene said on the message. "*I really did all I could.*"

Lydia believed her, but that didn't change the fact that, where Joey was concerned, she'd hit another dead end.

Lydia was working alone in the Psychology section, tidying up stray titles from tables and couches and spills on the floor, when she received a phone call from Raj.

"I need you to meet me," he said with urgency. "Can you come now? Lydia?"

Lydia ducked behind the Psych desk. Cluttered around the phone were a ceramic phrenology brain, a giant rubber-band ball, and a bearded GI Joe action figure with a peace sign Sharpie'd over his bare chest.

"Raj? Where are you, anyway?"

"The capitol building," he said. "Get here as soon as you can. And you're going to need a car."

"What's going on, Raj?"

"Just get here," he said.

"Is this an emergency? I'm in the middle of my shift."

"An emergency? Not life-threatening, nothing like that, but I need you, Lydia. Borrow a car. Please. I'll wait for you on the steps. Trust me. Please."

Lydia found Plath smoking against a brick wall up the block, reading *Poems of Nazim Hikmet*. A few butts were scattered around her feet, and their smoky scent conjured an image of the burned papers in the bottom of Joey's trash can. That felt like eons ago.

"How is it that you can look so *exhausted*," Plath said, touching the black ashy shrub of Lydia's hair, "yet still have that whole Fraggle Rock beauty thing going?"

"Found you."

"Let me guess: you want to borrow my car again."

"Is that okay?"

"What's mine is yours, sister. But what's with all the field trips? Sidelining as a drug mule?"

"Helping out a friend," Lydia said.

"That boy?"

"What boy?"

"The hottie with the hair and the smile."

"Raj?"

"I knew it!" Plath said, slapping her thigh with the book of poems. "You two-timing bird! So? Who is he?"

Lydia stammered. Then, in as few words as possible, she told Plath about Raj, and about their childhood, and about all the afternoons they spent together at his parents' doughnut shop.

"He's the *heir* to a doughnut shop?" Plath said. "Be still, my heart! Which one?"

"Heard of Gas 'n Donuts?"

"Just stop right there, Lydia. *The* Gas 'n Donuts? That stately pleasure dome over on Colfax?" Plath shook her head and lit another smoke. "I don't want to get involved, Lydia, but David is fucked."

Lydia laughed. "I'm not two-timing anyone."

"*Yet,*" Plath said, holding up her cigarette. "And there's something else, as long as we're talking about your stable of beefcake. Is it true that last night you had a steamy date with Hi Guy? Sounds like trouble. Everything okay?"

"Just trying to figure some things out."

"Which is why you need the car." Plath unspooled the Volvo key from her key ring and placed it in Lydia's palm. "It's up the block hogging a space. I'd offer to go with you but I know what you'd say: *I got this. I'm good. No thanks. I'm fine.* But really, Lydia, are you?"

"I don't know, to be honest."

"Will you talk to me?" Plath said, frowning. "Please? Just until I finish my smoke. Five minutes."

"I'm kind of in a hurry."

"Then let's get to it. Did you hear that Ernest quit? He said Joey's ghost ruined the best job in the world."

"I didn't hear," Lydia said, but she wasn't that surprised by the news. Once a comrade had vanished backstage it was often only a matter of time before they quietly slipped away altogether, to grad school or a publishing career if things were going well, and if not, to jobs whose advertisements had been stapled to telephone poles, slinging nutritional supplements or assembling toys at home. It could wear you down, which was why people like Plath were so admirable. They, like the store, survived.

"I'll never quit," Plath said. "Of course they might fire me."

"Why? For smoking seven cigarettes on a ten-minute break?"

"Touché."

Lydia looked up the block at the brick belfry and spire of the city's clock tower.

"What are you doing out here anyway?"

"Lydia," Plath said after a cold pause, "that is one question you should never have to ask a bookseller. Bright Ideas is not Victoria's Secret. It takes style to work here. We can't just *run errands* during breaks like we're all accountants. We must smoke on corners and read. We are decor." She dropped her butt casually to the pile already around her feet. "What's going on with you, anyway? Really. I'm worried. Ever since Joey's hanging, you haven't really been here. Psychologically speaking. Which is fine but, you know, maybe you should talk to someone, go sit in a circle of fold-up chairs in the basement of some church and drink coffee from a Styrofoam cup. Or screw the group and just tell me. Open up some."

Plath was right. For most of Lydia's shifts lately, whenever she'd come upon customers standing in front of shelves, holding slips of paper in their hands, she'd veered away from them without offering to help. Maybe she'd finally reached the point of hiding backstage.

"I'm just distracted," Lydia said. "My heart isn't in it these days."

"Your *heart*? Sweetie, you've got too much heart. Do yourself a favor and let it shrivel. Read some Henry Miller. Some Ayn Rand. Some Deepak Chopra. That'll shitten your outlook. And besides, you are the most *natural* bookseller I know. You're the bare-knuckled bookseller—you have the bookseller *élan*."

Lydia grunted. "I spend most of my time lately hiding from customers."

"Aloof is all the rage. When customers see you climb up from under a pile of books they know they are in good hands. The best hands." Plath peered into her cigarette pack but decided against it. "Listen. I guess I'm telling you that your presence on this planet is requested, okay?"

Lydia looked at Plath and wondered, not for the first time, how much she really knew about Lydia's life.

"Time's up," Lydia said, and rushed up the block to find her friend's car.

Within minutes of borrowing Plath's Volvo, Lydia had driven through downtown and parked on Broadway. As she walked toward the capitol, she could see traces of some earlier snowstorm in small curdled mounds along walkways and under trees, but much of it had melted, leaving soggy grass and slushy gutters and enormous puddles underfoot. The capitol's golden dome glimmered against the sky.

Raj, as promised, was standing on its western steps, beneath the trio of porticos. His hands were buried in his jeans pockets and he was wearing a light suede jacket that smelled like a goat when she hugged him. The light was dusky with dark clouds blocking the sunset, but she could still see prunelike swells under his eyes and she wondered if he'd been crying.

"You okay?" she said.

"Just great. Thanks for coming."

They sat down on the engraved step marked *One Mile Above Sea Level*. Raj touched the words with the tips of his fingers. "Remember coming here for a field trip when we were kids?"

"I guess so," Lydia said. "What's wrong, Raj? What did you call me up here for?"

Raj took a deep breath and spoke much more slowly than usual. "I got a call this morning from your counselor friend. From the records office."

"Irene? Why was she calling you?"

"You used me as a reference, remember, in your application for Joey's adoption certificates. Foster stuff. Whatever it was."

"But you already knew that."

"Yeah. I'm your *Primary Reference*, right?" he said, without any flirtation or humor this time. "And she told me your application had been rejected."

"She left me a message saying as much this morning," Lydia said. "But she shouldn't be involving you in it. I mean, why would I need a reference if my application was rejected?"

"That's not it," Raj said. "She asked me to come by her office this afternoon. She told me that your application had been rejected but that it had nothing to do with you using me as a reference. That *my* record was clear. That I shouldn't worry about applying for jobs or anything like that. That my record was *pristine*. Her word."

"She asked you to come into the office to tell you that? That makes no sense."

"None at all," Raj said. "She was trying to cover her ass in case— In case I got upset."

"Upset about what?"

Raj looked out over the traffic-clogged edges of downtown.

"Obviously I was confused," he said, "until Irene told me that *I* could always try to apply for Joey's adoption documents. That just because you'd been rejected didn't mean that I would be. But only if I wanted to, she was careful to point out. It's like she was dancing around something, but I was intrigued, and I thought it might help you out. So I went in."

"You actually went to her office?"

"I did," Raj said, "and she closed the door and asked me, point-blank, if I wanted to apply for Joey's adoption paperwork. But I had no interest in filling out an application, paying all the fees—I just wanted to know what she was up to. *It's really not hard*, she told me, then she handed me the application to show me how easy it was to fill out, and she flipped it to the second page and there's this list of checkboxes where I would state my 'relationship to the adoptee.' Only one of the boxes already had a checkmark next to it. And Irene was touching it with the end of her pen, tapping it, and looking at the door to make sure no one was coming, and looking at me, and tapping the page. *Tap-tap-tap*. She'd already checked the box for me. This is what I'm getting at—"

"What box did she check?"

"She was trying to tell me, Lydia, without actually telling me."

"What box, Raj?"

"*Sibling*," he said.

CHAPTER TWENTY

Raj hunched forward on the stone steps. Lydia rubbed his back.

"We don't know what any of this means, okay, Raj? This is a mistake. Irene was probably just trying to help me out, to work the system somehow."

She could feel Raj breathing deeply, pulling himself together. "Was Joey my brother?" he said. "Does that make any sense at all, Lydia?"

"I don't think so, Raj."

For a while they sat in silence. She could hear a couple of panhandlers fighting near the obelisk in the park and the clack of skateboards shredding the lip of the Civic Center fountain.

"Irene called him Joseph *Patel*," Raj said, pressing his temples with his fingers. "She said he got the Molina surname when his foster parents adopted him."

"Have you talked to anyone else about this, Raj?"

"What," he said, "like my *parents*?"

"It's got to be a mistake," she said. "Don't talk to them just yet. Or anyone, for that matter. Let me think."

"Irene said she recognized my name while she was reviewing your request."

"Maybe that's the problem. *Raj Patel*. Isn't that like the most common name in the Indian world? You're like the John Smith of whatever region that is."

"Gujarat. You know, the place my mom went to visit for nine months when I was a kid. Okay, not quite nine, but you get the idea."

"Oh shit," she said.

"Yeah."

"It's a mistake, Raj. Has to be."

"Lydia," he said, smiling with incredulity, "Irene encouraged me to take some time to think about whether I really wanted this, but when I said I wanted to know, she approved the application while I was sitting there. She even helped me to write up an affidavit in her office, then brought me down the hall to have it notarized."

"For what?"

"To request a sealed adoption record," he said. "Under 'Reason for Request' she told me to write *adoptee deceased* and *sibling is requesting*. Something like that. That was all. Then she checked some registry or calendar and said she could get me before a judge tomorrow. She does this stuff for a living, Lydia."

"Not like this she doesn't," she said. "She'd be out of a job."

Raj snickered. "The judge will still have to approve it before I'm able to see any original records, but Irene said she would help me if I was sure this was what I wanted."

"And are you, Raj?"

"Yeah. Totally. I mean, if—yeah. I'd want to know. This is just so fucking weird."

"I just can't believe she called you like that. Why would she—?"

"She thinks we're together," Raj said quickly. "That you and I are—together."

Lydia looked toward Raj, but Raj was looking away, toward the shiny plastic fortress of the art museum. On the walkway below the steps, a few sparrows fought over the corner of a hot dog bun.

"What was he like?" Raj said quietly.

"Joey?" she said. She thought for a minute. "Brilliant. Cool. Cute."

"But messed up," Raj said, "obviously."

"You could say that."

She could hear Raj sniff next to her and then exhale a long gust, the kind intended to clear cobwebs from the soul, to pry out its nails. Lydia didn't say anything more.

"You realize he brought us together," he said. "Not intentionally, but still, I saw your photo in the newspaper because he hanged himself at the bookstore."

"I know," she said.

"I could have helped him."

Lydia's hand shot out of her lap and clasped Raj's shoulder. She shook him gently.

"Hey. Let's not overdo this. We'll figure it out, okay? I'll talk to Irene first thing—"

"I've already talked to Irene," he said, "and she's told me all she's ever going to."

"But *I'll* talk to her, Raj, and—"

"You need to ask someone who might actually know something, Lydia. You need to ask your dad. He was around back then. And he's the only person connected to everyone involved. Including Joey."

Lydia felt the mile of height between this step and the earth's sea level begin to give way to space. She felt herself plummet. She felt herself fall. She felt air—

"That's why I thought you should drive here," Raj added, "so you could go straight from here to see him. So you could go to the mountains and ask your dad what he knows."

"I can't do that, Raj."

"You can."

Between gaps in the skyline Lydia could see the dark form of the distant mountains where Raj was trying to steer her. From this vantage the Rockies appeared as a spiky black wall, majestic and fearful, a remnant of an ancient time. She felt she understood those early roaming Denverites who'd hit that wall and couldn't take another step, so they stabbed some buildings into the prairie, rolled out some railroad tracks, and began their century of sprawl. It was so much easier to stay put.

"What I really want to do is go straight to the doughnut shop," Raj said, "and hear what my parents have to say about all of this. But I should wait until it's all verified, right? Besides which, if I go over there now—"

"You should *not* go over there now," she said, looking at how tensely he was clenching his fists. "I don't want to have to bail you out of jail."

"Please go see your dad, Lydia. If you don't want to go alone, I could go with you."

"No. Absolutely not."

"Or I can go see him by myself," Raj said.

"Just slow down, Raj. All of this has got to be a mistake. There's no point in me—"

"Stop saying it's a mistake," he said, with an edge in his voice that surprised her. He stood and looked at the sky and began to drop down the capitol's stone steps, one at a time. "I think you're forgetting something, Lydia: you weren't the only one in Joey's photo. *I* was in there, too. *Me*. Right at your side, as always. It's not a mistake."

Lydia watched Raj walk between the barren trees and across

the walkways in the direction of downtown. Once he was out of sight she wandered back toward Plath's car. Traffic inched brightly down Broadway, and she knew he was right: Lydia may have been blowing out birthday candles in the center of the photo that Joey had died with, but the ten-year-old Raj was at her side, as loyal as always. With small embarrassment, she recognized that Joey would have been more likely to die holding a photo of his big brother than a photo of the woman who sold him books. And Raj had been right about something else, as well: her dad—the source of Joey's photo—was the only person she knew who might just have the answers.

CHAPTER TWENTY-ONE

After leaving the capitol Lydia made a quick stop at her apartment to grab the birthday party photo and throw some crackers into her satchel. David was in the shower when she came in, and though part of her was tempted to disappear in there with him, she knew if she did, this journey would screech to a comforting halt. Besides, she was still hurt by the fact that he'd known about the Hammerman for years, yet had kept his knowledge secret from her. She knew that her reaction didn't make sense—it wasn't David's fault that he'd figured out her past, and she'd been just as secretive—but the betrayal she felt was real.

She could hear him humming to himself in the shower as she scrawled him a note on the back of a student loan envelope:

Going to see Dad in Rio Vista (if I don't chicken out). Be home tomorrow, latest. I'll call.

Wish me luck.

L

As she read the note she was surprised to notice the absence of a single word: *love*. She didn't want to think too much about why she'd omitted it, but it was an easy fix:

Wish me luck.

Love,

L

There.

The night was cold and windy as Lydia drove. Stars crowded the windshield, and ovals of ice glowed on the road like pools of oil. The drive was long, the mountains desolate. And then came Rio Vista.

Lydia hunkered low in the Volvo as she rolled onto Main Street. A lot had changed since she'd left town at seventeen—Elmo's Drugs was now a bistro pub, Hot Dog Heaven a massage therapist's office—and passing through the empty streets she felt little more than a maudlin familiarity. As she reached the long snowy driveway north of town that led to her father's cabin, she didn't see any tire tracks or footprints, which meant he hadn't left his property in a while. She parked and began to walk up the crusty slope, weaving a trail between pine trees and brush.

Up the stretch of hillside, twenty yards down from his A-frame cabin, she could see the light box of his workshop shining between the pines. The shop had been built with weathered lumber salvaged from a fallen barn, and from here it looked warm and inviting, the only glow on the entire frozen mountainside. Soon she was standing in a pile of snow and peering into one of its windows. The glass was so drizzled with dirt that it looked as if the shop had some sort of striped paneling covering its inner walls. She scratched an ice clod against the pane to see better and realized that the walls of the shop, all the walls, were lined with books. Thousands of them.

Her hand pressed the splintery siding. She felt a glint of hope.

As she soft-stepped into a slightly open door, the warmth of a woodstove poured through her and into the cold. Her father was standing at a long workbench with his back to her. He was wearing an oversized flannel shirt over a black hoodie, and the back of his hood was bisected by the elastic straps of a white work mask. His hands were covered by purple latex gloves and he was slathering some kind of stain over a row of wooden planks.

"I was wondering when," he said, pausing his brush but not turning around. His voice was deeper and hoarser than it had been on the phone, maybe because of the mask. "I guess I was wondering *if* more than when. But I'm glad you came."

She couldn't speak.

"I've been waiting for you forever," he added.

He still hadn't turned around. Maybe because she couldn't read his expression, she focused on reading the space around him. The shelves stretched from floor to ceiling, twenty feet high and equally wide, and they covered every inch of wall space except where they framed the windows and doors. It was as if his books had replaced the structure entirely.

"Are you making more bookshelves?" she said, mouth dry, fighting vertigo.

He set the brush in a black jar of spirits and ungloved his hands, keeping his back to her. She'd assumed he would be happy to see her but his posture expressed only reticence. Maybe he just couldn't face her.

"Almost out of space," he said, "for real this time." He gestured toward the planks he'd been staining. "Let's see, these are the new shelves for the bathroom in the cabin. Above the toilet. You think this is a lot, wait till you see inside."

"You have books in the cabin too?"

"Let's just say it got a little tight in there."

Lydia hadn't expected her father to be so fixated, so delusional. The thought of this man reaching deep into his memory to help her decipher the past seemed suddenly ludicrous. She shifted her satchel and unbuttoned her coat and cardigan.

"Are you ever going to turn around? You haven't even looked at me."

Without a pause he unsnapped his mask and faced her.

In Lydia's mind her father was the man she'd last seen well over a decade ago, snoring in his bed on the morning of her high school graduation, when she'd snuck out of the cabin with a map and a backpack and hitched a ride to the bus station in Leadville. Ever since then, his increasing age had always been abstract, something she associated with *Over the Hill!* birthday cards and Metamucil ads. Now it was perfectly concrete. He was into his sixties but he appeared at least a decade older. His face was spotty and dry and white whiskers furred his cheeks and neck. He was back to wearing black horn-rimmed glasses, but gauging from the scratched filth of his lenses he'd pulled them from a memento drawer. But most noticeable was how frail he'd become. The waist of his jeans was cinched by rope and his elbows dangled limply against his ribs. The man was rank, encrusted, but worst of all malnourished. The reality of this sent her screaming at herself: if she was going to cut him out of her life, she should've at least made sure he was healthy.

"Are you eating?" she said, nearly choking on the words.

"I'd be dead if not."

"How often?"

He leaned forward and squinted. "You doing okay? You look kind of worn out." He reached out a hand but stopped it midair.

"What are you eating?" she said.

"Back to that," he said impatiently, and shuffled head-down toward a large storage bin on the far side of the workshop, set like an island a few feet from the wall. Lydia followed. The bin held canned soup, beans, chili, pears. On the floor alongside it, at the base of a ticking woodstove, was a gray sleeping bag looking larval atop a mattress.

"Sometimes I live out here," he said, playfully swiveling a can opener. "Especially lately."

The sight of his tumbled canned goods added to the sadness she was feeling, so she walked along the bookshelves and tried to find her footing. He trailed behind her.

"You're getting a lot of reading done, anyway," she said.

"Actually not. I don't really have the energy, to be honest. Plus I'm long overdue for new glasses."

"Then why books?" she said, running her hand along the edge of a shelf.

"I guess I didn't know what to do with myself after you left. Then I started doing it and this is what it became."

"But where'd they all come from? You couldn't've bought all these."

"Courtesy of the Rio Vista State Penitentiary. Donations. Books come in from thrift stores, estate sales, libraries—a lot of books no one wants end up being sent to the prison, and those that the prison doesn't want end up here. This is the dreck that doesn't make it to those carts you see on sidewalks in front of bookshops. A lot are missing pages or covers or are moldy or torn. Sometimes they arrive on pallets. I think word got out that we'd take anything."

" 'We'? I thought you quit."

"I did. But I still go over about once a month and pick up whatever they discard. Which is most of them."

"To the prison?"

"I go at night. They think I'm nuts. But they're happy not to have to deal with them."

"It's quite a library, anyway," she said, trying to sound upbeat.

"I've begun to think of it as more graveyard than library. End of the line, you know. Where book-of-the-month club comes to die."

As they spoke, Lydia had been walking along the shelves, sliding out the occasional title. For all of their tatter and wear the books did have an overall tidy appearance. She noticed a few wooden rulers hanging from nails and realized that each book had been placed exactly one inch from the lip of its shelf. Staring toward the raftered ceiling, following the compulsive plumb lines of all those spines, Lydia felt a stitch in her neck. No wonder he had no energy for reading.

"I need to know something," she said, turning to face him, surprised at the boldness of her voice.

"Is it about what I think it's about? Let me see it."

It took her a moment to realize what he was talking about, and when she did she turned slightly away, as if to guard the satchel hanging on her shoulder. "You mean Joey's photo?"

"It's not Joey's photo," he said. "It's mine. He obviously took it off me, but—"

"I don't want to talk about the photo," she said, eyes closed, palms flattening the air much more intensely than she'd intended, "or Joey. Not now. I want to talk about what you did at the O'Tooles'. Or *to* the O'Tooles."

"What did Moberg tell you I did?"

"Why was your blood on Dottie's body? Let's start with that."

"Because I cut my goddamned hand."

He turned around and began tugging the purple latex gloves back onto his fingers. Their sight made her stomach swim.

"I want to hear what you did."

Tomas craned halfway around and stared at her for a long time. "Are you seriously asking me this?" he said. "Because I've been waiting a long time to have this conversation. I'm likely to tell you more than you're here for. I've been in that kind of mood since I quit the prison."

"I need to know."

"Fair enough," he said, ripping the gloves off again. "But don't say I didn't warn you."

CHAPTER TWENTY-TWO

For a couple of seconds Tomas stood dazed in the O'Tooles' kitchen, squeezing Lydia to his chest and listening to the ticking of the clock and the breathing of the house. A few feet away, the cabinet door beneath the sink was still open—the contact paper inside dotted with his daughter's blood—and in his dread he understood its invitation, as if it were a doorway to a better dimension. The linoleum was spread with bloody tracks turning watery from the snow he'd dragged in underfoot, and at their center was the hammer he'd been holding a few minutes earlier when he'd stormed through the house, searching for Lydia. Its wooden handle was so syrupy with blood that it had stuck to his palm.

In his arms Lydia whimpered and lifted her head. He could see her scanning the kitchen with glassy eyes and he didn't want any more of this awful house being absorbed into her mind, so he pressed her face into his neck.

—Don't look, he said. God, don't look. We gotta go.

But when he reached the mudroom and unlocked the front door, he could feel her faltering in his arms, growing heavy and boneless, and only then did he realize how seriously in shock she was. Her pajama bottoms were wet and one of her feet was bare and felt sculpted of ice. Her face was crusted under a mask of blood and she was chattering so badly he thought her teeth might crack.

—Are you hurt? Lydia?

—i'm freezing.

The little window in the front door showed a gray morning blowing drifts, and even the draft from the jamb made her curl against him. It had been a few minutes since he'd called 911, but the streets were clogged with snow so he knew they wouldn't be here any time soon.

—We gotta go outside. We'll find a neighbor and get warm.

—i'm too *cold*.

He hugged her tight. He could hear the wind ripping down the street and ticking the windows with snow.

—Okay. Okay.

He set her on the little wooden bench by the door and grabbed a coat off one of the mudroom hooks—Dottie's, nylon, light blue—and made a cape around her shoulders.

—Let's get you out of here.

—i don't want to go outside.

She hunched on the bench with her hands in her lap. It occurred to Tomas with a terrible clarity that right now she'd rather climb back beneath the sink than go anywhere else on earth, and though this reality was among the saddest he'd ever faced, it paled next to the horror of a different realization—one that slammed so forcefully into his chest that it nearly knocked him to the floor.

A pair of green mittens was there on the bench, right next to his daughter.

He braced an arm against the mudroom wall.

—what's the matter?

—Nothing. I'll grab you a blanket. Then we go.

Over the back of the couch in the living room a gray blanket was tented into the girls' sleepover fort, but he walked right past it and stood in the mouth of the hall, clenching his jaw, just down from the body pile.

Two days ago, during Thursday's lunch break, Tomas had crossed the O'Tooles' frosty lawn, holding the knitted green mittens that Carol had left in the library the afternoon before. Bart's yellow pickup was nowhere in sight, so he stepped forward and knocked on the door. He was wearing brown slacks and a quilted brown coat, and only when he was standing on the stoop did it occur to him that he should have done more to dress up, but he reassured himself that Dottie wouldn't mind. Smoke rolled out of the chimney next door, but otherwise there were no signs of people. This was good. Of course he wished he was gripping a fistful of carnations, but the mittens he held were better. They gave his presence here some purpose.

He knocked again, harder this time.

Dottie answered in her bathrobe, a red, silky number with an embroidered dragon crawling up the slope of her left breast. She didn't say anything, just smoked her cigarette and looked bored. Tomas could feel warmth pouring from the open doorway.

—Are you alone? he said.

—I am.

—I'm here for something.

—I gathered that.

He handed her Carol's mittens, then unzipped his jacket pocket and began digging around inside. Dottie glanced at the street.

—Slow down, she said. Close the door behind you. It's freezing out.

Inside, Dottie rested the mittens on the mudroom bench. Tomas followed her into the living room but stopped when they passed the kitchen. In there, next to the sink, a bottle of Coors sat on the counter. A toolbox sat on the floor by the back door.

—Is Bart home?

—Yeah, she said, blowing smoke in his face. He's gonna take a bath with us.

Tomas coughed into his hand as she strolled down the hall and into the peach-and-blue bathroom. The tub was filling in there, bubbles curling beneath a silver flow.

—Get in here, Mr. Giggles.

Dottie dropped a few bath beads into the water. Tomas stood next to the sink, his hands folded politely over his stomach. On the back of the toilet was a boom box with big round speakers and a cord that had to stretch over the sink to reach the electrical socket. Dottie pushed Play and flutish pop came rocking out. The small space of the bathroom, coupled with a broken treble knob, made the music sound tinny.

—*Aqualung!* she shouted.

—What?

—Never mind.

She turned it down a bit and let her robe fall to the floor, then slipped into the sudsy water.

Tomas looked at the bath rug. At the smear of blue toothpaste on the wall above the sink. At the steam billowing against the cold bathroom window. Finally he looked at Dottie, allowing his eyes to ingest everything—her wet skin and soft flesh, her puffy nipples barely underwater, her reddish pubic hair swishing gently between her thighs. She was still smoking, but with great languor she reached out her arm and dropped the butt into the toilet and it hissed and made the hot room smell ashy.

—You coming in?

—In?

—We need to be quick.

Her hand softly grabbed him behind the knee. He could feel his slacks getting wet and he could feel, in his jacket pocket, the knot of gauze that he'd brought just for her.

—I have something.

—Is that a bandage? she said when he retrieved it, her face quivering between a smile and a cringe.

Tomas untaped Rose's ruby ring from its bundle, wishing that he would've done this right, with one of those blue velvety boxes with plush satin that resembled a tiny coffin.

—It's for you, he said.

When Dottie held the ring up to the light, sudsy water slid down her arms. For a second, seeing it in her hand reminded Tomas that he'd recently promised it to Lydia, and he felt a short, inconvenient tug of shame.

—Is this really for me? she said. It's a flower?

—It's a rose.

—It looks old. Expensive.

Dottie slid it onto her pinkie but the ring was too big, so she moved it over to her pointer. There was already another ring there, Tomas noticed—silver and turquoise—and a gold braid on her middle finger, as well as bejeweled bands on each ring finger. He'd known from the start that she loved jewelry, but at the moment he felt a bit threatened by how crowded her fingers seemed.

—It's a little loose, she said, splaying her hand against a pillow of bath suds. But I like it.

—That's not all, he said, and he couldn't help but smile as he pulled out the page he'd ripped from the library's copy of *High Country Realtor* magazine this morning. The page held a real estate listing for an A-frame cabin on acres of pine a few miles north of Rio Vista. The cabin was isolated from town but close enough to hear the river and feel the shake of passing trains. And it was cheap. Really cheap. A few weeks ago the ad may have slipped past him, but these days the future had settled itself in the center of his thoughts, and in the center of that future was Dottie.

Her hand came dripping out of the suds and lazily grabbed the page.

—The one on the bottom left, he said. The cabin. In Rio Vista.

Dottie looked at him. At it.

—We'll have some things to figure out with the layout and everything, he said, but I think we should go for it. It has room for a hot tub and a great view of the Divide. The girls will have to share a room but they won't mind. Are they too old for bunk beds?

—The girls? You mean Carol and Lydia?

Tomas froze when he saw the look on Dottie's face. Her lips tapped together, then turned into a smile that crinkled her eyes. Water dripped from the ad in her hand. At first the joy he felt was inconceivable, like nothing he'd experienced in a decade or more. She appeared as happy about this prospect as he was, and he thought he might actually yelp with joy at the symmetry that for so long had been missing from his life—

But then she began to laugh. She reached out her arm and dropped the ad and laughed.

—Are you completely clueless, she finally said, or is that part of the act?

—What?

—Whatever happened to good old-fashioned cheating? You really thought I'd just run off with you? Is that why with the ring? That's so sweet. I mean it, Tomas—you are so sweet!

Tomas couldn't speak. He became aware of muscles constricting in his face.

—C'mon, she said. Don't get hurt feelings. You had to know I wasn't going to *elope*, for Christ's sake. We're not teenagers.

He saw the soaked ad for the cabin stuck to the linoleum and felt a slow surge of knots popping up his spine until finally there was nothing left to do but to erupt—so he did, and he watched his hand swipe the boom box so hard that it skittered right off the back of the toilet and arced through the air, its cord stretching over the sink, lobbing toward Dottie in the tub, flute rock blasting, and when her arms shot up to cover her face the boom box bashed into her elbow, tearing her skin, and then it hit the rim of the tub and splashed through her thighs and into the water with a *thunk*. The music stopped underwater. Tomas thought immediately of electrocution, of voltage, and in a panic Dottie tried to stand out of the tub but her feet slipped and she bashed her tailbone on its edge before plunging back in. A wave sloshed to the floor. Blood dripped from her elbow.

Tomas looked at the black electrical cord. One end was still plugged into the wall above the sink, but the other end had popped free of the socket in the back of the boom box as it had fallen.

—It came unplugged, he said. It shouldn't have shocked you.

—It didn't. I don't think.

—That's good it didn't.

He realized he was smiling. Dottie pressed a washcloth against her bleeding elbow. Water beaded on her face and she blinked hard.

—Could I have died?

—Well, he said, somewhere in Japan there's an engineer we should be thanking.

—What?

—For making the cord as short as he did. Everything's okay.

—*Everything's okay?*

Dottie rose to her feet and ripped a towel from the rack and tightened it roughly over her body, as if suddenly angry at her nudity.

—It was an accident.

—You fucking loser.

—Dottie?

—You fucking loser. Get out of my house.

Tomas stood still for a long moment. Then he walked into the hall and plunged his fist straight through the drywall opposite the bathroom door. He worked his fist out of the wall and crumbles of gypsum rained on the carpet below. He felt no reaction, no pain—just the satisfaction of punching.

—Get out of my house! Dottie screamed. Get *out*—

Tomas turned down the hall and before he knew it he was out on the sidewalk, feeling stunned, walking away from Dottie's house, rubbing his dusty knuckles in the cold.

Less than forty-eight hours later, Carol's green mittens were there on the bench, right next to his daughter.

He braced an arm against the mudroom wall.

—what's the matter?

—Nothing. I'll grab you a blanket. Then we go.

Over the back of the couch in the living room a gray blanket was tented into the girls' sleepover fort, but he walked right past it and stood in the mouth of the hall, clenching his jaw, just down from the body pile.

The hallway carpet was soggy in spots and umbras of blood marked the walls. Across from the bathroom, he could see the place where Dottie had hung a family photo over the hole he'd punched. The photo itself was faceup on the carpet below. It was several years old and showed, behind a sunburst of broken glass, the O'Toole family smiling and wearing matching white turtlenecks and freshly feathered hairdos—

And now they were together in the doorway down the hall, just visible from the spot where he stood. Tomas tried to avoid looking at them, but their gray limbs clung to his vision like a burr. He wanted to go back to the beginning, to jab his finger into the exact moment that led to this unraveling, but as he meandered through his memory all he found were more insistent images of Dottie: Dottie leaning over the library counter to laugh at his misbuttoned dress shirt. Dottie phoning him while drunk on Gallo wine at three in the morning. Dottie dipping her finger into his strawberry sundae at the Dolly Madison shop on Sixth Avenue.

Dottie in her suds, putting on his dead wife's ring. The ring he'd engraved years ago with the words *A rose for my Rose*. The ring that would point to him.

As he stepped deeper into the hall, pieces of glass snapped on the carpet beneath him. He could see Dottie's arm flopped out from the pile, just near the bedroom's doorjamb. Through the sour haze he reminded himself that he needed that ring, that leaving it behind was not an option, so he knelt near the bodies and planted his palms on the carpet to scootch closer. He heard something pop. Pain raced through his hand. He held up his palm and watched a red bead roll down his wrist and soak into his cuff. When he wiped the blood away he could feel the itchy tip of a glass splinter in the pad beneath his thumb. He must have gasped, because he could hear Lydia squirming on her bench in the other room.

—daddy?

—Stay put. I'm coming.

The splinter came straight out when he pulled on it—a sharp shard, the size of a snapped toothpick—followed by a small tide of blood. He pressed his hand to his thigh and felt the cut pulsing there, bleeding into his jeans, but his attention remained focused on getting that ring. Because if anyone else were to find it—

The air around him was thick and sour as he inched toward the bodies. He found it difficult to breathe and felt a pressure in his ribs so strong he thought he might rip down the middle. But finally he could see, splayed at the base of the doorjamb, Dottie's small hand, darker and fatter than it had ever been, adorned with a bevy of rings.

He reached toward her, blood beading on his fingertips.

CHAPTER TWENTY-THREE

Lydia sat cross-legged on the floor of her father's workshop, stunned by the weight of his words. The concrete beneath her was icy cold, and her back pressed against a low shelf of paperbacks. She wanted to stand—wanted to walk out of her father's life once and for all—but thought her legs would crumple beneath her if she tried.

He pulled a stool out from under his workbench and offered it to her, and when she shook her head he settled atop it and nervously patted his kneecaps.

"Did you love her?" she said.

"I gave her your mother's ring, if that's any indication."

"How long were you two—?"

"It wasn't anything like that," he said. "She was an unhappy person in an unhappy marriage. I thought I could make her happy. To be honest I think she was just lonely, trying to entertain herself. Like dragging yarn before a cat."

"So you did."

"Love her?" He tried to continue but his words got stuck and he had to cough. Somewhere inside of him a bone cracked. "It's embarrassing to admit, but yeah. I did. I really think I did. Clearly the feeling wasn't mutual."

Lydia glanced around his book-lined workshop and felt herself beginning to understand.

"Is that why you did it?"

Tomas didn't answer.

"Is that why you left me alone in the mudroom? So you could take the ring off her finger?"

"It made sense," he said.

"*It made sense?* Are you kidding me?"

"At the *time*," he said, breathing loudly. "Look. You might not remember this, but when we arrived at the hospital, within minutes of getting you situated in Pediatrics, Moberg steered me to an empty room on a quiet wing a few floors up. He took away my clothes and boots and had me wear a pair of scrubs. I still had your mom's ring turned around on my pinkie, but when I realized they were about to photograph my hands right there I asked to use the bathroom and slid it into my teeth. They took my fingerprints and took photos of the scabs on my knuckles and the cut on my palm. They drew my blood."

"Which was all over Dottie's skin."

"You're starting to sound like Moberg," he said, holding up a finger with warning. "When it was all over I went back into the bathroom and crumpled the ring into some paper towels and hid it away with my keys and wallet and haven't uncrumpled it since. But you've got to understand why I had to get it. For days I slept in a chair by your hospital bed, and every time I woke up he was standing there, Moberg, ready to start in on me again. I just wanted to take you out of Denver, to get us going on a new life, but that was the last thing he was going to allow."

"He thought you were guilty."

"He was *making* me guilty," he said. "He was *making* me a murderer, Lydia. The police had no suspects, none, and as the days went by I could tell that I was fitting that role rather adeptly.

They even brought in this bureaucratic crone to talk to me about moving you into foster care. *It might be in your daughter's best interest*, she told me. Children were their mother's job, right? Not the domain of some psychopathic single father. They even brought the hammer into the room, sealed in an evidence bag, and wanted to know why my prints were all over it. I told them I'd run through the house with it—"

"Searching for me. I remember."

"It was the first thing I saw that morning so I grabbed it. Moberg asked me why I didn't grab a kitchen knife or a rolling pin and I told him because there was a goddamned hammer in the sink that was obviously up to the job. He didn't like that one bit, but then Moberg wasn't ever interested in the truth. He'd concocted this elaborate web around the murders and placed me at the center of it. All he wanted was an answer to the unthinkable. You still want to know *why* I had to get that ring? Just imagine if he'd known how hard I'd fallen for Dottie. Just imagine what would've happened to me, with her dead like that. Just imagine what would've happened to *you*."

Lydia resisted the urge to push off the floor and escape down the snowy slope to Plath's car. But she forced herself to calm down, and to remember that she'd come here for a reason.

"You lied to the police."

"And?"

"And you don't get to do that," she said, raising her voice.

"Listen, for a split second in that house, I was lucky enough to have seen myself as others would've seen me. A detective like Moberg or a jury of my peers. To them I would've been the jilted lover, standing over Dottie's body with blood on my hands and brain on my shirt. I would've been the loser who two days before had proposed running away with her, then tried to electrocute her in her bathtub when she rejected me. I punched a goddamned hole in her wall. They would've had close-up photographs of my knuckles on a tripod in the courtroom. And here's that beautiful Dottie in the hallway with her head bashed in, wearing your mother's wedding ring. So please don't talk to me about the *right thing to do*. It was the *only* thing to do. I'm just lucky I had the foresight to do it."

His voice echoed in the workshop before recoiling to silence. Lydia felt her shoulders bowing in.

"The Hammerman got away."

"Yes he did. But that had nothing to do with me. One ring wouldn't have mattered."

"It might have."

"It would've mattered in all the wrong ways."

"It *mattered*, Dad. Moberg wasted years focusing on you, decades, when he could've been finding the Hammerman. *All of it* mattered."

"That's been Moberg's problem all along," he said. "He's been searching all these years for *this*. For *motive*. For a *reason* to pin those murders on me. If he found that ring, he would've had his reason—don't you see that?"

Tomas took off his glasses and wiped his forehead and eyes with his shirttail. His face contorted wildly and Lydia saw that even with all the time in the world to distance himself from that period of his life, it still carried the potency to wreck him.

"You want to tell Moberg what happened, you go right ahead," he said, slapping the air, finished with her. "I've got goddamned work to do."

Tomas started moving scrap wood from a pile beneath his workbench and stacking it near his table saw, readying his next batch of shelves. His pants were slipping and he tugged them up. His beard held speckles of sawdust.

"What'd you come here for, anyway?" he said, lifting boards

and setting them back down with no clear purpose. He huffed and inhaled slowly. "I mean I'm glad to see you, but—"

"I came here about Raj, actually."

"About Raj?"

"About his parents."

"What about them?"

"I don't know exactly. There was something going on back then that we can't quite figure out. Between them."

He turned around and crossed his arms and leaned against the workbench.

"*We* meaning you and Raj? You two are in touch?"

"We are."

"Raj," he said. "Well. I like Raj. How's he doing? I like that guy."

"Honestly? Not great," she said. "He wanted me to ask you— we wanted to know, I guess, if you ever noticed anything going on with them. With his parents. In their relationship. Back then."

"You mean when—"

"I mean before we disappeared to Rio Vista."

Tomas rubbed his hands together, a sound like swishing sandpaper. "They were a miserable couple, I'll tell you that. But that's nothing new. And they were all Raj, all the time, which isn't the worst thing. You saw that firsthand, of course."

"I remember them fighting a lot."

"You remember correctly," he said, and his sight panned from the floor to Lydia and back, "but it was more like Mr. Patel fighting and Mrs. Patel shrinking. She was lovely and friendly, and he was an asshole and a pig, and I think that pretty much says it all. I vaguely recall some fight about her wearing jeans, or maybe her jeans were too tight. The word *Jordache* comes to mind. She should've left him, anyway, but I'm guessing that wasn't an option for her."

"Because of their families?"

"Maybe that," he said, "or maybe just their dynamic. The only thing Mr. Patel controlled as much as his wife was his perfect little boy. He was so overbearing he'd never have let her out of the marriage."

"So you never heard of them having any other kids?"

Her father's head visibly jerked.

"Kids?" he said. "Besides Raj? Definitely not. She wouldn't put another kid through that, I don't think. No, that would be a deal-breaker. Why are you asking me all this?"

"I don't know," she said, and she could feel herself curling around Raj's secret, as if to protect him.

"I'm just glad we got out of there in one piece," he said.

Lydia sighed. She'd come here to find a path into Raj's past, but that path had dropped into oblivion. She felt light-headed and tired to the bone.

"I should go home," she said, lifting herself from the floor.

"It's too late to drive to Denver," he said, and began to ramble about snow tires and highway salt and plowing trucks in the manner of someone whose conversational skills had been so neglected that all that remained was a feral kind of monologue. She had the impression that he was glad to veer away from all this talk of the past.

He pointed at the mattress on the floor in the corner. "You can sleep right there next to the woodstove. It's the warmest spot I've got at the moment."

"That'll be great."

"I'd offer you your bedroom but it's been taken over by reference books."

"This is fine."

"I'll run up and get an extra blanket. Plus there's a few greeting cards you never got."

"Greeting cards?"

"One's from your eighteenth birthday. One's from Valentine's. I think I stopped writing them after that. Should still be ten bucks in the birthday card."

"Should I come with you?"

He paused as he was walking out the shop door. "Sure. I suppose. Only if you want." Then he ducked into the night.

Because of her father's hesitation, Lydia walked slowly up the pitted path he'd tracked in the snow, keeping a distance between them. A partial moon had emerged over the mountains and its faint light made the snow glow, exposing fat pines and gnarled clumps of brush. The night was freezing but it felt good to move.

No lights were on, inside or out, so his A-frame appeared crystalline in the moonlight. Alongside the cabin's small porch were stacks of cardboard boxes half-covered with a tarp, presumably packed with books awaiting shelves.

"Just be a minute," her dad said when he opened the front door. "Wait out here. Don't need you getting hurt."

She didn't quite understand what he'd meant until a light inside came on and she could see, through the open front door and the two windows that flanked it, that the cabin had been . . . remodeled. It looked for a moment as if he'd enclosed part of the entryway, and maybe even added a narrow hallway down the center of the main room. Then she realized that she wasn't seeing walls or halls, but *aisles*.

Let's just say it got a little tight in there, he'd said earlier, and now she understood. The main room was cross-sectioned by bookshelves that ran the length of the cabin, high enough to meet the ceiling and just narrow enough for a person to walk between. When she ducked her head to look down one of the aisles, she saw that the walls of the hallway and kitchen beyond were also covered in books, just as his workshop had been. She could only imagine what the bedrooms and bathroom looked like.

In her absence, he'd turned the cabin into a library where nothing was ever read, nothing ever checked out. *More graveyard than library*, he'd said.

The floorboards creaked and groaned under the weight of all those titles as he marched around somewhere inside.

When he appeared again in the doorway he wouldn't look at her, and she could tell he was embarrassed by their home's transformation. She realized she might very well have been the first person to ever see it like this. He handed out a folded wool blanket and a wad of brown paper towel.

"You know what that is, don't you?" he said, gesturing to the wadded paper. "Your mom's ring."

"I don't want it."

"I should never have given it to Dottie. I was keeping it for you."

"I really don't want it."

"You can give it away or pawn it. Just please take it. Please."

She tucked it into her satchel. He crammed his hands in his pockets and looked at the glowing sky. A thought occurred to her.

"Is it possible," she said, standing next to him in the cold, "that Dottie actually loved you? Because I was thinking she kept the ring, didn't she? She was wearing it when she died. So maybe she put it on because—"

"Romantic," he said, "I know. Except she only kept it because it was worth something. Another flashy ring for her flashy fingers. Had nothing to do with love, Lydia, believe me." He may have winked at her in the dark. "Not that I'm bitter."

Before leading her back toward the workshop, he stepped into the cabin to shut off the lights. Through the icy window she took one last look at the tight warren of shelves he'd created, at the mass of books that had pushed him out of his home, and finally understood what he'd been doing all these years: trying to return to a time in his life that was forever out of reach.

Not unlike Joey, she thought.

In the morning, Lydia awakened on the concrete next to the woodstove, covered by a blanket and snarled inside a sleeping bag. A soft blue light brightened the workshop windows; a crisp Mount Princeton loomed against the panes. Last night her father had set up the space and fluffed her dirty pillow as carefully as a parent at a slumber party. When she finally drifted off he'd been fiddling around at the workbench, tinkering under a dim single light. She didn't know where he'd slept, if he'd slept.

"Wakey-wakey," he said. He was perched on his stool in the middle of the room, hooded against the chill.

Lydia blinked into her palms and stretched the arches of her feet. Her father was holding something in his hand, and she realized it was the birthday party photo she'd packed in her satchel on the way out of Denver.

"Is that . . . ?" she said.

"I took the liberty. I wasn't snooping."

"You couldn't wait?"

"You still sleep like a hedgehog, like you're trying to disappear into your own belly. I didn't want to wake you."

She crawled from the sleeping bag and pulled her satchel protectively into her lap. Her first thought was to catalog its contents to see what else her father had unearthed, and she wondered about the sunflower notebook that held Joey's messages, and whether he'd—

"I didn't look at anything else," he said, "if that's what you're worried about."

She set her satchel down. Her father squinted at the image, pale faced.

"This is definitely the photo. God, I remember helping you pick out your birthday outfit and decorating the cake and everything. Ten years old. We had no idea what was coming."

His eyes crinkled and he coughed into his chapped fist. Lydia tried to swallow but couldn't.

"Is Joey really dead?" he said.

"He is."

"And Joey really had this on him when he died?"

"He did."

"He was one of the few, you know? In all my time walking those corridors, Joey was one of the few." And then he went on to explain to her the way he'd met the juvenile Joey in that isolated cell on that isolated block of the isolated level three, and how Joey must have cribbed the photograph from his desk on that quiet Christmas Eve.

"He was so promising," her father continued, "and then to finally finish his prison sentence and instead of getting his life together he goes after *you*? I just don't get it. It makes no sense whatsoever."

Lydia resisted her desire to point at Joey's maybe-brother Raj admiring her in the photo. She wasn't ready to get into all of that, not with her father.

"The only explanation I can come up with," he said, "is that after all those nights of me and him talking, maybe Joey felt like he knew you. And he knew that you'd treat him right, which I'm sure you did."

"You talked a lot about me?"

"You could say that," he said, clearly understating the point.

"I even told him that once he got out he could look me up, that I might be able to give him shelter until he got on his feet, but he said he was going straight back to Denver. He seemed happy to be getting out, I have to say, more hopeful than I'd ever seen him, so I felt okay about him heading into the world all alone." He tapped the photo against the back of his knuckles. "Can I keep this?"

"All yours."

"I'll take good care of it," he said. Then he stood and dug around for a roll of tape on his bench and taped the photo to the edge of a shelf. "What the hell happened to Billy Pilgrim?" he said contemplatively, under his voice, like a person who'd had a lot of practice talking to himself. "What the hell *happened* to Billy Pilgrim?"

For the first time since she'd arrived in Rio Vista, Lydia felt herself smile. He almost sounded like her dad.

CHAPTER TWENTY-FOUR

For nearly an hour Lydia had been driving away from Rio Vista, grateful for the isolation of Plath's car. The highway near Fairplay rolled between mountains, over a snowy basin peppered with pines. She found herself so enervated by the visit to her father that more than once the car drifted over the center line until she snapped alert. She wanted to focus on the connection she and her father had finally made, yet she couldn't stop thinking about Dottie O'Toole and the ring he'd tugged from her finger. The act was impulsive and had taken only seconds, yet it had rippled through the decades like a shock wave.

Lydia was scheduled to work at noon, so when she caught a glimpse of a gas station she pulled over to call Bright Ideas and let them know she was running late. As soon as she hung up she realized she should probably also call David to let him know she was safe.

No one answered at home, and when David's extension at work went straight to voice mail she set the receiver down without leaving him a message. Of course she loved him and knew that for years he'd been doing all he possibly could to create a home with her, yet she also felt that this—being here, in this desolate mountain gas station, after spending the night on the floor of her father's shop—felt *separate* from David, different from the life they shared. Instead of calling back she found herself retrieving Raj's number from her little notebook and dialing it.

"So how was it, seeing your dad?" Raj asked as soon as he answered. "You two are okay?"

"I'm not sure yet," she said.

"What does that mean?"

"He had a thing for Mrs. O'Toole, apparently."

"Every dad had a thing for Mrs. O'Toole."

"Where was *I* during all of this?"

"Being ten," Raj said matter-of-factly.

Lydia looked around the gas station. For the first time she noticed the woman working at the register, wearing a down parka, chewing on a meat stick, reading a romance novel on a stool.

"Did you learn anything else?" he said.

"He didn't have much to say about your parents, Raj. No gossip about a love child. Sorry."

"Worth a shot, anyway."

"Yeah." She could hear his breathing begin to slow, his hope deflating. Her attention drifted back to the woman at the register. She was perched in front of a wall of colorful cigarette packs and for a second Lydia imagined the packs were books, wordless and deadly, and she imagined herself standing before them, working a rural roadside job, as if this would be the trade-off were she to disappear into the mountains and leave all of this messy personal history behind. She couldn't help but think about the years of nights her father had spent roaming the halls of the prison—empty nights, it seemed, except perhaps for his time with Joey—and the price he'd paid for escape.

"What about you, Raj?" she said. "Anything happen on your end?"

"Quite a lot, actually," he said. "More than quite a lot."

"Here I am blabbing. So? What's the word?"

Raj explained that he'd just come in from bouncing around a bunch of different state agencies downtown. "I met Irene at the courthouse this morning. She gave me a Danish, and twenty minutes later we were standing in a meeting room with a judge and a stenographer. She talked to the judge briefly, going over the files she'd sent him, and then he asked me one question: 'Why do you wish to unseal Joseph Molina's adoption file?' And I replied, 'I'm his brother.' Three words. I thought I was going to have to elaborate, but then the judge said he'd been provided with a death certificate for the adoptee, Joseph Molina, and the Vital Records office had validated our familial relationship, and he saw no reason why he shouldn't unseal the records for a living sibling. That was it."

"Thank you, Irene," Lydia said. "Are you sure about this, Raj?"

"I'm definitely sure," he said, as if it were a proclamation. "Part of me still thinks that maybe it's all a mistake, but it's getting harder to believe that, you know? What were my parents thinking? I mean, what the hell? I barely slept last night I was so pissed. This is not the kind of thing you hide from your child."

"But you didn't—"

"I haven't said anything to them," he said reassuringly, "and I'm avoiding them to make sure I don't, but at some point they're going to look me in the eye and explain."

"Avoidance is probably a good plan. For now, anyway."

"Are you around later today?" Raj said, sounding frail. "Irene is hoping to have the files couriered to me late this afternoon. Speaking of, I might need to borrow some money. I'm sorry, I just had to have it rushed, and there were all these fees, and I can't ask my folks—"

"We'll figure out the money," she said. "Or maybe you'll have to get a real job."

"Not all of us can be booksellers," he said.

"Truer words have never been spoken."

Raj laughed. Lydia's hands were cold, and a bad taste stained her mouth, but hearing his laugh made her feel better. Out the gas station window, a pickup truck with a happy hound in its bed parked by the pumps. She knew she should hang up and get back on the highway, but she didn't want to be alone with her thoughts, so she was glad that Raj kept talking.

"Lydia? I know you need to go, but you don't have a picture of him, do you? Of Joey?"

"I don't, Raj. I could ask around the store, maybe Lyle or Plath, but I kind of doubt anyone would. He wasn't really the spotlight type. Why?"

"I still don't even know what he looked like. Did he look like me?"

With his green eyes and tawny skin, his black hair and lanky frame, Lydia had always been ready to assume, with little to no consciousness, that Joey was Latino. And learning his last name, *Molina*, probably only shored up this assumption. But in retrospect, he could just as easily have been almost any flavor of American, a kid whose portrait—dressed in black, standing on a Denver street with the Rockies in the background and bits of leaf in his hair—might have found a home in a *National Geographic* coffee table book, something called *A Day in the West* or *The Americans*. He could've been anyone, from anywhere.

"He looked like Joey," Lydia said. "That's just how I think of him. I know that's not helpful."

"I guess I've just been feeling bad," Raj said. "I mean, if Joey had been living here in Cowtown all these years, I probably

278

walked right past him on the street a dozen times, and I guarantee you that I didn't offer to buy him lunch or dump some change into his palm. The kid was my brother, you know?"

"You probably never even saw him, Raj. He was born to disappear."

"That's exactly the problem."

Lydia could hear Raj drawing air on the far end of the phone, and she realized he was more upset than he was letting on.

"Irene asked me if I wanted a photo of him from his police record," he said, "so that will be in the files she sends. But you know, I just keep thinking how awful it is that I only learned about him after he killed himself, and that my only photos of him will be of his body bag or his mug shot. What's wrong with the world if those are the only images we have of this kid? Where's his baby book, you know? I could've been his big brother, Lydia, for real. Instead of this."

Lydia didn't know what to say, so she sighed in agreement.

"I'm just glad he met *you*," Raj continued. "That before he died he had a chance to know you the way I know you. That helps some, Lydia, just knowing that you were there for him. You were, weren't you?"

"I think so."

"That helps, Lydia. See, I just . . ."

Raj trailed off, and she wondered if he was crying. She wished she was there next to him, but in a way she was glad that she wasn't.

"Raj?"

"I'm fine," he said after a bit. "Just come see me when you get back to town. I won't do anything until you get here. My fucking parents, man."

"I'll get there as soon as I can."

Lydia let the pay phone receiver crash into its cradle. She

stood there for a minute, eyes wandering over the gas station's rock candy and elk jerky, its belt buckles and butterfly knives. Before heading out, she retrieved her father's wad of brown paper towel from her satchel and rested it quietly atop the pay phone. The woman behind the register looked up and yawned, then returned to reading her romance.

CHAPTER TWENTY-FIVE

After her shift at the bookstore, Lydia called Raj and agreed to meet him on the sidewalk in front of the Terminal Bar & Cafe, a slouching brick dive a few blocks north, where he rented a tiny apartment above the bar. On her walk over, she was thunked by a fat, cold raindrop, and soon more drops spotted the cobblestones and concrete. When she arrived, Raj wasn't out front, but she soon found him sitting on a trashed vinyl bar booth in the alley, ignoring the rain. He was watching a pair of damp workmen carry an etched mirror out of the bar and slide it into the back of their truck. One of them gave Lydia a quick once-over as she approached, but otherwise the mood was funereal.

"Another one down," Raj said, but he didn't take his eyes off the workmen gutting the bar beneath his home.

Lydia understood. The Terminal was an epic dive with an epic history—Cassady, Kerouac, Waits—and the rumor among her comrades was that it would soon ditch the Coors taps and wonky pool table and be reborn as a sleek seafood bistro. A massive dumpster was parked against the curb out front, and it overflowed with the Terminal's discarded bar stools and vinyl booths, its kitchen mats and condiment dispensers—all of the artifacts the new owners didn't want.

"It won't be long before we're all evicted, anyway," Raj said. "Used to be no one wanted to live down here, now everyone does. How are you?"

"Wiped. Still no courier?"

"He must be running late," Raj said. He explained that the courier was supposed to deliver the package of files from Irene by five o'clock, but he hadn't called or shown up yet. "Do you mind waiting out here with me? I just don't want to miss him."

The orange vinyl wheezed when she plopped down next to him.

A faint ribbon of tangerine light glowed above Union Station, but otherwise the dusk was dark and cloudy. Soon the air had chilled enough to change the rain into a wet snow. Lydia and Raj scooched the booth closer to the alley's brick wall. The workmen took one look at the sky and called it a day.

"I don't know what I'm going to do," Raj said, "if Joey's files verify that he's my brother. I don't know how I'm going to face my parents. How could they not tell me?"

"Let's just wait and see, Raj."

Raj closed his eyes and leaned back into the booth. He was wearing black jeans and a gray coat and he didn't seem to notice the snow.

After last night's visit to her father's workshop Lydia thought she might feel stronger in her core—more in command of her feelings and her history—but now she felt as she always did, only worse. Nibbled by dread and in dire need of a toothbrush. There was no way around the fact that her father had tampered with the crime scene at the O'Tooles' and may have obstructed the investigation, but she couldn't fathom the possibility of his facing charges or a jury or even reporters. She couldn't risk that, no matter how wrong he'd been. And she especially couldn't send him out of her life right at the moment he'd reentered it. She really didn't know what to do.

Raj stood and began rocking on the balls of his feet. His boots ended in a smeary reflection of city lights.

"I don't know how I'd do all of this alone," he said with an unexpected formality.

"Don't worry about it, Raj. Have a seat."

He remained standing, squinting through the snowy drizzle at the dark frame of his apartment window above the bar. Below it a row of empty kegs were stacked against the building like bullet casings.

"I just keep thinking," he said, "about how cool it is that my brother and your father managed to find each other in that prison."

"I know what you mean."

"And in a similar way, you know, just tracing things out, how if Joey was alive I wouldn't be here with you. Does that make sense?"

"Yeah, but that's kind of a road to nowhere, Raj."

"I mean it, Lydia. More than anything I wish Joey was sitting here with us, enjoying this crappy snow—of course I do. But it was his death, his body bag in the newspaper, that caused me to find you again, right?"

"Right."

"I'm pointing this out because I want to make sure I don't squander Joey's value on this planet, you know? I feel like he led me into something rare here, whether he meant to or not, and I can't let that go to waste just because I'm too embarrassed to share my feelings."

"Raj," she said, "it's a lot to process, and there's a lot we don't—"

"Okay," he said, interrupting her. "I'm just going to say it: you and I, Lydia, we *need* to be together. We *need* to see what's right in front of us. This is no accident, Lydia. Our whole lives have been adding up to *this*: me and you, here and now. Just listen to it."

Lydia felt something stir inside her, and she did listen: to the traffic splashing in the distance, to a train clacking along its tracks, to drips plinking on the fire escape and in the gutters. For a second, she considered giving herself over to Raj's words, but doing so felt overly complicated and, in light of David's constancy, unnecessarily cruel.

"I can't think about this right now, Raj."

He turned away from her and stared at the row of empty brick storefronts across the street.

"Because of David?" he said. "At least tell me it's because of David and not because I'm chubby or gross or something."

"Raj, you're a total catch, trust me."

"The loneliest catch in the world," he said, but he sounded only half-serious.

A pickup truck splashed past and its driver tossed a cigarette out the window.

"We've always been close, Raj, even when we weren't together. And we'll keep being close. So let's just lead our lives and see what happens, okay?"

"Sure," he said, and though she could tell he was disappointed, she also knew she was right: this was not the time.

Lydia's hands were wet and a pool of slush had gathered beneath her feet.

"You can wait in my apartment if you want," he said.

"I'm happy right here."

When the courier finally pulled up in front of the Terminal, driving a little eighties Metro or Yugo, Raj ran to the curb to meet him. The courier stepped out of his little car and into the snow casually, sporting an anemone of dreads and wearing a ripped striped sweater.

"You're kind of late," Raj said.

"Traffic, man. Speer Boulevard. I mean, what's the point of even driving, you know? Move me to the mountains, give me a horse."

The man's car was double-parked, its hazards flashing. Lydia felt a swallow of anxiety as Raj took the package of files from the man and bobbed it dreamily in his hands. It was bound in some kind of waterproof sleeve and sealed with a string-and-button clasp. Lydia imagined Joey burning a similar package in his trash can on the day he'd hanged himself.

"I need a signature for that," the guy said, handing him a clipboard and hunching over it to block some snowfall.

Raj snapped out of it. "Sorry."

"I'm used to it, man. I deliver results for medical tests, divorce papers, all kinds of heavy shit. I bear *news*, man." He took the clipboard from Raj and shined a little flashlight on his name. "May your news be fruitful, Raj Patel. May your news bring peace. Later."

Lydia and Raj watched the courier's taillights disappear, then both walked toward the side entrance in the alley. Raj stopped beneath a light fixture bolted to the bricks and began ripping into the package. A Post-it note with a scrawled message from Irene was on the outside, but he didn't even bother to read it before opening the file.

"I can't see anything," he said, lifting the pages close to his face and blinking. "It's like everything is underwater."

"Here," Lydia said, and took the file from him, and leaned in close enough to read.

"What's it say? Were we right?"

She nodded, mouth dry. She could hear little persistent *ticks* and realized Raj was clicking his fingernails together.

"Raj. Are you seeing this?"

"What?"

"This," she said, holding a fresh photocopy that said *Certificate of Adoption* across the top, inside a border of scrolls, above the seal of the state of Colorado. The first thing she noticed was the way all the information was arranged in a grid of small rectangles, little windows, each holding different data, and she couldn't help but consider the resemblance they bore to Joey's messages. This was a copy of the certificate that was filed when baby Joey was adopted into the Molina family, soon after his birth, so a lot of the information recorded the details of Mr. and Mrs. Molina, as Lydia had expected, while the rest of the information focused on Joey's birth and birth parents. Those boxes also offered the details she'd expected—*Child's Name, Child's Gender, Place of Birth, Date of Birth, Time of Birth, Birth Mother's Name, Birth Mother's Maiden Name*—until she came upon the information about Joey's birth father.

"See that?" Lydia said, and her wet finger tapped the box that recorded the birth father's name.

"I don't understand," Raj said. He pulled the certificate from her hands and held it closer to the light.

Birth Father's Name: Bartholomew Edward O'Toole.

Lydia felt her shoulders tighten. She could hear the snap of drips hitting paper.

"Does that say Mr. O'Toole?" Raj said. "Under 'Birth Father'?"

"Yeah."

"What does that mean?"

"I'm not sure," she said.

"This isn't right," he said, huffing. "Irene sent me the wrong file."

"It's the right one, Raj."

"It can't be, Lydia. It *can't* be. Unless—"

"Yeah."

"Does this mean—?"

286

"I think so," she said.

Lydia felt snowflakes melting on her face. The file in Raj's hand fell to his side and draped against his thigh.

"Maybe Mr. O'Toole was just a witness or something," he said, "and they put his name in the wrong box." He looked at the sky. "They wouldn't do that, would they?"

"They wouldn't," Lydia said. "It says, 'Birth Father,' Raj. That means—"

"That means Joey wasn't my dad's baby," he said. "That means my mom—my mom and Mr. O'Toole?"

"That's exactly what that means."

"My *mom*?"

"I know."

"So she didn't go to India?" he said, incredulous, as he squinted at the letterhead on another sheet in the file. "She went to Colorado Springs instead, some place called the Sacred Heart Maternity Home. I'm surprised it doesn't say 'For Girls in Trouble.' My mom and Mr. O'Toole, for real?"

Lydia's blood felt thick as it squeezed through her heart. She sensed a thought forming that wouldn't quite emerge, as if it were trapped in a net just below her consciousness, trying to break the surface. How *sad*—maybe that was it—that Joey's dad was dead, probably before the kid was even born. Had he even known about Joey, and had Joey even known about him? How *sad*, either way.

Raj took a deep sniff and studied the paper, aiming for control. As his neurons scrambled to redefine everything he'd ever known about his parents, Lydia couldn't help but see him as the childhood friend who'd always shared the candy crammed in his jumpsuit pockets, who'd read endless books at her side, who'd always looked so worried when he walked up the porch steps to his own home. She ached all over.

"It'll be okay, Raj."

"Just give me a second," he said faintly.

Lydia was going to turn and wander away to give him some space, but when she took a step she felt a tug and realized that they were holding hands. She had no idea how long they'd been doing so, and he himself didn't seem to notice, but his grip fit within hers so naturally that she had to shake his wrist a little before he let up. As soon as his hand was free she regretted letting go. Her fingers felt colder now, unpleasantly damp and pruned, and the rest of her felt colder as well.

"I'll take you to breakfast tomorrow," she said.

Raj looked up from the file and seemed surprised to see Lydia still standing there, her hair soaked and flat. A small pop escaped his jaw. "Breakfast? Okay."

"Maybe hold off for a day or two before you talk to them."

"To my parents?" he said, brow raised. "My brother is dead, Lydia. And my mom was screwing Mr. O'Toole. I don't know that I'll ever talk to them again."

He returned to the cone of dripping light and didn't look up, even as Lydia walked out of the alley, past the cluttered dumpster, and off in the direction of Colfax.

CHAPTER TWENTY-SIX

Lydia sat in the Plexiglas bus shelter across the street from Gas 'n Donuts and watched the Patels closing up inside: Mr. Patel counting out register receipts, Mrs. Patel zigzagging a mop over the floor. The soggy snow had been falling for hours now, so the entire city seemed covered in a coat of sopping cotton balls, and each time a car drove past, slush sprayed Lydia's shins and knees and sometimes face. Something about actually *tasting* Colfax in her mouth felt appropriate for this reunion.

It was a welcome sight when Mr. Patel finally carried a blue padlocked bank bag to the store's side door. He pulled on his coat, looked cautiously toward the sidewalk and again toward the alley, then quickly walked to the white Monte Carlo parked next to the shop. He started it and let it idle, then pulled out a snow scraper and dragged the brush back and forth over his slush-covered windshield. When he walked around the front of the car to wipe off the rest, crossing the headlights and tapping the scraper against his thigh, Lydia felt sick to her stomach.

A moment later he drove away. Mrs. Patel was finally alone.

Lydia jogged straight across the street and rapped on the Gas 'n Donuts window. Still pushing her mop, Mrs. Patel shook her head almost violently and offered a muffled shout of "Closed! Closed!" She was wearing a creamy knit sweater over a brown sari, and her left hand was wrapped in a dirty mitten of gauze. Seeing it, Lydia recalled Raj mentioning how she'd burned herself recently but had refused to miss even a day of work.

She stood below a painted sign that read *Free Glazed with Fill-Up!* and rapped the glass again. Mrs. Patel approached the window, shaking her head and then softening as she began to recognize Lydia.

"Lydia?"

Mrs. Patel fiddled with a ring of keys, struggling to grasp the right one through the gauze.

"Lydia?"

She barely had the door open before embracing Lydia and pulling her into the shop. She was still beautiful, though her beauty now had more character to it, as her hair had grayed straight through and she'd gained weight across the middle, and the thin wrinkles on her face gave it more texture and depth. She had ashy circles beneath her eyes and an ashy blemish on her cheek. "Raj said you were back in town! I'm so glad, Lydia. But what brings you here so late?"

It was difficult not to smile, not to return Mrs. Patel's embrace, but Lydia stood stiff.

"You might not be so glad," she said, "when you find out why I'm here."

Mrs. Patel leaned back and her smile straightened out. She looked like a woman who lived in a world where unwanted babies had to be buried in the dark.

"Raj knows about Joey," Lydia continued. "We both know about Joey."

Mrs. Patel went pale, then began shoving her mop over the checkered floor, kicking a wheeled yellow bucket before her. A gumball machine rattled when she mopped its base. "Please close the door behind you when you leave, Lydia."

"Joey just wanted a family."

Mrs. Patel nodded grimly. Then she plunged her mop into the bucket, stirring gray waves. Lydia stepped forward and gripped the handle.

"Please sit," Lydia said, and gestured toward the old booth where she and Raj had spent so many childhood hours. The speckled Formica, the creamer bottles, the sugar spouts were all the same.

"Rohan will be back soon," Mrs. Patel said. "You cannot be here when he arrives."

"Then please start talking. Or we can wait for him and talk then. I could even call Raj over. He's really upset."

"You have no idea."

"Mrs. Patel. Please."

Mrs. Patel had recently washed the tables, and they were still slightly damp and smelled of bleach. She expertly ripped a few napkins from the cubed dispenser and dried the surface beneath their arms. Once she settled in across from Lydia she didn't say anything for a minute, just stared out at the traffic on Colfax and nodded, as if finally giving herself permission.

It started with a haircut.

A young mother with a baby on her hip had come into Gas 'n Donuts one slow afternoon when Raj was starting fourth grade, and as Maya Patel filled her box of doughnuts she found herself strangely drawn to her. The woman was slender, with skin the color of coffee, and she wore a gold-colored waitress uniform as if it were a gown. Her hair was shaved nearly bald and she had big plastic hoops dangling from her ears. The woman cooed to her baby as Maya rang her up, and after she left, Maya watched her stroll up Colfax until she became small and disappeared.

The woman had seemed so *tall* to Maya, so *proud*. She seemed to know *exactly* who she was.

For the next few days, Maya was unable to clear this woman's presence from her mind, and soon she felt an urgent need to do something with herself. She'd always had long, lush hair, and spent fifteen minutes every morning and evening brushing it out, and she was careful to only use shampoos with scents that appealed to Rohan. He was a big fan of her hair, though he only showed it about once a week when he made love to her, leaning on his elbows and immersing his face within it, sometimes even holding it between his teeth like a ribbon as he emptied himself inside her.

Many times Maya had caught Rohan watching the women of Colfax, especially the ones who went braless in the sun or who wore short skirts and corky sandals, and she convinced herself that he would be pleasantly surprised if her appearance was to take a bold shift in their direction. She wouldn't wear a tank top or anything too slinky, but she did buy a pair of Jordache jeans to wear instead of, or perhaps beneath, her sari, and even visited the stylist at the Glamour Guru salon down the street. He ran his comb through her hair, studied her from different angles, and recommended going short.

—*Very* short. Mrs. Brady short. Dorothy Hamill short.

Maya shuddered but agreed.

During those first days after the haircut, when Maya and Rohan passed each other behind the doughnut shop counter, he would barge though the space and make her step to the side, or he'd lift his hands, palms out, as if she were contaminated.

—I didn't marry a boy, he told her. We'll share a bed again when your hair is long.

These were his words to his wife of a dozen years, the mother of his child. Here she thought he would be aroused, but instead this marked the beginning of a long famine in their bedroom. Many of those nights, she slept alone on the couch.

A month or so after the haircut, in the depths of her marital misery, the corroded pipes in the doughnut shop crawl space burst. This was in the fall, long before the first deep freeze of the season, and Bart O'Toole spent the next two days working beneath the floors, lugging around his toolbox in that quiet way of his, and carrying lengths of copper pipe in and out of the storage pantry where the hatch to the crawl space was located. Rohan was at his side for most of the work, making sure he got the job done right, yet Bart still managed to throw looks at Maya all the time. She wasn't sure if Rohan ever noticed, but she certainly did. Every time she turned around, this handsome, soft-spoken man was looking at her, but it felt more like an offering than a stare, as if he were rolling his gaze gently at her feet and asking her to pick it up. For so long in her relationship Maya had felt herself teetering between invisibility and repulsion, and here was this lean blond man with blue eyes and a mustache—the opposite of Rohan, she thought—pouring his desire on her. She felt like that woman on television, the one in the street throwing her hat in the air.

When the work was finally finished, Rohan inspected the job and clapped Bart on the back and that was supposed to be it. But early the next morning, before the shop had even opened and just after Rohan had left to drop Raj at school and pick up a new spray arm for the dishwasher, Bart O'Toole knocked on the glass door. Three minutes later he was in the crawl space, clanging around with his hammer and flashlight, and his toolbox sat on the floor outside the hatch. The shop would be opening in twenty minutes and there was work to be done up front, yet

Maya poured him a cup of hot coffee, the first pot of the day, then crouched on the floor next to the crawl space. Bart was on his back on the cold dirt in there, directly beneath some junction between pipes, trying to unstick an old valve that he'd soaked with penetrating oil the last time he was there.

—Nothing urgent, he assured her, just a precaution.

Maya found that from where she crouched she could see him from the neck down, and as he inched his way deeper into the crawl space, his shirt shifted and his belly became exposed, its faint trail of hair disappearing under his Coca-Cola belt buckle. Just as she was about to look away she realized with a ripple of pleasure that she didn't need to look away at all—that because of the angle of the crawl space, he couldn't see her seeing him—and she wondered if this was like the nudie booths she'd heard about at the adult shops down Colfax, the ones she was sure Rohan visited, where the men could drop in quarters and peer into two-way mirrors and see naked women on old blankets and red pillows, bobbing to music, and the women couldn't see the men out there at all. Above the clang of pipes, Maya watched Bart's slender body for what felt like a long time until, without warning, he'd scooched toward the opening and caught her consuming him with her gaze.

—Coffee, she blurted, and handed the lidded paper cup in his direction.

He sat up on an elbow.

—I don't get this kind of service at home, he said. That's for sure.

—At home? Pshh. Who does?

Bart took the coffee from her and screwed it gently into the cool dirt inside the crawl space, but Maya's small hand remained extended, and he studied her fingers for a long time before reaching out and touching them. Within seconds they were on the tiled kitchen floor, mouth to mouth, breathing hard and fitting themselves together.

The crawl space hatch was sealed shut and Bart was out the door with his toolbox a full three minutes before Gas 'n Donuts opened.

After, Maya thought she would feel guilty, or terrified, yet all day long she could feel herself smiling, and when she closed her eyes she could still feel Bart sliding tightly inside her, his hands clutching the back of her head, right where her hair was the shortest. A few times she went into the kitchen and stood over the tiled space, as if to remind herself of their union. One of those times, Rohan appeared right behind her.

—Customers!

He clapped hard in her ear, startling her out of her trance.

And that was basically it for Maya and Bart. There was one other encounter, a few days into October, a snapshot of late-night stupidity in the front seat of Bart's plumbing truck in the lot behind the shop while Rohan was doing his nightly bank drop-off. Maya's sari got caught on a door latch and ended up with a small tear and a grease stain that would never fully come out, and Bart had clearly been drinking beer, and their sex felt awkward and ugly, more like an invasive trip to the doctor than a sensual tryst, and that marked the end of the affair, if these two encounters could even qualify as such.

Months passed. Maya's misery remained. When she realized she was pregnant she went into a panic and did everything she could to seduce Rohan, to try to blur the calendar in his mind, but her hair was growing slowly and he was adamant about their abstinence.

—When you stop looking like a boy, he reminded her.

Maya didn't go to the doctor, didn't tell a soul.

* * *

Mrs. Patel's eyes widened at the sound of a car splashing through the alley behind the shop. She appeared relieved when it moved on.

"Rohan will be here soon."

She scooted out of the booth and grabbed her keys from her sweater pocket.

"I want to know what happened with Joey," Lydia said.

"If you know Joey, you know the rest. I went away. I had a baby. I gave him up. I came back. Now, please. I have to finish."

Mrs. Patel was clearly upset. She fiddled through her key ring but never singled one out.

"Will you exit out the back, please?" she said. "I can't have Rohan driving up and seeing you through the windows. I don't need the anguish, Lydia. Out of nowhere you come in here, digging through our lives. Please. Just leave."

Lydia was feeling fogged by the confrontation and saddened by Mrs. Patel's predicament. Yet she couldn't shake the feeling that she was missing something, an elusive fragment that she couldn't pin down. She wasn't sure what else to do, so she followed Mrs. Patel past the empty display cases and coffeepots and through the kitchen's swinging door. Only half of the lights in the kitchen were on. She remembered its stainless steel counters, its stacks of silver bowls, its walls of white tile, but it seemed far more dingy now, and everything was filmed with grease. Marching solemnly behind Mrs. Patel, she was bothered by how this visit had turned out and was thinking she should probably call—

On the counter next to the deep fryer sat an assortment of cleaning supplies.

Lydia stopped walking. Mrs. Patel stopped as well.

"Lydia. Please. He'll be here."

Just near a mound of rags, Mr. Patel had left one of his frayed hairnets, a squirt bottle of degreaser and another of vinegar, a wire scrub brush, and the pair of wadded latex gloves he always used to clean the fryer's racks and frame.

Lydia's memories rolled over each other like pieces of glass in a kaleidoscope.

She could picture Mr. O'Toole's name, typed inside a tiny box and tucked into a file downtown: *Bartholomew Edward O'Toole*. Joey's father. Mrs. Patel's lover.

—i know.

She could picture Mr. Patel in the slush outside a little while ago, walking in front of his headlights with a window scraper in his grip.

—i know.

She could see the Hammerman's hand, slapping off the light switch.

—i know.

His hairy wrist tucked into a white latex glove.

—i know.

His white latex glove gripping a hammer.

"I know," she said, barely audible.

"There isn't time for this, Lydia. This way."

"I know what your husband *did*."

"Lydia."

Her thoughts came so fast and with such force it was hard to contain them with her voice. She heard herself begging. "Tell me!" She clung to the edge of the counter to stop herself from falling. "Tell *me*!" Mrs. Patel went pale and covered her mouth with her gauzy hand. "Tell me *now*, or I'll get Raj and you can tell *him*!"

* * *

At three months along, Maya had begun to wear looser clothing and had found ways to hide her nausea, but she still hadn't told a soul about her pregnancy—not Bart O'Toole, and certainly not her husband. But that would change one evening in January, just at the start of the biggest cold snap of the season. The stock show was going on over at the Coliseum, and there were more pickup trucks than usual carving through the snow on Colfax, and even more drunk cowboys waiting for the bus in sheepskin jackets. It was long after dark and the three Patels were at Gas 'n Donuts hours after closing because the BBQ Depot down the block had had a surprise visit that morning from a food inspector. Rohan was concerned that they would be inspected next.

As Maya scrubbed every surface and double-checked expiration dates in the pantry and fridges, Rohan lowered himself into the crawl space to make sure that the pipes that Bart O'Toole had replaced a few months before were holding up against the cold. Raj had been very gloomy lately, upset by Carol's pushy takeover of his best friend, and tonight was especially bad because Lydia and Carol were having a sleepover and hadn't invited him. Maya grew so tired of the complaining that she made Raj go out and clean up the trash around the dumpsters in the alley. As he stepped out the back door, Maya could see snow tumbling through the lamplights, and when she turned around Rohan was emerging from the crawl space hatch, holding two items in his hands. In his left, the cold cup of coffee Bart had screwed into the earth, untouched these past three months. In his right, the hammer that Bart, in his horny haste, had accidentally left in the crawl space.

As Rohan straightened out and stared at her with icy silence, Maya realized that she was cupping her belly, as if to protect the life growing inside. Rohan clearly suspected that Bart had been there, in that dark and quiet place, without him, which meant that Maya had been there, in that dark and quiet place, with Bart. Maybe because of this, the words poured out of her before she could stop them.

—I'm pregnant.

Rohan looked confused for a minute, just as he did when he was puzzling over the columns of digits in his account binders. He seemed bigger than usual, wider through the shoulders. He pointed toward the bump of her belly with the hammer in his hand.

—Are you sure? he said.

—Fairly. Yes.

Rohan looked at the small initials scratched into the base of the hammer: BEO.

—Mr. O'Toole?

—Yes. Three months. About.

—Bart O'Toole?

—I've been planning on telling you. I was thinking I could take Raj somewhere for a while, until—

—Take Raj?

—Just for a while. I was thinking—

—And go away? No.

For months Maya had been anticipating this conversation and she'd always envisioned it as being more chaotic—more dangerous—but Rohan was so calm and cold, it was as if he was storing up his energy. It felt strange to wish he was more upset.

—How many times? he said. With you and him.

—Only twice.

Rohan stretched out his arm and touched the flat head of the hammer to her abdomen, and began to press, gently at first, then with a slight springiness, as if stoking a fire.

—Only?

—Rohan. Please.

She tried to step back but he followed her belly with the hammer, taking slow steps toward her, and she could feel its cold metal against her tummy and its forked end sharp through her shirt. He was pressing with more force now and she was feeling nauseous and scared, really scared, but in that instant Raj shoved open the back door of the shop and came trundling into the kitchen, eating a dumpling of snow out of his woolly glove. Maya and Rohan watched him glide through and disappear into the seating area out front.

Maya believed that if Raj had not chosen that moment to come in from the alley, Rohan would have killed her then and there. Instead he dropped the old cup of coffee in the trash and went into the storage room for a new hairnet and a flashlight and a pair of the latex gloves he used for cleaning. When he came out, he was wiping the hammer's handle on the sleeve of his coat.

—Where are you going? she said to his back.

He yanked open the shop's rear door and became a dark silhouette against the glow of falling snow.

—Somebody's daddy forgot his hammer, he said.

CHAPTER TWENTY-SEVEN

"Carol wasn't supposed to be there," Mrs. Patel said, pulling a Kleenex out from beneath her stretchy watchband and holding it to her nose. "I don't know what happened in that house, Lydia, I don't *want* to know. But I do know that Carol was supposed to be at *your* house. Not there. It's all Raj talked about, being left out of your sleepover."

Lydia leaned into the stainless counter, feeling like she'd swallowed her tongue. Across from her in the doughnut shop kitchen, Mrs. Patel picked threads off her bandaged hand and dropped them to the tiled floor. The sight made Lydia dizzy, as if she too were unraveling. She looked around and nothing was what it had always been. The buzzing industrial fridge, the dripping sprayer above the sink, the stovetop with its faint blue pilot lights—all of it was a grainy version of itself. The world she'd known for all these years was not the world around her.

"You need to sit," Mrs. Patel said, and slid an upturned bucket toward her feet, but Lydia shook her head. Mrs. Patel opened the back door and propped it partway with a brick. Out there the alley was sloppy and dark. "Then you need some air."

Lydia's clothes were still damp and the fresh chill seeped through her skin. She thought about how so many people—

Moberg chief among them—had spent years seeking an answer to the Hammerman, and the whole time it had been sealed in a file, waiting to be brought into the light: *Birth Father's Name: Bartholomew Edward O'Toole.* This single bit of data could have broken the case, except it hadn't even been recorded until Joey's birth in Colorado Springs, six months after the murders. No wonder Moberg had missed it.

"You knew all along what your husband had done."

"Only after," Mrs. Patel hissed. "I had no idea what he was going to do. I'm not even sure *he* knew what he was going to do. Not exactly."

The day after the murders, Mrs. Patel learned about them by gluing herself to the local news channel. Her first thought was to turn Rohan over to the police, but in a fog of fear and panic, she reasoned that doing so would only hurt Raj. She convinced herself that it would be better for her boy to live a false life under the adoring gaze of his father than to live under the odious shadow of what he had done, and equally important, what she herself had *caused*.

"Because make no mistake, Lydia," Mrs. Patel said, "*all of this* was my fault. Their blood was on *my* hands. Make *no* mistake about that."

Mrs. Patel seemed as if she was about to shriek, or curl into a crying fit, but instead she turned and brushed some remnant flour off the counter behind her.

"Please just let this go, Lydia."

"I can't do that."

"You are *alive*," Mrs. Patel said. "Maybe you've never thought about the risk he took by not killing you."

He walked into that kitchen covered in blood, Moberg had told her, *holding a dripping goddamned hammer, and let you keep your life.*

"Of course I've thought about that," Lydia said, sickened.

"And what about Raj?" Mrs. Patel said. "Do you understand what it will do to him if he finds out?"

"*When* he finds out. I do."

"You say you do," she said, shaking her head, "but you don't. You have no idea how bad this will be for him."

Mrs. Patel slumped forward, apparently resigned. Lydia could hear traffic splashing past on Colfax.

"You're not protecting your son, Mrs. Patel. You're protecting your husband. *The Hammerman.*"

"I am protecting my *family*," she said, as if her silence were a maternal duty.

Mrs. Patel peered out to the alley, checking for her husband's car. Then she moved the brick and closed the door and sat on a bucket near the dishwashing station.

Lydia's mouth was parched and her ears were ringing, but she forced herself to focus.

"When did you decide to track Joey down?" she asked.

Mrs. Patel looked at her strangely and furrowed her brow.

"When did I *decide*? You've never had a child, Lydia, otherwise you wouldn't ask me that. I *decided* the moment he left my arms."

Something changed in Maya as she held her newborn in the delivery room in Colorado Springs. Joey had coppery skin and a head of soft black hair, and he smelled more lovely than any flower on earth. Though he'd only been outside of her body for minutes, he seemed so attuned to her presence, so *alert*. She knew that in giving him up she was doing the only thing she could; but after a few hours, when a pair of women came in and unpeeled him from her chest, she reached for him with

303

horror, and her skin went cold in the empty air. And the thing was, her skin never stopped feeling cold, ever again, as if her infant Joey were some kind of phantom limb.

She needed to know that he was okay. That was all.

Which was why some years later, as his eighteenth birthday approached, Maya made a trip to the Vital Records office, without Rohan's knowledge, to see if Joey had also expressed interest in meeting.

—It may never happen, Irene had cautioned her. It usually doesn't.

But Irene's skepticism turned out to be misplaced. A few days after Joey's eighteenth birthday, Maya received a certified letter from the Vital Records office stating that Joseph Edward Molina had requested and been given her contact information.

In the days that followed, Maya nearly lost her head. She began checking the mail all the time, not only out of eagerness and excitement, but also because she was terrified that Rohan might intercept a letter from Joey and learn that she'd been secretly rummaging around in the past. And then one morning in the shop's mailbox she found an envelope from her boy, *Joseph E. Molina*, tucked between a utility bill and an appliance catalog. She rushed into the bathroom to read it.

The last news she'd ever heard about Joey was that he'd been taken in as an infant by a generous couple who ran a household bursting with other adopted kids. This meager bit of information had always been a source of comfort to Maya, which was why the return address on Joey's letter hit her with such sadness and shock: it had been mailed from a state penitentiary in the mountains. She was so mortified that she could hardly rip the letter open, and when she did, Joey's words only reinforced her horror: Her baby was in *prison*.

The letter exchange began. Rather than chronicle each step

or stage of his life, Joey shared wide swaths of his experience in the foster system, beginning with his broken adoption from the Molina family, but left out his struggles with depression and his inability to feel close to anyone. He asked her a lot of questions, most of which she ignored, especially the ones that concerned his father. *He passed away before you were born*, she wrote, and that was the first and only reference she ever offered about Mr. O'Toole.

More than anything Maya wanted to go see her young son in prison, to embrace him and stroke his cheeks and begin the long act of apologizing for casting him into the world. Yet she also knew that it was unrealistic for her to make even a single visit. One day was all she needed, but it was too complicated to coordinate the lying and the transportation. What reason could she give to her husband for being away? That she was attending a conference? In what? Doughnut making? Gas pumping? That she was having a spa day? She could not come up with a single believable reason to be away from Rohan.

Why would that boy, she asked herself, even want a mother like her?

Even so, Maya loved exchanging letters with Joey. Although she worried that their contact might threaten to upend her life at the doughnut shop, she also realized, with no small degree of guilt, that there was a certain safety in his imprisonment. Joey was her child, yes, but he was like her child in a playpen in a distant part of the house, occupying her heart but not threatening to interrupt her dinner party, tyrannical though it was. This allowed her to encourage their relationship in a way she might otherwise have not. In her letters, she chronicled Raj's various school achievements, their daily routine around Colfax—things Joey would ask Tomas about during their nights on level three, Lydia realized, without ever mentioning his newly discovered mother—and put an upbeat spin on her life. She hardly mentioned Rohan.

After a year and a half or so Joey was due to be released, and Maya was worried. In her last letters to Joey in prison, she stressed the importance of keeping their relationship a secret, of giving her the space to figure out how he fit into her present life. She had an older son who didn't even know of Joey's existence, and a husband who was unaware that she had tracked him down. It was *imperative* that he stay away.

And for a long time Joey did. Maya talked to him briefly on the phone sometimes and encouraged him to keep out of trouble and to do well in his rehabilitation programs. She told him that she hoped, one day, to meet him in person—just not now. Never now.

But the postponements went on for too long, and both of them knew it. Joey grew tired of Maya avoiding their reunion and she grew tired of trying to keep him hidden. She began to dodge his phone calls, and sensed a side of him that she'd been happy to ignore before—that of a solemn, desperate boy whose very desperation made people want to avoid him.

At that point, Maya began to receive calls from Irene, who wanted to know if there was anything she could do to facilitate the meeting. Apparently Joey had made a habit of stopping in to see her and begging her to do things that were well beyond her authority. Maya told Irene she had no business calling, that it was bad enough that Joey wouldn't respect her wishes.

She knew what Rohan was capable of. And she knew that she'd made herself available to Joey when she was really not available. Her feelings were real, but she had no room for that boy in her life.

Just a few weeks ago, Maya finally agreed to meet Joey for an early dinner at a Mexican restaurant on South Broadway. All afternoon at the doughnut shop, she faked groaning trips to the bathroom, then asked Rohan if he could possibly finish up the shift while she went home to rest. He reluctantly agreed, and she hopped a cab straight to the restaurant.

On the cab ride over, she vowed to tell Joey, in no uncertain terms, that he should try to create his own life, separate from her. But when she reached the restaurant and stood on the sidewalk outside, peering through the window at Joey's quiet table, her heart fell into her feet. Seeing her grown-up baby for the first time in person—with his thick black hair, his long arms, his slender neck—she was floored by how unmistakably he was her son.

Through the window, Maya watched Joey rub his teeth with his finger and stir his salsa with a tortilla chip. Every few seconds he'd touch a button on his suit coat or the knot of his tie, clearly uncomfortable in those grown-up clothes. She'd last seen him in the delivery room when he was less than one day old, and she realized that all of his days since then had been turned over to the world, and even from here she could see that the world had not been merciful.

She wanted to scoop him up and protect him, but that was impossible, so she turned up the sidewalk and walked away from the restaurant, sobbing, and made it home before Rohan had even locked the shop.

Maya should have expected it the next afternoon when Joey showed up at Gas 'n Donuts. He was wearing his black jeans and his black hoodie and he sat on a stool at the counter. Raj had stopped in for a short visit and was sitting by himself in the corner booth, looking through the want ads. Rohan was in the storage room in the back, emptying giant pillows of flour into five-gallon bins. With his scrawny frame and nauseating quivers, Maya first mistook Joey for an addict, but when he pulled back his hood she recognized him immediately. Her first reaction was one of not fear but excitement. She gasped. Raj looked up from his newspaper. Maya was standing next to the coffeepots behind the counter, so only ten feet separated her from her youngest son. As she began to walk in his direction, Joey's green eyes brightened and she was filled with the same love she'd felt when he was born.

And then she heard Rohan's voice coming from the kitchen doorway.

—Maya!

Raj shifted. Rohan pushed the door fully open.

—Maya, I'll do this. Can you finish the flour?

Maya froze in place. She could feel the tiled floor tilting beneath her, sliding her toward the kitchen's swinging door. All of her feelings were consumed by fear as Joey's gaze shifted from his mother to this man, this burly stranger his mom must have loved.

Across the shop, Raj set down his newspaper. From his booth he would've been able to see the back of the scrawny young man at the counter, and his father walking over and leaning into his face.

—Out.

Maya hovered before the door. She could have stepped forward and said something. She could have acknowledged her younger son. But instead she disappeared into the kitchen. She told herself she was remaining silent in order to protect Raj, but choosing him over his baby brother only made her feel worse. When the door closed behind her, it felt as if it had closed upon her life.

Ever since Joey's birth, if she shut her eyes and concentrated she could *smell* him, like he was still that infant in her arms, and that was what she did right then, all alone in the kitchen. Even from there, she could hear the squeaky spin of the counter stool as Joey stood and ran toward the exit. The bell rang against the glass as the door shut behind him.

—He's a thief, Rohan said to Raj.

Maya leaned against the tiled wall for a long time after Joey was gone, forcing herself to recall every detail of his face, his hair, his clothing, his gait, and after a time she heard Raj gathering his things, zipping his knapsack, and heading out as well.

—Tell Mom I'll call, he said.

The bell rang against the glass, and her other son was gone.

Rohan turned over the *Closed* sign and came into the kitchen. He'd clearly known who Joey was the moment he saw him, or maybe the moment he saw Maya looking at him. He even seemed to have expected him, which made her wonder if he'd intercepted one of their letters or phone calls. She didn't dare ask.

—How long have you two been in touch? he said.

Rohan was so calm, standing there, that Maya thought the years had maybe changed him, that maybe he would allow Joey to have a place in their lives. She must have seemed happy when she told him that she and Joey had been writing letters for a few years, but that this was really the first time they'd seen each other in person.

Rohan nodded along until she was finished.

—If I see him again, here or anywhere, I will kill him, and then I will kill you.

—Rohan. He needs a family, that's all. We could provide that.

—You act like you don't believe me.

His calm was reassuring, so she tried to plead with him.

—Rohan. He's my child.

—Okay.

—He's my *son*.

—Okay already.

309

He nodded with what seemed to be understanding, then held out his hand to her, open palmed. She was nervous but she took his hand and allowed him to walk her gently over to the stainless steel mixing station, with its vats of sugar and flour, its deep fryer and cooling racks and industrial mixer. He stopped there, then held her bicep with one hand, her forearm with the other, almost as if he were leading her onto a dance floor—except then he tightened his grip and plunged her hand into the bubbling oil of the deep fryer. Her eyes opened so wide that she felt like her lids had peeled back over the top of her head. She watched her fingers loosen as he pulled her hand, dripping and glistening, out of the golden oil. Stars stirred in her vision. Skin slid off of her hand like an unfurled glove.

—Do you believe me now? he said.

Now she could feel it, her entire hand blaring an unfathomable noise. She was unable to breathe, let alone respond.

He let go and walked toward the shop's rear door, just as he had that night twenty years ago.

—*Please* don't hurt him!

—Get that hand fixed before we open tomorrow.

In the shop with Lydia, Mrs. Patel fiddled with her gray gauzy mitten.

"*Please don't hurt him,*" she said. "That was all I could offer my son. That was the extent of my motherhood. Four words. *Please don't hurt him.*"

After Rohan left the shop Maya made two phone calls: one to get the taxi that would take her to the emergency room because her husband had just driven off in his Monte Carlo, and the other to Joey, who had just arrived at his group-home apartment and picked up his ringing phone. He was silent as Mrs. Patel spoke the last words she would ever say to him.

—I never want to see you again. I never want to hear from you. I never want to read your letters. Am I making myself clear?

—Mom?

—Don't call me that. It's not your fault, but some people are just not meant to be born. If I could undo you, I would. I promise you, I would.

As she set down the receiver she could hear him saying, *Mom?*

"That hurt far more than my hand ever could," Mrs. Patel said to Lydia. "But I didn't know how else I might protect him. Rohan would be glad to kill him."

Lydia imagined Joey hanging up the phone, then sitting in his empty apartment with his pile of books, ignoring Lyle's calls and his landlady's knocks. His whole life he had turned to books as his only solace, so it made sense that in preparing to undo himself he would do the same: fall into their pages, disappear into their windows, expose his soul on his way out of life.

She could have asked Mrs. Patel for more details, but she knew enough. After that final phone call, Joey had spent two or three days carving his messages, and each piece of a page he sliced inched him ever closer to death.

io

We

U.M.

or

eth

ant   his,

L.

dia

but   I'd

On

tha

vet

hew

or

ds

. Any

mo

reth.

ey

have been

tak

in

. A long

with

my l

If,

Mrs. Patel looked drained and scared on her upturned bucket. She seemed to be asking Lydia for forgiveness, or at least for understanding. But it wasn't Lydia's to give.

"You don't even know why I'm here," Lydia said.

"Because you and Raj found out about Joey," Mrs. Patel said, but there was a lilt of doubt in her voice. "I will make it up to him, Lydia. Maybe now that Raj knows, we can find a way. I *will* make it up to him."

"You can't," Lydia said.

"I can, Lydia. I just don't know how yet."

Lydia had been so caught up in this knot of secrets that she'd nearly forgotten why she'd stepped foot into the Vital Records office last week in the first place: to track down Joey's mother in order to share the news of his suicide. She deserved to know, Lydia had told herself then. After all, his mother had been seeking him out.

"You can't make it up to him," she said, "because Joey is dead. He hanged himself in the bookstore where I work."

"No, he didn't."

"Check the newspaper. Joey hanged himself. That's why I'm here, Mrs. Patel. I came to tell you that your boy is dead."

"He's not, Lydia. I saw him when? Three weeks ago? Less than three weeks. What is today?"

Lydia could see her struggling with her own denial, but the certainty of her words had broken through. Mrs. Patel's mittened hand clutched at a phantom spot on her chest.

"Joey's heart was already broken," Lydia said, "and you broke it again. He couldn't recover this time."

"I will make it up to him."

"It's too late."

Lydia opened the door to the alley. She heard voices out there and in a moment of terror expected to see Mr. Patel—but it was only a homeless couple, pushing a shopping cart through the slush. Just beyond them, across the alley, was the rusty old ladder bolted to the side of the motel. It hurt to remember Raj in his buckled jumpsuit, climbing rung by rung to its top and pouring a curtain of powdery creamer as little Carol held out her pack of matches below.

Lydia was glad that it wasn't Mr. Patel she'd heard in the alley. He'd killed Mr. and Mrs. O'Toole, and he'd killed her friend

Carol, and he'd killed the broken Joey—or at least caused him to die—and it only took one look at Mrs. Patel to see all the damage he'd done to her as well. Before she could face him, or call Moberg or the police, she promised herself she'd first speak with Raj, empty herself of all these secrets, and maybe even figure out a way to shield her father from the secrets he'd kept as well.

"I will make it up to him," Mrs. Patel said.

"Joey deserved a better mother than you," Lydia said, buttoning her coat and stepping out the door.

"I will make it up to him," Mrs. Patel repeated, but Lydia was already trudging through the alley slush, glancing at the ladder, thinking about the fiery flower—warm and alive—that her friend Carol had conjured from the air.

EPILOGUE

On the night before Thanksgiving, Lydia's ghost appeared on television.

At the time, she was in the kitchen, pulling down boxes of stuffing and cans of yams and periodically slapping the cold pimpled turkey thawing in her sink. From where she stood she could see Raj in the other room, wearing a gray wool sweater and cut-off army pants. He thumbed the TV remote.

"Maybe nothing good is on," she said.

"Something good is always on."

Raj had offered to come over and help get the meal ready, but since he didn't have cable yet in his new apartment he'd gone straight for her remote. To save a little money, Lydia had planned on getting rid of cable when David moved out six months ago, but Raj had been coming around often enough that she'd postponed making the call. He would watch just about anything, the cheesier the better, but she usually didn't mind. For all the perks of living alone, one downside was how long the nights could sometimes feel with no one there to grasp.

Her dad would be coming over for the holiday tomorrow as well, his first trip to Denver in two decades. Lydia hadn't seen him in person since last winter's visit to Rio Vista, but he'd been calling every Sunday like clockwork and she was usually glad to hear his voice. Most of the time they kept their conversations away from anything too substantial, but at one point during the summer, after a few beers at a Bright Ideas barbecue, she'd bravely suggested that he turn his cabin into a used-book store, since he had plenty of inventory already and Rio Vista could sure use a—

He hung up the phone before she even finished. Their calls continued, but neither of them ever mentioned the used-book store idea again. By way of an apology, she mailed him an assortment of reading glasses.

Lydia had hoped to invite David over for Thanksgiving dinner as well, but he wouldn't even return her calls, and she really couldn't blame him. The original plan last spring—hers, anyway—had been for them to try living apart for a while, just as a test, to see what would happen if they had some distance between them. After discovering that he'd known for years, in silence, about Little Lydia, she'd been spotting his faults all over and losing her ability to overlook them. If the two of them were meant to be, she reasoned, they'd be drawn to each other again like a pair of cranes or vultures, ready to mate for life. David begrudgingly agreed, and she helped him get set up in a studio apartment near the University of Denver, a bit closer to his office.

Those first weeks of separate living had invigorated them as a couple, as if the arrangement had merely given them a new place to have sex and a new neighborhood to grab coffee. But something happened once the first month wore off. David gradually stopped inviting her over to his studio, claiming perhaps rightly that spending all of that time together felt too much like cheating on their agreement, and within another month he'd come right out and accused her of *trying to have it both ways*. He had plenty to offer, he said, and if she didn't want *all* of him, she couldn't have *any* of him. It hurt how right he was. By the time Halloween rolled around, he'd gone totally cold.

David would not be spending Thanksgiving with Lydia and her father, but she was comforted by the fact that Raj would be there. And Raj was comforted, too. For the first time in his life, he had nowhere else to go.

Ten months ago, the day after leaving Mrs. Patel at Gas 'n Donuts, Lydia had been organizing a pile of board books in the Kids section when Plath approached, wearing flip-flops and a skirt she'd made from a shower curtain. She held out the morning paper and bit her lip.

—If it's another picture of me, Lydia said, gesturing to the newspaper, I don't even want to know.

—You look tired, Plath said. I'll come back.

—What is it?

—It's bad. Really bad. Murder-at-the-doughnut-shop bad.

Lydia was supposed to meet Raj for breakfast this morning, but he hadn't answered her calls. She assumed he'd spent all night poring over Irene's files and needed to catch up on his sleep, but now her heart began to pound.

—What happened? she said. What murder?

—Late last night at Gas 'n Donuts. That's your friend's place, right?

Lydia felt herself falling into a panic—thinking first about Raj, then about Mrs. Patel, then she was unable to think at all. She grabbed the paper out of Plath's hands.

—Who got killed? *Who*—?

—The guy who owned the shop, Plath said. Your friend's dad. He's dead.

Lydia's hands were so shaky that Plath had to spread open the pages for her to read: *Local Business Owner Slain in Late-Night Robbery.*

—You okay? Plath asked.

Lydia frantically read the article. She learned that after dropping his deposit bag into the after-hours slot at the bank, Mr. Patel had returned to Gas 'n Donuts to pick up his wife and finish locking up. When he stepped out of his Monte Carlo, someone emerged from the darkness behind the dumpsters and shot him multiple times in the back, then in the head. The police were speculating that the shooter wanted the deposits and panicked when it was discovered that Mr. Patel had already been to the bank. A passing driver may have seen someone walking away on foot, but no further information was known about the assailant.

—Maybe you should go over to the doughnut shop, Plath said, pay your respects.

—I don't have any respects.

The Hammerman was dead, and Lydia's immediate reaction had been to rush to a phone and try calling Raj again to find out if he knew, what he knew, and to see if there was anything she could do to help. All afternoon his phone rang and his answering machine didn't pick up, and even when she stopped by his apartment on the way home from work no one answered the door. She considered calling Gas 'n Donuts or his parents' house but couldn't bring herself to punch the digits.

Early the following morning, as a few yawning BookFrogs lined up at Bright Ideas for their day's wordy intake, Lydia stood at the newsstand, combing through the paper for any updates. She'd barely dented the Metro section when Raj came rushing across the floor and landed smack in the center of her embrace.

—Raj, my god, your *dad*.

—I know.

—How's your mom—?

—They got her, he said.

320

—What?

—The police. They got her.

Then he collapsed into sobs and had to plant his hand against the magazine racks in order to stop himself from falling sideways.

—They *took* her, Lydia. They took my *mom*.

Raj didn't tip over, but he did end up with one arm around Lydia's shoulder as they hobbled to a table in the coffee shop.

Raj had been at his mom's side nonstop during the thirty-two hours since the shooting, but it wasn't until the two of them had been called into the station near City Park for yet another informational session that one of the detectives, a young guy with big ears who seemed embarrassed to be there, came into the room and asked Mrs. Patel if she wanted to enlist a lawyer. Then he presented the old Montgomery Ward .22 rifle that Mr. Patel had kept under the Gas 'n Donuts counter for years. The rookie had barely even placed it on the table before asking Mrs. Patel if she had any idea how it had ended up in the dumpster behind the shop.

She did, she told him. And yes, she would very much like that lawyer now.

Years ago, it was Mr. Patel who'd advised her that in the event of a life-threatening situation, she should yank back the slide, aim the rusty rifle, and pull the trigger until the tube was empty. *Spray and pray*, he'd called it, and that's exactly what she had done behind the dumpsters that night, just after Lydia left the shop: waited for her husband to step out of his car, then fired. Three bullets hit his back, two hit his head, and five hit the car—though not in that order. Then she ditched the gun and called the police.

—They let me stay with her for a while as we waited for the lawyer, Raj said, and she told me everything.

—Everything?

Raj wouldn't look Lydia in the eye.

—Enough, anyway. It won't be long before she tells the police everything, too. It's like she wanted to get caught.

Lydia considered asking Raj what he'd meant by *enough*, but he seemed so distraught that she knew this wasn't the time. She thought about the last words Mrs. Patel had said to her, on the slushy night of the shooting as she exited the doughnut shop: *I will make it up to him.* To Joey. Her lost son. She'd tried.

There at the coffee shop, Lydia bought Raj a pastry and a bottle of juice. They sat together for a long time, mostly in silence, and when he left the store that afternoon, he put on a pair of sunglasses and gave her a clumsy kiss on the cheek. On the way out he bumped into a table of books.

For Lydia, Mr. Patel's murder had reaffirmed something that she'd been gradually facing up to her entire life: the Hammerman would always be with her. He occupied an immeasurable space inside her that would never be altered by the outside world—not by rifle shots or a therapist's couch or a child's tiny grip on her finger—and, paradoxical though it was, the reliability of this had always offered her some strange semblance of identity. Even if Mr. Patel was forever gone, the Hammerman would always be out there, and Lydia would always be that girl beneath the sink.

Always Little Lydia.

Which was why what happened to her on the night before Thanksgiving felt so unexpected. She'd been in the kitchen, drinking a glass of the wine that Raj had brought, plunging her hand into the turkey and trying to pry out a bag of giblets that were still frozen to its cavity, when Raj abruptly stopped changing channels.

"Are you seeing this?" he said, his voice eager and unsteady. "Lydia? Quick—come in here!"

Lydia was up to her elbow in the turkey but when she looked at the television she could see a static image of the O'Tooles' small, familiar house. Without washing her hands she stepped toward the couch. She felt her skin tighten and everything but the screen faded away. A buried phrase crackled from the television: *Little Lydia,* the voice said—only it had been sifted through an accent and surrounded by rolling Spanish: *Leetil Leedyah.*

"What is this?" Raj said, turning to look at her. "Should we turn it off?"

"Turn it up."

"It's in Spanish," he said, looking at the remote. "Some kind of ghost-hunting show. Do you even get this channel?"

"No idea."

Most of what appeared on the screen was filmed through an obnoxious green night-vision camera that tracked through the O'Tooles' house in the dark. In the center of the green, a flashlight halo dragged over the carpet and the walls and the pictures and the doors. The production values were painfully low, yet she could see that the O'Tooles' orange shag carpet had been replaced by a speckled brown Berber and that all the fixtures had been updated. Otherwise the layout of the home was almost exactly the same, as if the new family were working from the blueprints of the old.

Raj covered his mouth with his hand.

"Oh my god," he said. "That's inside *Carol's* house?"

Lydia could only nod.

The host of the program was a histrionic thirtysomething with slick black hair and a black leather jacket. As he walked through the house, he whispered into the camera, periodically raising a finger and allowing his eyes to roam from wall to wall, floor to ceiling. He opened closet doors and peeled back the shower curtain, and occasionally the screen would cut to

323

a close-up of the Ghostometer, a ridiculous contraption that looked like a mix between an old-fashioned radio and a pasta colander. An outdated oscilloscope screen attached to the device showed a glowing flat line of inactivity, at least until he carried it into the hallway, just near the master bedroom doorway. The host looked at the camera with wide eyes when the beeps grew frantic and the display showed a flurry of green waves.

"I guess that means there's a ghost," Raj mumbled.

Lydia felt her heart pounding and every few seconds she felt someone blowing gently on the back of her neck. As the host continued down the hall, the screen showed grainy photographs of each of the O'Tooles, one at a time: Bart first, then Dottie, and finally Carol. Then the camera focused on a girl with straight black hair, twelve or thirteen years old, wearing a pink sweatshirt and fidgeting in an overstuffed chair. The girl obviously now lived in Carol's old house, and she was being interviewed about a ghost who lived in her hallway—the ghost that this show was apparently there to find.

As the girl spoke to the camera, the voice of a translator crowded over her words, but she could still be heard faintly in English beneath:

Sometimes, she said, *in the middle of the night, I can hear someone crawling fast through my hallway. Only no one is there when I look.*

Lydia's first reaction was to feel terrified for this girl, but when she saw the smile on her face—like she was trying not to laugh, like she was doing this on a dare—she realized that this was more about entertainment than fear.

One night, the girl continued, *I was getting a drink of water and I could hear someone breathing inside the sink.*

The screen cut to a night-vision view of the O'Tooles' kitchen. Slow and unsteady, the camera roamed over the humming refrigerator, the scuffed baseboards, and finally, the cabinet beneath the sink. Lydia could hear the voices of the girl and her translator behind the images.

The story I heard at school was this one girl hid under there all night. She didn't get killed because she was so hidden. But in the morning no one could find her. Like she just disappeared into thin air.

Leetil Leedyah.

On the screen the host's hand reached out, opening the cabinet beneath.

It was apparently inconvenient for the producers to show the famous photograph of Lydia being carried off the neighbor's porch by her father, surrounded by police and paramedics; that would break the paranormal narrative they were creating. What they showed instead was the host's hand lowering the Ghost-ometer into the dark space beneath the sink. Inside, below the disposal, she could see grimy pipes and a pair of crusty shutoff valves. The space was crowded with cleaning products and a roll of trash bags, and her stomach dropped at the thought of folding herself tightly enough to fit inside. Predictably, the machine's oscilloscope lit up, splashing green waves, screeching beeps, proving undeniably that there was a ghost under there.

Lydia felt her body stiffen. She could sense Raj swaying against the couch.

She was in there forever, the girl's voice continued, *and then she was just gone.*

On the screen a hand pressed closed the cabinet door: *ke-tick*.

"I can't watch this," Raj said, grimacing. He lifted the remote. "Can I?"

"Please."

In an instant the television blinked to black. Raj tossed the remote to the couch and closed his eyes.

"Raj? You okay?"

"Not at all," he said. "You?"

"Me neither," she said, holding her elbows. "That was weird."

"Really weird. I'm never watching television again."

She laughed uncomfortably and after a moment Raj did, too. Then he slowly reached out and took her hand and pulled her into an unexpected hug, despite the turkey juice sticky on her arm.

"You're not a ghost," he said.

"No?"

Lydia smelled his clean skin and felt the warmth and comfort of his body. And though she wanted to close her eyes and feel the promise of this moment, she couldn't help but look beyond his shoulder, hoping to see for one last time the girl he'd just erased from the screen.

ACKNOWLEDGMENTS

My deepest thanks . . .

To my kind and nimble agent, Kirby Kim, who rescued me from his slush pile, dusted me off, and led the way forward without a flinch; to Cecile Barendsma, Brenna English-Loeb, and the rest of the team at Janklow & Nesbit, whose expertise and professionalism are unmatched.

To my editor, the talented and generous John Glynn, who patiently guided this story into the light; to Laura Wise, Nan Graham, Roz Lippel, Jeremy Price, and the rest of the team at Scribner, whose commitment to artistry and excellence is a gift to readers everywhere.

To the organizations that have helped me in so many ways along this path, especially Tattered Cover, Brookline Booksmith, Yaddo, Centrum, the Vermont Studio Center, Write on the River, the D.A.M. writers' group, Artist Trust, and the University of Idaho's MFA program; and to my many inspiring students and comrades at Big Bend Community College.

To Aja Pollock, who combed every word with her brilliant eye, and to Sean Daily at Hotchkiss & Associates for working to get this book onscreen.

To the individuals whose feedback and support, at various

times, helped to shape this book and fuel my persistence, especially John Bartell, Matt Blackburn, Mary Blew, Steve Close, Brian Davidson, Pete Henderson, Jamie Horton, Mary Ann Hudson, Jim Johnson, Greg Matthews, Minh Nguyen, Lance Olsen, Rie and Fran Palkovic, John Peterson, Joe Rogers, Nat Sobel, Julie Stevenson, Eric Wahl, Jess Walter, Judith Weber, and my all-time second favorite librarian, Lance Wyman.

To my teaching mentor, John Carpenter, who dropped everything to tell me about guns.

To Mark Barnhouse, whose books on the history of Denver brought me back in time.

To the nefarious Sullivan clan, in all your sprawling glory, for the laughter and love that you spread; and especially to my mom, Ann Sullivan, who took me to my first writing conference when I was in grade school, and who wrote stories in the bathtub because that was the only place she could find any peace and quiet.

And most important, to Libby, the one true love of my life, for all that you are, all that you create, and all that you give; and to Milo and Lulu, our bright little bibliophiles, who used to sit in my lap as I wrote and now are making their own stories in the world.